Where the Clouds Sleep

Robert G. Makin

Where the Clouds Sleep

Sons of Aaron Publishing

Palm Coast, Florida

Acknowledgments

No book or work of this kind can be done without the encouragement of friends, family and fans. I'd like to thank Sophie Tredor for her encouragement and keeping me on track during the development of the story. I'd like to thank Pam Reed for her indefatigable urging and questioning "When's the next book coming out?" Okay Pam. Here it is.... Geez!

Of my many friends and family who helped me make this book possible, none contributed more significantly than Schneider National Carriers, without whom I would never have driven across the valley where the clouds really do sleep until late most mornings, the New River Gorge in West Virginia. Schneider also provided me with more than adequate time to muse about developing the plot lines and characters and then motivated me to take the time to do the actual writing.

The editing marvel, Jonni Anderson, has beautifully designed four of my five books. She handled formatting of the cover design and smoothed over some of my rough edges in the book writing business. Thanks, Jonni.

The cover artist, Briana Serna, painted the cover art for *Faces of Inanna* and *Where the Clouds Sleep*. I find her work amazing. Thanks for your help, Brie.

Robert G. Makin

This book is dedicated to Bert

Contents

Where the Clouds Sleep

Robert G. Makin

Chapter One

Pinned to the rocky ground, Trudy's realization of betrayal and her screaming fear struggled for dominance. She had trusted him! Odd, that the pain of a small pebble pressing into her right shoulder blade should capture her attention, while her whole being suffered the invasion of one sick man's evil. His hands pinned her wrists over her head while he forced her thighs open with one knee. Trudy screamed. He released one hand that was holding her wrist and slapped her face with passion. His whispered, "I told you to be quiet," was barely heard as she screamed again. This time, he struck her with his closed fist. With one hand free, she clawed frantically at his face, but her arms were not long enough to reach it.

"Shit!" he exclaimed, releasing the other hand. Both hands now circled her throat, strangling her next scream into silence.

ᙗ ᙘ

Trudy Griffin liked walking home after Junior Varsity Cheerleading Practice. The coming fall football season looked good for her classmates. They had a heavy turnout of volunteers among the boys. The high school kids worried that they would not put on as good a show as the graduates of the year before, but Trudy was sure they would do just fine. Jack Thiebault and Daryl Lewis were coming up from their Junior year, with added weight and a year's growth. They were as big and as fast as last year's graduated stars, at least Trudy thought so. The team ended last year nearly leading the state in victories. This year they would do even better. Part of her enjoyment of her walk home included admiring the blue chicory flowers alongside the road. She was picking some to bring home with her when Beamer pulled up beside her in his hot little BMW coup convertible. It was blue with white trim and had the top down. Her classmates didn't know his name. They just called him "Beamer" because of the BMW. That was a play on words. Before he got the BMW, they always called him "Beaver."

"Hey, kid. Beautiful day for pickin' chicory. Ain't it?"

Trudy recognized Beamer, although she hardly knew him. He graduated some years ago and had a job at the quarry. She watched many times as he drove by in his shiny sports car, wondering what it would be like to ride in such a marvel of mechanical beauty and genius. Sometimes he waved at her as he passed. But now... *Oh my god! He stopped! He's talking to me!* She lowered her head slightly, shy as a rabbit on the verge of springing into the bushes and out of sight. But she didn't. *I'm going to be bold! This might be my only chance for a ride in that car! ...and it's Beamer! Oh my God!*

"Don't you be talkin' to no strangers!" Her dad's voice echoed in her memory. "There's bad men out there that take advantage o' little girls."

Well! I'm not a little girl anymore, Daddy. I'm twelve years old. And I know Beamer. He went to our school. And he has a BMW! He's not a stranger!

"Hi, Beamer." Trudy raised her eyes to look at him. His oddly narrow head accentuated the wide toothy grin. She lowered her eyes again. *Too much to look at all at once.* Then she raised her eyes again and said, "I thought Mom would like some of these pretty blue flowers. Dad says they improve the taste of his coffee. Everybody will like them. Want some?" She held up a handful of blue blossoms with a big grin of her own. "They almost match the color of your car."

"Sure. I got a gum band right here. I'll jist string 'em together." He reached into his small glove compartment and produced a rubber band as she approached the car. "I was just headed up to Chad's Knob to watch the moon rise. It's a full moon an' it's gonna be a big one. It won't even be dark when we can start to see it. Wanna come along?"

Trudy handed the bundle of chicory blossoms to Beamer. *Oh my God! He's offering me a ride in that car!* "My mom's expecting me home. If I'm late, she'll get worried."

"We won't be gone long." Beamer's grin grew even wider as he leaned back into the driver's seat and waited.

Trudy took a step back, away from the car. "I better not. It's getting late. I need to get home." *What am I doing? ...saying no? This might be my only chance.*

"Well. I sure like watchin' that moonrise over Chad's Knob. The most beautiful sight in the world. I'm startin' school up in Pennsylvania in the fall and I moved into an apartment there last week. I just came back to Copperhead to watch the moonrise over Chad's Knob, one last time, before I have to start school. Be a shame if I had to do it alone. You sure?"

I guess if I go, I won't be all that late. Mom will understand. Dad will fume, and after supper, all will be forgotten.

"I guess I will, but I have to be home before dark." Twelve year old Trudy Griffin's decision was more final than she could possibly have imagined. As she climbed into the BMW, she brushed her strawberry blonde, shoulder length hair behind her, kicked some dirt off her white sneakers before entering and glanced at her short cheerleader's skirt, wondering if she was showing too much leg. As she settled into the right bucket seat, she self-consciously tried to stretch her skirt lower on her legs with a sidelong glance at Beamer. As he pushed the floor shift lever into first gear position, the back of his hand brushed her naked thigh. *I think he did that on purpose. That rascal.*

"My mom says I'm pretty mature for only twelve years old. But I'm going to be thirteen in about five months. What do you think?"

Beamer quickly glanced at her naked thighs for a second too long, then at her budding breasts, barely apparent through her cheerleader tee shirt, then at her eyes. He returned his attention to the road and muttered just loudly enough for Trudy to hear him. "Oh yeah."

ଓଃ ଽଠ

Marjorie Griffin stirred a pot of beef stew she had simmering on a four burner gas stove in the cottage she shared with her husband George and their daughter Trudy. A half a mile beyond the turn-off for Pigg's Cemetery Road, the cottage wasn't as isolated as George had wanted, but they had an acre and a half of land that could be cultivated, a detached garage and a shed large enough for some rudimentary farm equipment. George was proud of the rows of corn he had sprouting in back. The broccoli and beans patch just beyond wasn't growing as fast as he liked. She smiled at the thought of his fretting about it. "If I give them more water from the well, I'm afraid the water level may drop too much. There hasn't been much rain this year." She smiled again as she gave the pot another stir. She put a lid on it and walked to the front porch. *I wonder where Trudy is. She should be home by now.*

Just then, George came driving down their short lane from the

County Road. His red Ford Ranger kicked up a little dust as he came to a stop. As he exited the vehicle, he picked up a small bag of groceries he bought on the way home. "Hi Sweety. Where's Trudy?" George's broad shoulders were no match for the small grocery bag that, Marjorie thought, *sort of disappears into him when he carries it like that.*

"She ain't home yet, George. She'll be along shortly. She's such a good girl. She had cheerleader practice tonight. When she does that, she's a little later than usual, but she'll be along. How was work, today?"

"We're almost half way there," George remarked over coffee as they waited for Trudy to get home. Brochures for various colleges were spread over the table, between the plates Marjorie had set out for their dinner. "The money we've saved over the last few years is growing pretty fast. By the time Trudy is ready to pick one of these schools, there will be plenty. Has she decided what she wants to major in, yet?"

"Not hardly," George. "She's only twelve. Some days she says she wants to be a doctor. On other days, it's a lawyer. Sometimes she says she wants to teach English or French or elementary, or home economics. She's still a kid. When she's older, the ideas will form up and she'll make a decision."

"I got a chance for more overtime at the quarry," George ventured. "I'd rather spend my spare time home with you two but this is a chance to make that college fund grow faster."

"I had a call from my mom today." Marjorie brushed a wisp of her honey blonde hair out of her eye, shook the rest of it toward the back of her head and smiled. "I know how you love it when my parents show up, but Mom says they're coming up from Roanoke for a few days, at the end of the month. She says she can't get enough of visiting with her 'gorgeous granddaughter.'"

"Speaking of the gorgeous granddaughter, where is she? It's almost six o'clock." George slid his chair out from under the table, rose and, turning for the door, he said, "I think I'll take a ride on down the road and see if I can find her — give her a ride home."

Marjorie turned down the heat under the stew to keep it warm without cooking it more. Her wait began in a wooden rocking chair on the front porch, grew into pacing on the porch and at seven o'clock, she turned off the fire under the stew. *Jesus! Should I call the police?* She walked up to the end of their lane and looked down the County Road in growing fear. No traffic was in sight and no twelve year old girl with strawberry blonde hair and a cheerleader's uniform walking toward her. No red Ford Ranger could be seen either. She walked back to the house, went to the phone and dialed the sheriff's office.

"Oh she's just found some distraction and lost track of the time," she was told. "Don't worry, Mrs. Griffin. She'll be home soon." But Mrs. Griffin — Marjorie — was worried. Her daughter had never been late before and now her husband was out running around, looking for her and obviously had not found her. Otherwise both of them would be here.

CS &

The pain in Trudy's right shoulder blade grew worse but the pain between her legs almost made her forget about it. The rocks under her back became agony. *How will I explain these scratches and bruises when I get home? Oh my God! Am I going to be able to even get home? This guy's gonna kill me!* His hands on her throat had slacked their grip enough that she could breathe, but not very well. Her flailing arms with claws bared had scratched his arms, *but not very much, I'm afraid. Not enough to stop him!* She tried to scream again, but when she did, the hands on her throat tightened. Then they tightened more. —

Chapter Two

Billene watched him from her favorite quiet place, a large area concealed under the azalea bushes in front of their ramshackle cottage. It's where she always went - after - to hide and cry silently. The ground where she sat felt gritty and dirty, like sin. Glancing up at the sunlight filtering through the azalea leaves, she saw bug eggs on the underside of the leaves. A grand Daddy Long Legs spider crept past with its stilted gate, uncertain, it seemed, which way it wanted to go.

He hurt her more this time. She was bleeding. As a ten-year-old, she had been proud that her breasts were beginning to grow and that her stepfather, Joe Cleod, wanted her, but now as a twelve-year-old, she had begun to realize the danger he posed to her and to feel the shame of her reality.

Billene was freckled and thin, "lanky" some would say. Her long red hair always tangled in things and she wanted to cut it but Joe was against it and she always did what he told her to do. "The boys'll lak ya better with it long," he always said with a sort of jeer. "Ha-el, I lak ya better with it long," and his pallid gray eyes would grow cold, changing from the softness of the overly doting father he always liked to pretend to be, to the dominating, sadistic child molester that he was. "So don't be talkin' o' cuttin' it no more. Ya hear? Somethin' might happen to ya like what happened to yer ma."

The words chilled her, gave her goose flesh. The look in his eye, when he said it and the coldness in his voice confirmed what she had long suspected. Now she knew for sure. Her mother's death was not some serendipity slip on the part of mother nature or her mother's own clumsiness.

The story of her mother's "accident" had always puzzled her, like some vital part of the information was missing, but now the accident itself became clear to her, explained by the events immediately preceding it. Now, she finally understood, or thought she did.

Darla had gone to Beckley, about 25 miles away, shopping with some girlfriends. The plan was to have an early dinner together then come home, so Joe expected her to arrive around 6:00 or 7:00 P.M. Billene would have gone along but she was working on a project she wanted to finish for school. Joe's plan for the day was to go trout fishing in one of the small mountain streams up toward Chad's knob.

Joe actually had gone fishing but an all-afternoon drizzle brought him home early, around 3:00. He was bored, frustrated, wet, and had caught no fish. He parked his old white Ford Van at the foot of the porch and stomped into the house after throwing his fishing gear in a pile by the door. As he came inside he started tearing off his wet clothing, cursing the weather, the upstream breeze which he blamed for his poor luck with the fish, and the fact that he was having a hard time finding a clean towel. That he had been drinking all afternoon did not help him in his search for a towel. By now, he had all of his wet clothing off and was in the bedroom tossing things around and demanding a towel.

After a few minutes of his grousing, Billene, then ten years old, appeared in the doorway of his bedroom with a towel in her hands. He didn't see her at first, but then he did. She was wearing cotton print shorts and a white sleeveless blouse. She had her red hair tied back in a tight pony tail tied with a blue ribbon and was wearing a smirk on her face, thinking it funny that she had caught him naked. She was pleased that Joe also seemed to think it was funny. He sat down on the bed with a smile and said, "Bring that towel here Billene. You can help me dry off if you want to." She did not miss or understand the odd tone in his voice.

That was their first encounter and Joe lost track of the time. When Darla came home earlier than expected, only half an hour later, she caught them in the act. The hysterics were unbelievable. At first Joe didn't see her, but by the time she had laid her hands on the nearest weapon she could find and was approaching him from behind, Joe heard her and turned in time to fend off a blow from a heavy cast iron skillet.

As soon as the fight began, Billene ran to her own room and closed the door to hide. That was the last time Billene ever saw her mother. Within a few minutes, the screaming and sounds of a struggle stopped.

She heard them leave the house. Joe returned a few hours later alone, asking if her mother had come back yet.

Now, she watched him fearfully through the tangled growth of azaleas, flower petals all around her on the ground, withered a little. The azalea blossom season was over for this year and summer was about to begin. He had just returned from the mail box, out on their road, "Goshen Trail" by name, little more than a no-name dirt track coming up from Pigg's Cemetery Road, "The Bulleevard," as the locals affectionately called it, also dirt.

Goshen Trail wound four or five miles up through the heavily wooded mountainside to Chad's Knob, the bare stone top of the mountain. Few hardy souls lived along its reach and those were back in the woods, out of sight. Billene knew some by sight and none by name.

He was sitting on the top of the steps to the front porch, reading a letter. Billene thought this odd because he seldom did any reading on his own. He nearly always asked her to read his mail to him. She took pleasure in watching him struggling over the words, sounding them out like a first grader, *stupid for a grown man,* she thought. *I don't know what I ever thought I saw in him.*

But she remembered the first time. She had always envied her mother because of the attention her mom got from him when she was younger. She never knew her real father. He was sent off to prison somewhere near Morgantown, Joe told her, just before she was born. Joe Cleod was the only father she had ever known. She was six and a half when her mom, Darla, started seeing him. Darla was working nights at the Slipped Dysk Lounge just down the road, on the south side of Copperhead, West Virginia, about 2 miles away. Joe was a coal miner and made more money than Darla ever dreamed of, at least since Billene's real father, Bill Parsons, had to go to prison. Bill drove big trucks, coast to coast, "over the road," as Darla used to say. "Seldom seen the son of a bitch, but he sure was makin' good money."

Billene clearly remembered the day she first saw Joe Cleod. The Slipped Dysk Lounge was a concrete block building with peeling gray paint, a sloping flat roof, rotting soffits and a black wooden front door with a two inch gap between its bottom and the floor, big enough for rodents to freely enter and leave, much like those other decaying souls that had to actually open the door to enter.

The parking lot was mostly the gravel shoulder of the State Road and sported two motor cycles, a rusted-out pickup truck and a water-runoff ditch on either side, connected under the gravel by a two foot wide drainage pipe. The sign on the side of the building said in huge neon letters "Nude Dancing, Nightly, Cum As You Are."

As Darla's old Chevy *ka-chunked* into the parking lot, the door to the building swung open revealing a woman of about Darla's age, wearing a knee-length green coat. The woman's luxurious blonde hair was tossed by the afternoon breeze as she glanced at them, rushing to her pickup truck. Darla, slender, tall, strawberry blonde and light on her feet, jumped out of the Chevy and called after the woman, "Hey, Karen, why you leavin' sa early? Yer shift ain't up till five."

The woman called Karen stopped and looked at Darla mournfully, then ran to her and hugged her, sobbing. "My shift is up forever," Billene could hear her say. "I'm leavin' this place and never comin' back. This place is a hell hole and what they want me to do ain't worth no damn money. How can you stay here? You're not like them."

"When ya have a youngin' ta raise, ya do what ya have ta do," Darla replied solemnly, brows furrowed slightly. "At least I know Billene won't have to go through this. I'm gonna git her a education and she can leave Copperhead West-f 'ing- Virginia and get a decent job, maybe marry someone nice."

"Well, you do what you have to do, Darla. I'm outta here." The blonde fumbled in her purse for a cigarette.

"Where can you go, Karen? There ain't no work around for girls like us, but this."

"I'm goin' up to Parkersburg and maybe work one o' them truck stops. The truckers'll sure treat me nicer 'n at ole Horace. Good luck to ya, Darla. Maybe I'll see ya again sometime. Watch your back!"

The inside of the Slipped Dysk smelled musky with spilled beer, sweat and pool table chalk. It was dark. Though only two customers were present, Joe Cleod being one of them, the cigarette smoke burned Billene's eyes and throat and made her choke. The walls were covered with advertisements, signs of all sorts. One said, "Can't drink all day if you don't get an early start. We open at 8 A.M." Behind the large bar where Joe and the other man were sitting was a wall-size mirror, coated with tar from years of exposure to tobacco smoke, shelves of liquor in front of it and the slogan "I'd rather have a bottle in front of me than a frontal lobotomy."

The two men heard 6-year-old Billene and her mom come in and turned to see who it was. "Well, well. What have we here," said the man who would become Billene's stepfather. "Two of the prettiest ladies I have ever seen."

This was high praise to Billene, being called not only a lady, not only pretty, but one of the prettiest ladies this man had ever seen. "And jist look at you blush," Joe continued. "Why yer jist as cute as they come, ain't chou. Come here and sit on ole Joe's knee, now and le' me have a lookit' chou." Seeing the look of concern and distrust in Darla's eyes, Joe responded, "it's okay, Mama. You cin have ma other knee." And both men laughed vulgarly, exchanging knowing glances.

Watching Joe Cleod now, from under the azalea bushes, stumbling through a letter on the front steps to their falling down mountain cottage, Billene's perception of him was completely different than on that first day. He could still make her blush, but now the reasons were different. Her revulsion, hate and fear could still make her heart pound, like someone faced with a real copperhead snake the area was so well known and named for.

Billene remembered when she began hating Joe Cleod. It was the day after her tenth birthday. There was a strike at the mine, so Joe was home for several weeks without much to do but drink beer and harass the women, but Billene still thought the harassment was all innocent fun, then.

Billene had just returned from school to find Joe sitting on the porch in the midst of a case of empty beer bottles with a second case chilling in the refrigerator. His eyes were glazed. He had not bathed or shaved that morning and a lock of sandy hair stood straight up, as though he had just crawled out of bed, and maybe he had. Joe stopped shaving 3 weeks before, when the strike was called, so he had a growth of whiskers on his face with one side sort of smashed down by last night's pillow.

Joe was a thin man, but tall and finely muscled from the strenuous work he did for the mining company, "two miles down," as he liked to put it. His face was narrow as a result of being at one end of a very narrow head. Billene used to think this was charming, but now she thought that his blue eyes were a little too close together for him to be "all right in the head." This was an expression she overheard from Mrs. Overby, one of the ladies who worked in the kitchen at her school.

His mustache was habitual but since he quit shaving, his mustache took control of his mouth, hanging down over his lips, partially hiding his lips. Joe had a wide mouth for such a skinny face and his grin revealed big, white, straight teeth. This very grin charmed Darla right out of her pants the first night he came to the house. Billene could hear them thrashing around in bed, and she wondered why in the world they would choose to mess up the bed by wrestling in it when they would have so much more room on the floor.

When Joe saw her that day, after school, his famous grin appeared. She was not too charmed since he had bits of food stuck in his teeth. His mustache was clumped together with food and moisture from the last swigs of beer he practically sucked from the bottle in his hand. His shirt, on at least its fifth day, hung open half way to his waist, rather enhancing the smell, arising from his lack of bathing.

Still, he was the man who married her mother, who earned their bread, well, most of the time, and didn't he, after all, deserve a little recreation after endangering his life in the mines and working such long hours for them? *Of course he does,* she remembered thinking.

"Come 'ere, honey," he slurred through his soggy mustache. "I got somethin' yere' gonna lak." It was not the first time she had seen that look in his eyes, but there was nothing she could do. She walked up to him with the intention of giving him the usual kiss of greeting on the cheek then going inside to change her clothes and do her homework. As soon as she was within reach, she knew what was coming.

Billene had missed her mother badly after the accident, but never so badly as that afternoon, and now, while she watched him stumbling through his letter. *Who would write to him anyway?* she asked herself. *He doesn't know anybody who can write. Well, he knows me. Maybe he does know someone else who can read and write."*

Joe stood suddenly, looking around, *for me,* she thought. *Oh God!! He's looking for me again.* She sat very still hoping he couldn't see her under the azalea bushes; hoping she could avoid another bout with him. She quietly felt herself and looked at her hand. Still bleeding.

Joe began walking toward the road, crumpling the letter in his hand. Every few steps he looked around again as if watching for someone. Billene could see him as he approached the trash bags he had set out for pickup the next day. As he approached the bags, he paused and looked around for her again. Not seeing her watching him, he stuffed the letter inside the nearest trash bag, looked around again, just in case she might have come back into view, then headed back toward the house, coughing and spitting.

When he reached the front porch of the cottage, he again took a seat on the top step and reached for his now empty beer bottle. He lifted it to his lips, threw back his head as if for a long swig, then realizing it was empty, he heaved it with a curse into the woods surrounding the house on three sides.

The forest around their home was heavily littered with Joe's empties. When this bottle hit the ground, Billene could hear glass shattering. Before the sound of the impact, Joe headed into the house for another. Since the kitchen was in the back of the house, Billene knew that, for a moment, he would not be able to see the road. She counted a few seconds, then darted out from under the azalea bush, ran to the street and reached inside the trash bag where she had seen Joe hide the letter. It was damp already from the other trash, but she got it and quickly pulled it out, hiding it in the pocket of her cut-off jeans.

She could hear Joe coming back toward porch. His coughing was loud enough to announce his presence fifty yards away. She ducked behind some bushes, then slipped quietly down the Goshen Trail toward another secret shelter hidden among some wild elderberry bushes, next to the road.

She liked this spot, because Joe was less likely to find her there. She could hear any vehicles coming up the road and see anyone walking without being seen. All she had to do was keep quiet and watch, but this time, instead of watching, she pulled the crumpled letter out of her pocket and began reading in the fading afternoon light.

There was no date on the letter and no return address. As soon as she saw that it began "Dear Darla," she realized, "This fool don't know my mama's day-ed." Quickly, she turned the letter over to see if there was a signature. It was signed,

"All my love,
Your husband,
Bill Parsons."

My Gawd!! she thought. *This is from my real daddy.* She turned the letter back over and began reading.

"Dear Darla,

"I know it's been a long time, since I been away, up here in the pen. I ain't forgot I promised to never git in touch on account o' the baby. What I was accused and convicted of was jist horrible. I kep swearin' and swearin' I never done it but nobody believed me and I thought I was gonna be put to death. Hell, I been on death row for 12 years. Thank the good Lord that lawyer and all them anti-death penalty people kep gettin' them appeals goin.' They would o' fried my butt for sure, but wouldn't ya jist know it. After all this time, they come up with a new kinda evidence - they call it D-N-A. I got no idea what them letters stand for, but it's some kinda way they can tell one man's seed from another's. They tested my semen an' compared it to the semen they found in that dead girl's body and they say there weren't no chance of it bein' mine. They finally proved what I been tellin' 'em all along. I'm innocent. I never done that terrible thing to that poor Trudy Griffin, Ben and Lu-Anne's kid. They don't know who done it yet, but they know it twern't me.

"I'm comin' home Darlin.' I know you divorced me an' all, an' I don't blame ya.' Ya might even have a new man for all I know an' if ya do, there's nothin' I can do about it. I'll respect your choices, if you made some like that, but I hope ya didn't git married agin, cause I love ya Darlin.' But if ya did git married agin, I hope you'll jist let me see my little girl. Ya know I never even seen her, afore they arrested me an' by the time she was born I was already in the slammer. I ain't never even seen a picture of her. I bet she looks jist like you. You sure were pretty. I laid awake many nights in this hell hole dreamin' o' seein' you again, an' holdin' my little girl in my arms. Hell Darlin,' I didn't even know what you called her. I didn't even know my little girl's name - only that the baby was a girl.

"My ma used ta come up here to see me an' she tole me it was gonna be a girl. But you know my mama passed away after I come up here. I think my gittin' put away like this flat out killed her. God I miss seein' her. An' I miss seein' you.

"I'll be home real soon Darlin.'

"All My Love,

"Your Husband,

"Bill Parsons"

Billene was quietly sobbing as she finished the letter. "my mama called me 'Billene' for my daddy," she muttered to herself. "My daddy's comin'. Maybe he'll take me away with him — away from ole Joe Cleod. God! My daddy's comin'!"

Chapter Three

Copperhead's only sidewalk sagged here and heaved there, over huge roots of the old growth elms that lined the classiest road in town, or so thought Giuseppe "Chigger" Bartalucci, sarcastically. He was reluctant to call it a "street," since it had no curb, no gutter, no thought to drainage for when the heavy rains came. He was thankful for the elms. The shade guarded his fair complexion from the sun, not that the sun is so fierce in Copperhead, West Virginia, but fierce enough to give him a burn in just a few minutes, if he let it. The sidewalk appeared some thirty years ago because Danny Maguire went to the mayor of Copperhead and said, "I want a sidewalk on my damned street. Put one there."

So Jessica Lane got itself a sidewalk. The street took its name from Danny's mother at the behest of his father, Dan Senior. Dan Senior went to the Council and offered a substantial bribe if they renamed Tupper's Row to Jessica Lane. The Maguires usually didn't have to ask twice when they wanted something; not in Copperhead, West-by-Gawd!

Albert Maguire, Dan Senior's great grand daddy started the ball rolling when he won an old rundown coal mine in a poker game, back in 1800. The fact that it was in a remote, unsettle region, halfway to the top of Crayfish Creek, didn't faze him. That dilapidated hole in the ground evolved into seven very active mines over the next few generations. Danny Maguire was filthy rich and provided jobs for most of the people in that and three neighboring counties. When Danny Maguire wanted something, he usually got it.

Chigger turned left at the entrance to Maguire's house. The two story clapboard affair with the steep hip room sported huge, bulging bay windows on both sides of the centered front door. The white paint was in good shape, framing a large elaborately carved door with a gargoyle doorknocker, front and center at eye level. Smiling, Chigger knocked on the door with the knuckles of his right hand. He had heard the demonic laughter recording in the past, set off by moving the doorknocker. *I wonder who the old man wants me to kill, this time. He summoned me all the way from Palermo.*

Maguire liked Chigger Bartalucci. He always got the job done, no matter what it was.

The latch clicked and the door swung open toward the inside. The stiff-looking young man at the door eyed Chigger from head to toe, then said, "What's in the bag?"

Chigger knew this game, too. If he reached into the bag to pull out the bottle of wine he brought for Dan Maguire, he could be shot dead on the spot. He handed the bag to the young man and said, "A bottle of wine. See for yourself."

"You haven't changed a bit," Maguire greeted him. "Same tan blazer, blue twill shirt, army boots and Don Johnson Whiskers. I don't even think you've aged. How long has it been?"

Maguire had not changed, either: plaid flannel shirt and all. His full head of steel gray hair framed his heavy glasses. His stomach pushed slightly over his belt. His cheeks puffed as he talked and his beard had not been touched since Sunday morning when he attended Mass, something he never missed. They sat at Maguire's favorite desk, the kitchen table. Maguire pulled the corkscrew out of the wine bottle, smiling at the satisfying pop. "Fatascia Almanera Sicilia. What have you brought me this time?"

"It's Black Cherry, one of the most popular Calabreses in Sicily" Chigger answered as he poured.

After a few sips of the Callabrese, Maguire cleared his throat, a signal Chigger recognized as the pronouncement that something of import to Maguire was about to be made perfectly clear. Chigger had seen the newspaper lying on the table. Aside from the wine glasses and the bottle, there was nothing else on the table. Now Maguire pushed it toward him.

"About twelve years ago, a little girl here was raped and murdered. Her name was Trudy Griffin. She was a cute little thing. Her daddy is one of my supervisors. They arrested the wrong guy, a man named Bill

Parsons. He was one of my truck drivers in the quarry. He did twelve years before they found him innocent on the basis of DNA evidence. They busted the wrong guy, and almost executed him. I'm going to offer him his old job back, if he shows up here."

"Shit happens," Chigger eased his chair closer to the table to look at the newspaper. "Where is the guy now?"

"On his way back here, I suppose." Maguire cleared his throat. "He was just released a few days ago, with a huge settlement for the bogus incarceration. Since he left, there were no more murders around here, until last week. Check the paper." Maguire again pushed the newspaper closer to Chigger. "It couldn't have been Parsons. He was still in the slammer when this one happened.

"They found this one in the same place as the other one, way up on top of Chad's Knob," Maguire continued.

Giuseppe Bartalucci narrowed his eyes. With long, slender, white fingers and carefully manicured nails, he lifted the paper to read the article. As he scanned it, he muttered just loudly enough for Maguire to hear him. "You know what we do to guys like this back home in Sicily?"

"Yes." Maguire almost sighed the word. "I do know. I want you to find out who this guy is that did this to these little girls and make him disappear. I don't want this kind of scum running around loose in my neighborhood. I don't care how long it takes, but I don't know of anyone else on this planet who is better able to do this than you. Are you willing?"

Copperhead, West Virginia (Two weeks later)

Copperhead's only convenience store, The CCS, had been doing business in the same location since it had been built sometime around 1950. They sold gasoline, diesel and kerosene in the parking lot. Customers for groceries, cigarettes and other things crammed their cars together in what remaining space they could find. The large white painted wood clapboard building had two large windows on either side of the entrance, used primarily for advertising special sales and special items available from time to time, like different kinds of live fishing bait, fresh apples and sometimes apple cider. One small sign in the window on the left, in the lower right hand corner said, "Greyhound Bus Stop. Tickets available inside."

Mag Johnson was at the pump in front, filling her old Chevy Coup with gasoline. The sun stood high in the sky. The air bristled with the promise of high heat later in the day. A couple of baby thunderheads competed with each other at respectable distances for height and power. The Country and Western music blaring from a speaker in the area of the pumps was suddenly drowned out by the sound of a large diesel engine powering a Greyhound Bus up the hill to the CCS. It pulled into the front parking lot a little too fast, raising a cloud of dust that motivated old Mag Johnson to start shaking her fist and shouting at it, just as the cloud of dust hit her directly. The bus came to a stop and the door opened. Mag left her car and stomped into the store to complain.

One lone passenger descended the steps. He paused on the last step, raised his eyes to look around for a moment, as though smelling the air for the first time, then took the last step to the ground. His short cut red hair was mostly concealed by a baseball hat, brim pointed forward, that said, "Pittsburgh Pirates." His squared chin was set in determination, accenting a brow so habitually furrowed that even when he relaxed, the creases remained. The pallid complexion hinted at long incarceration and the lines around his eyes suggested this man had seen the worst life has to offer, and the best, but not recently. He placed his one item of baggage, a hiking pack, on the ground to unbuttoned the light vest he wore over a cheap but neatly pressed and clean long sleeved flannel shirt. He picked up the pack and walked into the store where he went directly to the cashier. When it came his turn, he looked the young woman behind the counter directly in the eye, which she evidently found disconcerting. He said, "My name is Bill Parsons. They told me you could tell me where to find a room."

When Parsons left the store, he walked to the street and turned left, heading for the south end of the small town and the Slipped Dysk Lounge where he had been told he could rent a room, short term. Bill didn't notice a man, seated in the shade to his left, as he walked away from the store. This man could have been easily taken for a homeless vagabond, probably passing through. He wore old faded jeans, so threadbare that his knees were about to burst through the cloth and amazingly well cared for army boots. He wore a full brimmed canvas hat barely allowing the observant to notice graying in the coal black hair at his sideburns; the very observant might also have noticed his hair was surprisingly well groomed for a man in such otherwise desperate condition. As Bill Parsons disappeared from sight, the vagabond stood. With long slim fingers and immaculately manicured nails, he reached for a heavy pack by his side. He shouldered it and went off at a very respectful distance from his quarry, Bill Parsons, pacing himself so that the distance between them increased gradually.

CR   BO

Earlier that same morning, westbound on I-64,
just west of White Sulphur Springs, West Virginia

"Look, honey. There's a deer."

"Where, Mom?"

Camila James Hardy slowed the car so her twelve year old daughter Angie could see - AND- to give herself more time for braking if the deer decided to step in front of the car. She pointed ahead and to the right. "No! There are six of them! Aren't they beautiful?" She reached up with her right hand to swipe a lock of blonde hair out of her eyes. "I'm going to have to cut this," she moaned softly. "It's getting in my eyes again."

"You sure don't see things like that in Boston!" Angie announced. "Is this what it's going to be like where we're going to live?" She was seat-belted in on the shotgun seat of the red four door 1993 Bonneville.

"I haven't seen the place yet," her mom answered in a disappointed tone. "Your dad said he'd send pictures, but he never did. It's on a road called Goshen Road, way up on the side of a mountain. I'm pretty sure we're going to see deer there."

"He's NOT my dad," Angie objected. "My dad was a hero. This guy's..."

"Oh stop that," Camila snorted. "He's a good man who works hard..."

"That's not what they're saying about him in Boston!" Angie was testing her newly learned lessons in sarcasm.

"You know that stuff isn't true! He's not like that. Oh look! We're above a really deep valley and it's all full of clouds!"

"It looks like they're all sleeping down there. Mom, do clouds sleep?"

"No." Camila considered explaining what clouds are and decided Angie probably already knew the answer to that. "We'll be in Copperhead pretty shortly. Your dad said he found a really nice house for us up on the side of that mountain. You'll probably see lots of deer, maybe even black bears."

"Is that where we're going to live? In the valley where the clouds sleep?"

"I suppose it is," Camila answered.

"Why would it take Bevin so long to find a house for us? He's been here three weeks, already."

"Look, Sweety, call him 'Dad.' Humor me. It'll make everything easier for everyone. He said his Aunt Marvelynn died and left him this house a little over a year ago. He wanted some time to get it ready for us. I think you'll like it. There's a creek and woods and lots animals..."

"Yeah," Angie interrupted. "...like snakes. Isn't that why they call the town Copperhead? What a name!"

"I suppose it's better than Rattlesnake."

Copperhead, West Virginia, provided a Grand Entrance for those coming from the south. It consisted of a large sign on the side of the road, broadcasting to the world, in large, copper-colored letters shaped like snakes, "You Are Now Entering the Incorporated Town of Copperhead, West Virginia." Just beyond on the right stood a dilapidated bar with neon lights flashing the words, "Cold Beer," under a larger sign that read, "Slipped Dysk Lounge." On the north side of the bar stood a long, one story building with many doors, obviously a motel of sorts.

"What a dumpy looking place!" Camila snorted. "I hope this isn't the only restaurant in this town." Unexpectedly, she slowed the car. "Isn't that man striking looking?" She pointed at Bill Parsons who had not quite made it all the way to the motel. "And look at that one!" Half a mile behind Bill, Chigger Bartalucci was still shuffling his feet to stay far enough behind to remain unnoticed. "The second one looks homeless but the first one looks like he has a story."

"They're just bums," Angie retorted.

Not far past the Slipped Dysk, Camila turned left on the County Road, up the mountain, then left on Pigg's Cemetery Road then left again on a poorly maintained dirt road called Goshen Trail.

ౘ   ౙ

That Evening, just Before Sunset

Giuseppe "Chigger" Bartalucci perched himself under the covered walkway in front of his room next to the Slipped Dysk Lounge, right next to the room rented by Bill Parsons, that afternoon. The week he had spent in the neighboring town, reading the archives of the "newspaper of record," taught him who was what in Copperhead. He learned all he could about the town, the people, the way of life and most importantly of all, everything that had been recorded about the murder that took place twelve years ago at Chad's Knob and the murder that had taken place two weeks ago in the same place. Then he returned to Morgantown and turned in his rented automobile, placed his luggage in long-term storage and took the Greyhound Bus back to Copperhead.

Chigger had been sitting on his small chair for almost an hour before the door next to his opened and Bill Parsons emerged, newly showered and in fresh clothing. Bill looked around, sniffing the air, then seated himself in the chair in front of his door. It was a plastic lawn chair, marred with mildew and dust, just like the one Chigger was using. Bill said nothing. He leaned back with his head against the motel wall and watched the traffic rolling up and down the hill in front of the building.

The Hit Man waited for what felt like a respectable amount of time, then he broke the silence with, "Good evenin' neighbor." The one thing Chigger hated about working in the United States was having to learn these regional dialects. He did it to avoid being recognized immediately as an outsider. His constant fear was a slip-up, so he talked to as few people as possible and tried to keep the conversation, if there was one, as short as he could. This time, he chose a Western Pennsylvania accent. If he admitted he wasn't from the immediate area, people tended to be more forgiving about his accent and less likely to recognize he was a born and raised Sicilian.

Bill Parsons shifted in his chair and glanced over at Chigger. "Good enough, thank ya and same to ya." He volunteered nothing more.

How am I going to finesse him into talking a little bit? Chigger wondered. "I wonder if there's any work around here? You know of any?"

Parsons obviously wasn't looking for a conversation. He shifted in his chair again, crossed his legs, then uncrossed them. He turned and looked at Bartalucci for almost a full minute, sizing him up, before answering. "If yer lookin' fer a job, I'd go to Maguire Enterprises," he said as he turned back to face the street. "They have an office about half a mile up the road on the right. They own quarries, coal mines. They have a trucking company with a couple of divisions — flat bed, dry freight, reefers — but their main line is hauling rock and coal. If there's work to be had, that's where it is. Old Mr. Dan Maguire is a good man to work for, too. He takes good care of his people. I'm going to go there tomorrow morning myself."

Chigger couldn't stifle the slight smile at the friendly words Parsons had spoken about Bartalucci's own employer. He began liking the man in spite of himself, but there remained a test. What sort of man is this? Good man? Bad man? Confused man? Pervert? What? The opportunity to find out was now walking down the street. There were four young girls. Their shorts were too short and their manner playful. Chigger guessed they were the right age for what he needed right now. They were probably on their way to some school function. There was a school about half a mile farther down the road. "Some girls, ain't they?" Chigger sniggered the remark. "Just the right age, eleven, twelve, thirteen..."

Chigger stopped in shock. Parsons was standing over him, glowering. "They're children! What kind of sicko are you?" He said it loudly enough that the girls stopped and looked, then paused longer to see if there was going to be a fight. Parson's stance obviously required a quick and decisive response. The Hit Man wanted no trouble here and especially with a man who had just proven himself respectable. Another door opened, two doors toward the lounge and a head popped out. It was a grizzled looking fellow of some heft, probably a coal miner with muscle from head to toe.

"Bill," Chigger began. "Calm yourself. Sit down."

Parsons remained standing, but backed off on his aggressive stance. Aware of the new audience, he spoke much more softly, "Time for you to answer some questions. To start with, how do you know my name?"

"Bill. Please. Sit down, so the audience goes away. We'll talk."

Parsons remained standing for a moment, then, still glowering at Bartalucci, returned to his plastic chair. The grizzled head two doors down retracted back into its room. The girls lost interest when Bill returned to his chair and they continued down the street and out of sight. Parsons turned to Chigger and said, "Okay. Talk."

Chigger cleared his throat, at least half in honor of Dan Maguire. "Dan Maguire and I go way, way back. He brings me in for special projects every now and then. Part of the project I'm here to work on this time is to find out who the real killer is whose work you got blamed for. Dan doesn't like it when his people get in trouble and punished for things they didn't do. He also doesn't like it that someone is shitting in his front yard. He wants me to make that stop. I made those remarks about those girls to test you. You pass."

Parsons kept his gaze fixed on the road in front of the motel. "Just how do you plan to go about finding who the real killer is? Sounds like finding a needle in a field of hay stacks."

"I have my ways. By the way, it won't help anyone if you mention to anyone that we talked."

Chapter Four

Summertime, and the livin' is easy, Billene mused to herself as she explored down the Bulleevard towards Pigg's Cemetary Road. *Catfish are jumpin'...* She glanced at the creek, down over the hill, beside the road. *No catfish in that creek. Maybe some trout, now and then...* The old house where Abigail Dyke died about a year ago had been empty since then, but now there was a blue minivan parked in front, with Massachusetts license plates. Billene marveled to see the house had been freshly painted. A man on the front porch worked at replacing the screen that through Billene's whole life had been torn, with large pieces missing. A movement, up ahead caught Billene's eye. *There's someone coming!*

She disappeared into a stand of sumac and elderberry beside the road. She watched. The sounds of a staple gun attaching new screen to the porch distracted her, but she kept her eyes glued to the road, sure she wouldn't be seen. A grackle shrieked overhead, a locust buzzed nearby, but she could hear the soft sounds of the stranger's footfalls as he made his way up the road, dislodging a pebble here, kicking a stone out of the way there. He was coming closer. His slow pace allowed him to study the ground as he walked, glancing from time to time at the creek down over the hill. He wore a floppy wide- brimmed hat, more or less concealing his eyes, but Billene could see that they darted everywhere. His worn army fatigue jacket hung loose and open in front, stretched slightly by the huge pack he had over his back. *Looks like a strong man... not big, but strong... who IS he?*

At that moment, he stopped, turned his head and looked directly at Billene through the sumacs and elderberry. *Oh God! He can see me!* He paused only for a moment, as though memorizing her, then looked away, continuing his study of the ground and the surrounding forest. When he reached the driveway to Abigail Dyke's house, he paused a moment longer, studying the tire tracks going into and out of the large yard. Then he continued until he was out of sight, up the road, toward Billene's home with Joe Cleod and, beyond, Chad's Knob.

Who is he? She waited till he was out of sight, then a few minutes longer, to make sure he was far enough up the road that he wouldn't see her when she emerged. *Who is he? No one comes up here — 'cept the po-lice, and then only when there's trouble ... like when they found that girl, up the road ... still don't know who she is ...er... was!* Billene shook off the chill of fear that swept over her every time she thought of it. *Coulda been me! I wonder if Joe Cleod did that! God! I hope it wasn't him.*

Picking her way slowly up the road toward home, she kept a wary eye ahead, hoping to not overtake the stranger by accident. As she rounded the first bend, she spotted him and leaped back, out of sight. Then, hugging the foliage alongside the road, she crept forward again, to spy on him as he made his way toward Chad's Knob. When he got to her home, he paused again, just as he had in front of Abigail Dyke's home, studying the tracks into and out of the entrance path to the home. Then he paused again, raised his eyes as though to look at the sky, or sensing something interesting. Then he turned suddenly and made direct eye contact with her again.

Startled and fearful, she jumped back out of sight and stayed out of sight for a full minute. When she peeked around the corner again, he was gone. Vanished! *Where'd he go? He couldn'ta made it up to the far turn that fast ... must be in the woods!*

Billene backtracked a few yards to a secret path she knew of that would bring her around to the back of her home. Still fearful, she watched ahead and around her all the way and when she got near the cottage, she slowed even more, trying to be absolutely quiet, picking her way through the beer bottles Joe had thrown into the woods all around the house.

There was no sign of the stranger behind the house. She inched her way around the side of the house toward the front. When she got there, she was appalled and terrified to find him standing on the spot where Joe normally parked his van. Joe was at work, so the van was gone. Billene watched a moment to see, if she could, what he intended to do. It seemed that he was studying the ground and the surroundings. She thought she could be away and up through the woods faster than he could, especially since she knew the paths, so she stayed a moment longer to watch. With horror, she realized he had seen her again. This time, he didn't break the gaze, just raised one hand in a silent greeting. Then he turned and began making his way back toward the dirt road. *What thin, long fingers. Does he use them to kill people?*

She stayed where she was, watching the man make his way to the road, then turn right, up the mountain, toward Chad's Knob.

She stayed at the house for the next few days, afraid to leave, especially when Joe left to go to work at the mine. The ground under her azalea bush was getting worn from her constant presence. From there, she could see both the house and the road. Her vigil was fruitless. The stranger didn't return, at least while she was watching. When her fear began to subside, she wandered down the hill again toward Abigail Dyke's house to see what was going on.

Now two vehicles occupied the yard, both with Massachusetts license tags. The second one was an old red Pontiac Bonneville, streaked with dust as though it had driven through rain at high speed but didn't get the dust completely rinsed off. Billene crept closer, wondering, wide eyed, who her new neighbors could be. They were obviously moving into the house. So rapt was her attention to the house that she didn't notice Angie Hardy approaching from farther down the road. Billene jumped when Angie announced herself, "Hi. I'm Angie. What's your name? Are you one of my neighbors?"

It was only then, and for the first time, that Billene noticed the tire tracks entering and leaving the driveway. They were old tracks, but still obvious, despite some rain that had fallen over the last few weeks. What was odd about them was the fact that one set of tracks turned right out of the driveway, or left into the driveway, from the direction of Chad's Knob. *Strange,* Billene mused. *Maybe they were exploring ...*

"Yeah. Hi. I'm Billene Cleod. I'm prob'ly yer only neighbor. I live about half mile up the road from you. You muss be from Massachusetts."

"How did you know that?" Angie demanded in a cute, friendly tone.

They became instant friends. Billene knew the neighborhood and Angie knew about outside of the neighborhood. They could talk endlessly, sharing their experiences of the here and the outside world. Billene warned Angie about the stranger and told her about the murder that took place just a few weeks earlier. "They was cops everwhere. State cops, county cops. They even had cars and SUV's that said 'FBI' on them. They was all over the mountain — specially up at Chad's Knob."

"Who got killed?" Angie wanted to know.

"No one knows." Billene paused to straighten her shirt. "She must a been from somewhere else. She wasn't from around here."

Billene was delighted when Angie asked her to come up to the house for some lemonade. She wanted a closer look at the place since it was getting fixed up, but she had been afraid to go closer with that strange man who was there. That thought got her thinking about the stranger she had seen a week or more earlier. *Who was he? He was no bum. Shoes were too new. The rest of him was pretty raggy. Maybe he stole the shoes.*

The house was better built and bigger than the one she lived in with Joe Cleod. It had two stories. The fresh paint made it look new and the screen around the porch was finished now. Some of the steps leading up to the porch were new and also freshly painted. When they walked in the front door, they were greeted immediately by Angie's mom, Camila James Hardy.

"Where have you been?" she demanded of Angie before giving Billene a second glance. "This could be dangerous around here. I want you to stay in the yard. And watch out for snakes. Who's your friend?" Letting up finally, she stood back, hands on hips, swiping a lock of blonde hair out of her eyes.

"Mom, this is Billene Cleod. She lives just up the road from us."

"You'll probably be going to the same school in the fall. My husband is going to be the assistant principal this coming year. Would you like to meet him, Billene?"

Billene glanced at the floor, shy, averting her gaze from the direct and powerful one of Camila Hardy. Glancing up and then away again, she murmured, "Yes, Ma'am. Thank you."

"It's okay to speak up, Billene. No need to be afraid of me. I'm trying to get a job teaching fourth grade. There's an opening, but you're way past that age group. I won't be your teacher, but Mr. Hardy will be your assistant principal." Turning her head toward one of the rear rooms of the first floor, she called out, "Bevin? Bevin? Come meet one of your new students."

"How about some iced tea or some lemonade?" she asked the girls.

As Camila busied herself in the kitchen, cracking some ice cubes and pouring drinks, Billene could hear footsteps coming from another room. The floor of the house was hardwood, tongue in groove boards, so they creaked. Camila showed up in the door of the kitchen at the same moment as Bevin "Beaver" Hardy showed up in a different doorway. "Here are the drinks, kids. I got one for you, too, Bevin. I'm assuming you're thirsty after all the work you've been doing."

Billene glanced up at Camila, smiled at her image in the doorway with the thick blonde hair, sleeveless print blouse and knee length shorts. Then she turned her gaze on Mr. Hardy. Her eyes grew wide. Her mouth dropped open and she took two steps back. He was a thin man, but tall. His face was very narrow as the result of being on one end of a very narrow head. *His blue eyes are a little bit too close together, for him to be all right in the head,* she thought.

"My goodness, child!" Camila swiped a lock of blonde hair out of her eyes as she held the tray for a moment with one hand. "Are you okay?"

Billene glanced at the front door, nervously judging its distance, then she turned her eyes back to Mrs. Hardy. "He looks like my step-daddy."

"Hell! We might be related!" Bevin Hardy took another two steps into the room. Billene retreated, about to run for it. "What's your step-daddy's name?"

"It's Joe Cleod," Billene answered, trying not to be obvious about gritting her teeth when she said it.

"Hell! Joe Cleod's my half brother! I haven't seen Joe in years. We lost touch. Is he our next door neighbor?"

"Yes sir," Billene grimaced as she glanced again, fleetingly, at the door. Then as the realization settled in, she glanced at Camila with fear, wondering if she would die in mysterious circumstances like her own mother did. Taking a deep breath she turned her eyes to Angie wondering if the same fate awaited her that Billene herself was experiencing at the hands of the half brother, Joe Cleod!

"Well," continued Bevin Hardy. "I haven't seen my brother in at least twelve years. I'll have to drop by and pay him a visit. Does he still work at the mine for old Dan Maguire?"

"Yes sir," Billene felt she was losing her voice. "He's at work now." She had to get away. Her feet wanted to run as fast as possible — through that door she kept glancing at, but she had to be polite and Angie was her new friend. She didn't want to hurt Angie's feelings by running out the door as soon as she met her parents. Besides, this man probably wasn't as evil as Joe. Mrs. Overby at the school liked to say, *We can pick our friends but we can't pick our family.*

She calmed down, had the lemonade and excused herself as soon as she felt she gracefully could. Then she ran all the way up the road to her cottage.

Chapter Five

At the bottom of the hill, below the high school, a lone brick building adorned a well manicured lawn with professional landscaping, including a low brick planter that ran the length of the front of the building. The planter contained mums, petunias and some other plants Bill Parsons couldn't identify. Fresh paint on the building's wood trim indicated a county budget that placed the appearance of law enforcement in high priority. In front of the building, a police cruiser blocked the entrance sidewalk that led up to the front door. This was no impediment to Bill, though. He had walked down the hill, past the high school, from the Slipped Dysk's motel, where he had spent the night.

The building had smoked glass windows, so he assumed he would be observed as he walked up to the door. It was a heavy pull-open, aluminum, also with smoked glass. The sign above the door said, "Sheriff's Office," and below that, "County Police." In finer print, under all of it, the sign continued, "Billy F. Rankin, County Sheriff." There were phone numbers. Bill noted the glass on the door had not been cleaned in quite some time. Neither had the windows to the sides of the door.

The last time, Bill Parsons walked through that door, he was in handcuffs. He had a bruise on his cheek where one of the cops had laid a fist during the arrest; sort of a vengeance blow, for the act he was accused of committing. Other bruises were less visible. The police were contemptuous, venomous in their treatment of him, convinced they had the right man, a vicious sex offender who had murdered and raped a little girl by the name of Trudy Griffin.

Bill had gone fishing, up Crawfish Creek, running alongside Goshen Trail, the road leading up the mountain, to Chad's Knob. He had a pup tent and sleeping bag and other camping equipment. He planned for it to be a two day outing and unfortunately, he had gone alone. The day was dreary but not cold. The fish were biting and he had caught enough that he decided to trek on home in the morning instead of spending a second day up the mountain. He pitched his tent between Goshen Trail and the creek and was awakened late that night by an automobile of some sort, driving up the trail. He wondered why anyone would be headed for Chad's Knob so late at night, but then he smiled, assuming it was some young couple looking for a safe place to park for a few hours; a little privacy...

A little later, he heard the vehicle coming back down the road. It didn't seem to be in any hurry and that would make sense because Goshen Trail, that far up the mountain, is no road for fast driving. He didn't even glance up to see if he could see anything. He just assumed the young couple were ready to head home and face the parents for being out so late. He smiled again and went back to sleep.

In the morning, instead of working his way down the creek, following the path he took, fishing his way upstream, he went out to the road and took the easier path, on the road, in plain sight. A police car came by, headed up the road, driven by Billy Rankin, himself, a lowly deputy in those days. Half an hour later, several more police cars came up the road at a higher rate of speed than might be regarded as safe, considering the condition of the road and the terrain. Billy Rankin was coming down from Chad's Knob. The police cars stopped in front of him and three burly police officers emerged, roughly placing Bill Parsons under arrest. An ambulance rushed by, slowing to get past the many police cars, and then continuing up the mountain toward Chad's Knob.

"What's goin' on?" Bill asked the arresting officer.

"You'll find out! You son of a bitch!"

Over the years Bill spent in the penitentiary, the anger seeped away. He lost everything. His new wife, Darla, divorced him. His life was over. Prison, he thought, would be where he would meet God.

Bill reached for the door handle on the sheriff's office door, grasped it and pulled it open. He had come to make peace. He bore the police no anger or ill will. The ill will he felt for so long, wore him out, wore him down and he finally let it go. Now he just wanted to come home to Copperhead, West Virginia. He grew up in this place. His father had worked the mines and his mom, a petite smiling lady with a knack for cooking, fussed over his clothing and homework. Now he had no mother or father. There were no aunts or uncles, brothers or sisters. He was alone in the world, except for his daughter who was now in the custody of a stepfather, somewhere. He didn't know who the stepfather was or where he might find his daughter. He knew he would not be able to claim legal custody and intended to avoid disrupting his daughter's life with his presence. But he had to know where she was living — that she was okay. He also wanted to be able to see what she looked like. It was all small stuff that he wanted, but he wanted it very badly.

The sheriff's receptionist wore a telephone headset. The light from a computer screen highlighted her face. A stack of correspondence on her desk was being systematically stamped with a signature stamp that said, "Billy F. Rankin." She continued studying the computer screen, while talking on her telephone headset and stamping signatures on the sheriff's latest political campaign for re-election. The nameplate on her desk said, "Sally Colletti."

After allowing Bill to stand there for at least five minutes, she concluded her phone call, but continued stamping letters while she glanced up at him and said, "May I help you?"

Bill shuffled his feet, cleared his throat and said, "I'm Bill Parsons. I'd like an appointment with Sheriff Rankin. I'd like to speak to him."

The friendly look in her eyes went blank. She continued to just look at him for a moment, then as though clearing her thoughts, she shook her head slightly, put down the signature stamp and said, "I'll see if he's busy. Maybe you can speak with him right now."

She dialed a single digit on the telephone. She said into the receiver, "Mr. Bill Parsons is here to see you. Do you have a minute?" Then she returned her gaze to Bill and said, "He'll be right out." Then she stood, walked around the desk and went outside. Bill waited and not very long.

Sheriff Billy F. Rankin emerged from his office with his service pistol drawn, just as two other officers came in the front door also brandishing firearms. Rankin had gained considerable weight. His belly hung over his uniform belt and he couldn't move very fast. He practically blustered when he said, "I never thought you'd be such a fool to come in here! You are under arrest for the murder and rape of the unknown female we found three weeks ago at Chad's Knob. We didn't have any trouble after you left, but now that you're back, we got another body. You have the right to remain silent..."

His treatment was again rough. He was bruised and battered when he landed in the county prison, one more time. His one permitted phone call was to his attorney in Morgantown. When he was questioned, he refused to talk to the police without his attorney being present except for one comment, directed to Sheriff Billy F. Rankin. "Sheriff. I come in here to make peace with you, to tell you that after all this time, I was no longer angry. But this is how you treat me! The anger is back and this time, my lawyer and me will pay you back in coin that you will understand. Maybe in the future, the county will look a little closer before it jumps to conclusions and acts on them. A man just can't be in two places at the same time."

An hour after his phone call, Parsons was not only released, but driven by a county patrolman to the nearest hospital, in Beckley, where his bruises and abrasions were photographed, documented and treated. Parsons drove home his promise for payback by writing a check for $100,000 to the campaign fund for Joe Perry, the candidate for sheriff who was apposing Billy F. Rankin. When Perry contacted him to thank him, Parsons said, "If you don't think that's enough, please let me know. Don't forget TV ads. I don't think Rankin can afford that."

Parson's lawyer, William C. Dagget, commented, "False arrest, assault and battery, defamation of character, liable and false imprisonment. It's a slam dunk. When that last kid was killed you were still in prison in Morgantown. And they still have you on the sex offenders registry after being fully vindicated! Let's go for twenty five million? Settle for fifteen? With a little luck, they'll even have to pay the attorney's fees. There's civil rights stuff going on here too. What a gift!"

03   80@

The excitement wasn't over for Bill, for that day. Before he was released from the hospital, two men showed up, dressed in jeans and button-down-collar shirts. They took seats outside his door without introducing themselves. Bill watched them with apprehension as the doctors and nurses completed their examinations and treatments. When he was permitted to rise from the hospital cot to leave, both men stood up and greeted him at his hospital room door.

"Mr. Parsons? I'm Mick Jaber and this is Marlin George. We work for Maguire Enterprises over in Copperhead. Mr. Maguire asked us to come over here to make sure you're okay. Are you?" Jaber moved to put his hand on Bill's arm in a gesture of friendliness, but Bill brushed it off in distrust.

"Why would Maguire have any interest in me?" He took a step back from them trying to decide if he needed a defensive posture. *What do these guys want?*

"Mr. Parsons. There's no need for concern. Mr. Maguire says Copperhead is his hometown just like it's yours. He knows you were seriously wronged and he wants to talk with you about making things right.

He just wants to talk with you. Will you come with us? After, we'll take you back to your motel, maybe get you dinner somewhere. Whadya say? Will you come?"

Bill swiped his hand across his nose, a nervous gesture. Mick Jaber seemed to be the one to do all the talking. He was around 5'11" with thick, closely cut black hair, broad shoulders — *he's apparently a muscle freak,* Bill guessed. Jaber's eyes were an intense brown, shadowed by thick, black eyebrows. The man he introduced as Marlin George was more on the paunchy side, also close to six feet in height. *Big guys!*

"I drove eighteen wheelers for Mr. Maguire, nationwide, before all the crap happened. He was a good boss. Fair. I'll talk to him."

The drive back from Beckley was uneventful, filled with truck driver stories. "Man! First time I was in Barstow... Yeah... I quit goin' to Brooklyn. Got wedged under a bridge there. The bridges are marked wrong. They say twelve feet of clearance but they're usually fourteen feet — but sometimes, they're really twelve feet. The truck was thirteen and a half... Vince Lombardi rest area is full of lot lizards. I'll never forget..."

Maguire was his usual self. It was Friday. His five days' growth of beard was almost long enough to require clippers. "'Scuse the beard," he smiled as Parsons walked in. "I only shave before Mass on Sundays. One of the perks of bein' the boss. No dress code." His smile broke into a grin as he invited Bill to his favorite desk — the kitchen table.

More small talk followed, during which Maguire offered Bill, alternately, a glass of wine, a shot of scotch and a beer. "Never touch the stuff," Bill answered each time, "but thanks. Some of my family had a problem with it. I always thought the best way to avoid the problems was to just never drink."

Finally, Maguire cleared his throat. Even Parsons knew that was the signal to listen, even though he had never spoken with Maguire, one on one, before that day. Maguire stood, turned his back to Bill and gazed out of the window into the rear yard. "This is my home, Bill. I got grapes growin' out back this year. Maybe I'll make some of my own wine, come fall. I got azaleas growin', over there —" he pointed. "Come see. They bloom nice in the spring."

Parsons rose from his seat at Maguire's favorite desk and joined him at the window. "I like my home, here, in Copperhead, Bill," Maguire continued. The people here are my family — all of 'em. Most of 'em work for me in one way or another, so I depend on 'em for my bread and butter just as they depend on me to provide jobs." Maguire paused, glanced at Bill, then back out the window. "Bill. About twelve years ago, someone shit right in my lap. I didn't much like that. Someone did wrong to my family and then made it worse by doing wrong to another member of my family — you."

Maguire returned to his favorite desk and poured himself a glass of wine. He sat down while Bill returned to his seat. Maguire took a sip of his wine. "It's Fatascia Almanera Sicilia," Maguire remarked with a wide smile, as he put the glass back down on the table. "It was given to me by a good friend who I asked to come and help me clean that shit out of my town."

Parsons listened in silence. The persona of the famed Maguire was well known in Copperhead and the nation over, on the highways where his trucks delivered cargo. Maguire's reputation was quite good for his philanthropy, his organizations, but just why he was so feared was never quite clear to Bill, so he listened and kept his mouth shut.

"After you went to prison," Maguire continued, "there were no more murders or rapes. Everyone thought they had the right guy, because of that. We were wrong. Everyone was wrong ... and you sat in prison, for nothin,' for twelve years." He raised his eyes and looked directly at Bill and with heavy emotion he said, "Bill, I can't give you the twelve years back. I can't give you your wife back, but I can help you now and this is how."

"But there's nothin' you can do," Bill shuffled his feet under the table, then crossed and uncrossed his legs. "It's done. What's done is done."

Maguire's brow furrowed deeply. His eyes turned to a steely hardness and the tone of his voice dropped to almost a growl. "Oh, but there is, and I'm doing it."

So intense was the change that Bill almost drew back. The change was from the demeanor of a kindly benevolent, economic leader to that of a cornered Tasmanian Devil. *Geez! I hope he never gets mad at me!* Bill's thought was spontaneous and involuntary, then he wondered if Maguire was armed and if he should flee the house.

"The first thing I need to do is protect — YOU. When this comes down, if you're in the neighborhood, you'll be blamed. I've arranged for a driving job for you. It's out of Oshkosh, Wisconsin. I know you don't have to work, but this will protect you. You'll be hauling freight between Chicago, Kansas City and Minneapolis. What this will do is prove where you are, all the time. The electronic log books and your appearance at loading docks in that region will eliminate any possibility that you could be blamed for anything that happens here ...and somethin's goin' to happen."

"Mr. Maguire, I came back to Copperhead to make peace with the local police department, but the most important thing I want to do here is find my daughter. She..."

"Your daughter is fairly safe. It could be better, but it's good enough for now. I know where she is. I'll make sure she stays safe. When this is over, I'll make sure you get to meet her, maybe even get custody. Ya gotta trust me, Bill."

"How long?"

"Can't say." Maguire brushed a crumb off the table. "Maybe a few weeks. Could be a few months. When it's done, you're probably gonna hear about it, even way up there in Oshkosh, but I'll send for you before that."

Chapter Six

Half a mile down the hill from Chad's Knob, on the dirt road whose name was Goshen Trail, Giuseppe "Chigger" Bartalucci studied the bushes alongside the road. Something was not right. It didn't look right. He cleared his mind and focused into the forest. *Something is there that doesn't belong. And there is something with the bushes... Ah yes — this twig is out of place. It doesn't float freely, as it should. Something passing brushed against it and it is now hung up over the twig next to it. That's what's wrong.*

Chigger slipped between the bushes as smoothly as a deer, disturbing nothing. There were wild raspberries, other thorny vines. There was vervain, blooming with its purple flowered stem, and numerous ground plants, low to the ground, that he neither crushed nor bent. No twig or tree branch snapped back as he passed. His movements were absolutely silent. With each step he paused to scan for movement, color or any other sign that meant something was present. He saw nothing, but he could feel it.

My teacher, the Keetowah would be proud of me. Giuseppe Bartalucci joined the Italian Military as a young man, the branch called *Esercito Italiano* — general Army stuff. From there he moved into the Carabinieri, or military police. His superiors recognized uncommon talent and moved him to a secret branch of the Italian military, camouflaged with the name *Commando Raggruppamento Subacquei Incursori Teseo Tesei.* They were commandos, but Giuseppe's group was special with special teachers and special techniques. The Keetowah belonged to the Cherokee Nation. He said his name was too difficult for Italians to pronounce. "Just call me Sam." The Keetowah was recruited from the American Forces after World War II. He liked Italy and Sicily, so instead of going back to his "occupied nation," he stayed to teach.

Giuseppe became so skilled in the art of being invisible that he was loaned to the American Forces, to teach as well as to learn. There he learned that he loved studying dialects, perfected his imitation of American English and met Daniel Maguire.

The Keetowah taught him to understand the language of the birds and the squirrels, to recognize the difference between a warning call, a mating call and simple joyful chatter. It was a warning call he heard now. A mockingbird was giving its threatening hiss. Not far off, above him, a mockingbird was announcing its nest was close, there were young in it and he better not get any closer. He returned the warning with the sound of a loud kiss, repeated three times, about ten seconds apart. It was a reassurance that he meant no harm. The bird stopped hissing and watched him with distrust.

He slowly sank to his knees, wondering if the mockingbird had warned someone else of his approach. He stayed in position for about twenty minutes to make sure nature had time to settle down and get used to his presence. Moving on, he took pleasure in watching the other wildlife around him, all the time watching for the presence he felt in the forest. His movement was slow and methodical, silent. He wanted to see and not be seen, the highest skill of the sniper. But no sniper was he today. He was gathering information, studying the area around Chad's Knob, searching for any sign or clue that would give him guidance. On one of his long pauses, he gradually became aware that directly in front of him stood an extremely well-camouflaged hut. The roof and walls were woven branches, apparently water-tight and probably warm against the winter winds. It hid under what appeared to be a carefully contrived deadfall. Shocked that he got so close without recognizing it, he froze in position for another twenty minutes before approaching to investigate for a door or entrance of some sort.

He found what he was looking for, an opening low to the ground. One would have to crouch very low to enter it. Its covering was like the walls around it, woven branches with gaps plugged with mud. He was considering looking inside when a voice behind him caused his heart to leap in surprise; shocked that he had been caught without knowing another was so close. That was something that just didn't happen to Chigger Bartalucci!

The voice demanded loudly, "Freeze, stranger! If you so much as twitch a whisker, I'll blow your beatin' heart right out of your skinny body."

Chigger slowly stood, lifting his hands away from his sides to show that there was nothing in them and to express submission. When he came fully erect, he raised his hands over his head and said, "I meant no intrusion, sir. I apologize for my presence."

"Turn around, stranger. Let me see who got so close to my place without my knowin' it!"

Chigger slowly turned to face his potential antagonist. The man stood about five feet eight inches tall with straw colored, graying hair that had not seen a scissor or knife in decades and a beard to match it. His homemade Ghillie suit was so effective that Chigger could have looked straight at him from five feet away and not seen him, except for the barrel of a twelve gauge shotgun aimed at his chest, protruding from the suit. The man had moved the material out of his face so he could see Chigger better and were it not for that movement, the hair and beard would have remained invisible.

"Why are you here?" the Ghillie suited figure demanded.

"I will tell you," said Chigger. "How long have you been in this place?"

The Ghillie suited figure sat back on a stump behind him, the shotgun never wavering. He scratched under an arm pit, spit to one side and said, "I asked first, but out of hospitality, I'll tell you. I haven't moved off the top of this mountain since George H.W. Bush was president. How long ago was that? I've lost track. Now you. Why are you here?"

"Then you've been on this mountain for at least twenty-five years. How can you do that? Life is hard, alone, isolated like this."

"Quit beatin' around the bush," Ghillie suit snorted. Why are you here?

"May I lower my hands? I am not threat to you."

"Lower 'em. But I got you covered. If you make any odd moves, I'll shoot you in a heartbeat. We're far enough up the mountain no one will even hear the gun shot. Answer."

"Someone has been killing little girls on this mountain and leaving their bodies over here at Chad's Knob. I'm here to find out who that person is and to make sure he NEVER does it again. That's why I'm here."

The point of the shotgun dropped to a non-threatening position. "I'll be damned," Ghillie suit muttered. "so that's what he was doin' up here. And that's why there were so many cops and dogs afterwards." Ghillie suit's demeanor hardened suddenly from the reflective back to the aggressive. "How do you know it ain't me?" The gun barrel came up again.

"I don't think you were in White Sulphur Springs three weeks ago. Were you?"

"Ghillie suit started chuckling. "Hell! I don't even know where that is.""

"And I don't think that, twelve years ago, you went into town and snatched a girl on the way home from school, either. Did ya?"

"I don't think so," Ghillie suit answered with a wry smile. I'd probly remember somethin' like that. But I'll tell you what. I seen that guy come here many times. He comes under a full moon. After that time, years ago, I didn't see him for a long time, then he showed up, about three weeks ago, as you said, under another full moon. Same guy. Older, but the same. Must have been away for a while. Before that time, years ago, he used to come up here pretty regular. I can always hear him drivin' up the road.

"How'd you sneak up on me so easy, anyway? Nobody can do that."

Chigger smiled, memories flashing through his mind of his old teacher. "My teacher was a Keetowah."

"Hell," bellowed Ghillie suit. "I'm a Keetowah! Maybe that's how I caught you. The voice of the mockingbird warned me. Then I heard your kisses. I knew."

Chigger shifted his feet. "Mind if I sit down?"

"Sit, but you can't stay. I don't entertain visitors. Gotta say it's nice to see another human face that isn't tryin' to kill me."

Seated on the ground, Chigger ventured, "If you don't mind my asking, I'm pretty sure that when the police were up here and the FBI were here, they used dogs to search the woods. How did you avoid the dogs?"

"I shouldn't tell you my secrets. Your Keetowah should have told you. Well-trained dogs lookin' for a man, don't chase deer piss and rabbit shit." He held up one foot to reveal a smooth bottomed handmade deer skin shoe that appeared to be streaked with brown and black. "Deer skin don't smell like a man and soaked in deer piss and rabbit shit, the moccasins smell like deer piss and rabbit shit, not like a man. I also stayed off of Chad's Knob, so they didn't pick up any scent from me at all."

"I'll be living in the woods nearby, till the man comes back," Chigger told the Ghillie suit.

"I ain't gonna git involved in this," Ghillie suit muttered. "But I'll tell ya this. If you're asleep and you get awake to the sound of the mockingbird's kiss, that's your heads up. He's either there or on his way. And he don't come 'cept when the moon is full."

"When this is all done, can I get you anything? If you've been up here on the mountain, you must have some need of supplies. Can I send anything for you?"

Ghillie suit smiled and stood. He pointed the twelve gauge shotgun at the sky and pulled the trigger. The sound it made was a sharp 'click.' He gave it a pump to re-cock it and pulled the trigger again. It went 'click' again. "Twelve gauge shotgun shells would be nice, and maybe a gallon of gun oil?"

"They call me Chigger." Chigger held out his hand to shake. "Ghillie suit grasped his hand and said, "Spook."

ଓଃ   ଥ

Daniel Maguire sipped a glass of wine as he watched a deer nibbling at a blossoming rose in his back yard. He could hear his wife moving around in the kitchen. Despite his offers to hire a cook, she insisted on doing the cooking. Tonight it was to be sauerkraut, mashed potatoes and a pork roast. Maguire liked his wife's sauerkraut *(as long as she doesn't do it too often)*. He smiled at the thought. Life was normal. An axle had broken on one of his quarry trucks that day. He closed one of his coal mines temporarily to replace some of the reinforcements holding the Earth above the heads of the miners. The phone hanging on his hip represented the only change in his life in the last few weeks. It was a cheap truck stop variety that had no name or address registered to it. All it had was a number and no matter how carefully anyone checked, they would never find out whose hand held it. Maguire purchased two of them in Parkersburg using cash — no credit card trail. The one thing that COULD be traced was the location — *damned GPS — or triangulation!*

The phone he cursed in his thoughts now tweeted once, softly. He opened it to find a simple text message. It said, "1. 2?"

So. Chigger has a suspect — maybe two.

Chapter Seven

Camila James Hardy stood in her classroom door. She still waited for word on her fourth grade teaching job application, but summer school was okay, for now — *even if it is seventh grade arithmetic.* She brushed the ever present lock of blonde hair out of her eyes that she kept meaning to trim. *It's sexy* was her justification for putting it off. Angie was home with strict orders to stay in the house — "Ya never know what perverts you might meet out here on this dirt mountain road."

"Ah Mom! It's safe enough. Perverts don't come out in daylight. Besides who would come up here, anyway?"

"That little girl they found a few weeks ago up there on Chad's Knob was just about your age. You stay in the house."

"Mo-om!"

"Read or something."

Camila heard a door slam down the hall and probably around a couple of corners. The echo reverberated through the halls. Plaster covered concrete walls, pock marked with banks of lockers, overlooking a linoleum floor over a concrete slab — *great for uplifting acoustics! Why can't they give schools a softer ambience? No wonder the kids are so ratcheted up all the time!*

She heard other doors opening and closing — the other teachers arriving. Her class had thirty two students. The day was typical and humdrum. Attendance. Exercises. Personal assistance. *They don't look like much. No wonder they flunked math last year.* Some were intent on success while others acted out, as they probably did in class all the previous year. *Kids! I wonder what my teachers thought of me.*

Bevin showed up around mid-morning. His assistant principal job got him summer school duties — a chance — they said — to get his feet wet, meet some of the students and the other teachers. "Learn your way around. Summer school ain't much but it'll gitchou the flavor of the community. You'll feel more at home then, when school starts in the fall."

She heard the knock on the door; it opened to reveal the grinning face of her husband, Assistant Principal Mr. Bevin Hardy. She smiled at the interruption, glad to see him. *He always looks so fresh. Of course, it was ME who ironed his shirt. Great teeth, Mr. Bevin.* He introduced his companion for the morning, Ms. Sherry Paulus, assigned to him by Principal Jim Gibbons, to fill him in on the things he was seeing, with the added task of reporting back to Gibbons as to her impressions of Hardy — strengths, weaknesses, foibles — etc. Sherry Paulus was about fifty percent Native American — a Conoy, part of the once proud Shawnee Nation. Although Sherry never made the claim, Gibbons believed she was a Shaman and a psychic. Her wide, fierce brown eyes and don't-mess-with-me demeanor led many to believe that. Her practice of Indian healing methods and the fact that they were usually very effective, reinforced this perception among her peers. Today she wore a loose-fitting heavy print blouse, brown loose-fitting slacks and sandals. Her very thick black hair was drawn into a single tight braid that dangled half way down her back.

He introduced himself to the class while Sherry took up a position beside Camila, her arms crossed, studying the situation. Bevin then went around the room greeting each student, paying particular attention to the girls, mock flirting. Jeannie, not one of the brighter ones, even remarked to him, "I like you Mr. Hardy. When I grow up, I'm going to marry you!"

He straightened up, glanced at his wife with a smile and said, "You might have some competition there."

Sherry leaned toward Camila and without smiling muttered, "We best keep an eye on that one."

Camila forced a smile and retorted to Jeannie, "I believe he might be taken. Check the wedding ring on his left hand, Jeannie. If you look closely, you might even notice that it matches mine." Camila shook her head slightly — *Wow! Why the sudden burst of jealousy? She's only twelve years old. What's the matter with me? Keep an eye on her? Why?*

Mrs. Hardy watched in amusement as her husband schmoozed the children, interacting with humor and wit, or so she thought so. Camila joined in where she could, trying to offer positive input on behalf of the children, especially for the ones who seemed the most withdrawn. *Nothing like a little praise to bring out the best in a frightened child.* Sherry Paulus remained planted in the front of the room, arms crossed and brows furrowed, watching carefully. Camila noticed that some of the children seemed vaguely afraid of Sherry and avoided eye contact. The children in the front of the class even turned their backs on her, watching the action behind them with the new assistant principal. Others of the children seemed to know Sherry and greeted her warmly when she entered the room behind Bevin.

When the visit was over, Sherry left first, followed closely by Camila's husband. As Bevin left, Jeannie half stood in her desk, waving. "Goodbye Mr. Hardy. You remember, when I grow up..."

Lunch was too short. Camila packed into The Teacher's Room with several other teachers and tried to join in the conversation as she inhaled her lunch.

"How's the new experience going?" one teacher asked

"Great," Camila tried to reply with her mouth full. "Mr. Hardy came by around mid-morning with Ms. Paulus to introduce himself to my class." *Trying to avoid rubbing it everyone's face that I'm married to the assistant principal.*

"He's your husband, isn't he?" Camila cringed. They knew.

"Yes," she replied after swallowing. "We were really lucky to be able to get these jobs so quickly. Of course, he was hired before we moved, but my getting the summer school position was pure luck."

"That Sherry's a trip. Isn't she?" This came from a middle aged, thin man named Mr. Layton.

"Well," Camila began, "I didn't really get a chance to get to know her, but she certainly is striking." *Sherry is downright strange. Best to keep my mouth shut till I know my footing, if I will ever know my footing in this place.*

"She's amazing," Layton continued. I came to work one day with a sprained wrist. She said, 'let me fix it.' She put her hands on it and the soreness just vanished. Indian magic, she called it."

"She's also a major computer geek," a Miss Carlisle chimed in. "If you have any problems with your computer, she's the one to ask for help — first. Your husband grew up here, didn't he? I bet she knows him. She grew up in Copperhead, too."

CB   BD

Billene, much farther up the mountain than the school, worked her way down the road, past Abigail Dyke's home, all the way to Pigg's Cemetery Road. *What a strange name for a road,* she mused as she tossed a rock over the side of the road, trying to hit the creek. Flowering time was over for the trees and most of the bushes around her. Some goldenrod flashed its bright yellow flowers and chicory punctuated it with its blue petals. *Joe likes chicory in his coffee sometimes. Maybe I should get some for him.*

She paused after rounding one bend to watch a large rattlesnake slither into the bushes as she approached. *Damned snakes is everywhere.* She threw a rock at the snake, striking its side. The snake stopped, coiled and hissed at her. She was far enough away that it didn't concern her. She threw another rock, hitting it again. The snake started rattling and opened its mouth, wide, revealing large fangs. She knew the snake would not come after her. Rattlesnakes tend to be defensive and territorial, not aggressive like moccasins can be, much further south. She knew about moccasins because Joe talked about them sometimes. She took a seat on the ground and watched it. In a few minutes it stopped rattling, and continued on its earlier course.

"You're very brave." A voice startled her. She jumped involuntarily and the voice started giggling. "I didn't mean to frighten you. Sorry." It was Angie Hardy, from up the road.

"If I was brave I woulda picked it up and petted it," Billene replied. "Rattlesnakes is nothin'. Ya jist have to give 'em plenty a space an' they'll leave ya alone. Now, copperheads is somethin' else. They don't warn ya. How do ya'll like yer new house?"

"It's boring," Angie announced. "In Boston there were cars coming past all the time and people on bicycles. There was a park nearby with a small lake and in the summertime people would come and sail model sailboats in it and remote-control motor boats. There were ducks and wild geese, sometimes. There was always something going on. Here, there's nothing." Angie slapped her hands to her sides in emphasis.

Billene was not deterred. "Ever seen a rattlesnake in Boston? I mean a real, honest to God, live, wild, rattlesnake?"

Angie came closer and as she passed Billene, looking tentatively in the direction where the snake had disappeared, she answered, "Well. No. Do you see them very often?"

"Not often," Billene pushed herself off the ground. "But often enough, an' if ya ask me, that's too often. I got no use for 'em; copperheads, neither."

Just then they heard the sound of a truck engine laboring up the hill. "That's my stepdad," Billene muttered as she headed for the side of the road. "I don' like him seein' me, if I can hide. You should come, too."

"Why should I hide from him?" Angie wanted to know. "If he's my uncle, I'd sort of like to meet him."

"You do whatchou want." Billene vanished in the undergrowth beside the road, watching carefully to avoid disturbing the rattlesnake or some other disagreeable creature, but she stayed close enough to the road to be able to see what was happening, to be able to jump out to protect Angie, if she needed it.

Joe Cleod's white van rounded the bend, coming into sight. Angie stood by the side of the road watching it. Billene, concealed in the bushes, watched too. The van stopped beside Angie and Joe's face appeared in the right side window. "Well. Ain't chou a perty sight. Where'd you come from? I'm Joe Cleod."

Angie put her hands on her hips, cocked her head and said, "I'm Angie Hardy. I'm your new next door neighbor and my stepdad says Joe Cloud is his brother."

"Bevin? Izat Bevin? Heeza one 'at moved inta ole Aunt Abby's house?"

"That's his name," Angie answered. "He married my mom a couple of years ago. My real dad was killed in Vietnam. He was a hero. Did you have to go to Vietnam?"

"Nah. Neither me nor Bevin went. By the time we was old enough, the war was pretty well windin' down. No Vietnam fer us." Joe's tone dropped, signaling to Billene that he was about to come up with something — not nice. "Where is Bevin? I'd shore like to see 'im."

"He's the new assistant principal at the school. He's there today. So is my mom. It's summer school."

"So." Joe cleared his throat and looked around to see if anyone was in sight and he said, "You alone, today? Come on, git in the van, I'll drive you up to your house."

At that point, Billene knew she was needed. She knew his tones so well. Billene stepped out of the bushes and called out, "Hi Joe. You home from work early today?" Billene didn't know if Joe would harm Angie or not, but she wasn't taking any chances. This was no way for her to meet her new neighbor Joe Cleod.

"Well hello, Billene. Whatchou doin' way down the road like this?" She could hear the disappointment in his voice and hoped there would be no reprisals later.

"Jist goin' fer a walk, same as Angie, here. I had to chase a rattlesnake further into the bushes."

Angie's eyes grew big. "There was a big rattlesnake. Billene was throwing stones at it. It coiled all up and was hissing at her."

"Yeah," Joe fidgeted in the van. "She shore can be hell on 'em snakes.

Why don't both of ya git in the van an' I'll give ya both a ride home."

"Hey thanks, Joe," Billene hedged. "We were enjoyin' the walk. I wanna bring home some chicory for your coffee, and I ain't picked it yet. You go on ahead an' I'll see ya a little later."

How 'bout you, good lookin'? Ride home?"

"Don't do it," Billene hissed at Angie.

Without understanding, Angie took her cue. "I'm going to stay and help Billene. I don't even know what chicory looks like. I guess Billene will show me."

"Well." Joe slid back over to the driver's seat. "I guess I'll git on down the road. By the way. It's Cleod — not CLOUD."

As Joe's van disappeared around the next curve, farther up the road, Angie turned to Billene and said, "Why are you afraid of your stepfather?"

Billene lowered he head, a little bit like a bull, and moved toward a clump of chicory beside the road. "This is chicory. You can recognize it by these blue flowers. Some say it goes well in coffee. Want some? All ya have ta do is rinse it off a little bit and make sure they ain't no bugs in it."

Angie stepped closer. "Why are you afraid of your stepdad? I've never seen anything like what just happened here. Why are you afraid of him?"

Billene turned her attention away from the chicory and looked Angie right in the eye. "I ain't afraid of him for me. I'm afraid of him for you. He done me all the harm he can *(I think he killed my mom)*. I don't want him to do no harm to you. He's evil." She returned her attention to picking chicory, tears running down her cheeks. Angie was the first person to ever hear a word about Joe Cleod from Billene. The release was too much. The repressed fear and loneliness, the isolation with the horror of regular submission to rape, refused to stay hidden after she made that one quiet opening: *he is evil.* The tears came, but she would say no more about it.

Angie just hugged her till the tears began to subside to a gentler sobbing. "My mom wanted me to stay in the house today. She said there are perverts around Why did she say that?"

"There was a girl's body found up on Chad's Knob, just a few weeks ago — that's way up at the end o' this road at the top o' the mountain. I heard she was from White Sulphur Springs. That's far from here. No one knows how she got there. She was raped and murdered. Yeah. There's a pervert around here, somewhere. No one knows who, 'cept, maybe, me. But Joe wasn't outta town. He didn't bring her here."

Billene had stopped sobbing. Angie released her. "We came through

White Sulphur springs on the way here from Boston a few days ago. I know about where it is. You're right. It's far from here."

Chapter Eight

Diary of Sherry Paulus

Dear Diary,

The monster is back.

He didn't recognize me. I've gained weight. My hair is longer and I now wear glasses, sometimes. I have breasts and my thighs are now those of a woman. I am no longer the starry-eyed, skinny, twelve year old girl that he raped and tried to murder on Chad's Knob, nineteen years ago. He has forgotten me. I have not forgotten. He stole my life. He ruined me. My Conoy/Shawnee/Algonquin blood still boils with rage!

I remember the story my father told me of Catahecassa, the Great Shawnee Chief and his young son Quaskey (Black Hoof). Quaskey had trapped many beaver and traded the pelts with an American Trader for a horse. He named the horse Wind Flying. Wind Flying stood seventeen hands. His legs were long and muscular. He could outrun any of the other horses in the tribe and when he did, his tail and mane would fly in the wind like the flags Quaskey had seen on the White Men's forts. Many had tried to trade with Quaskey to get that horse, but Quaskey loved the horse and refused to trade. When the British came to try to enlist the Shawnee People against the Americans, they stole his horse!

Quaskey was not fully grown, but he was fully enraged. He gathered his weapons together, determined to set out all by himself, and kill all white men, not just the British. The Great Chief Catahecassa of the Wapakonetan Shawnee found his son, about to set out on foot. The Great Chief put his hand on his son's shoulder and said, "You are a boy. Not all white men are evil, just as not all the Real People, our people, are good. When you become a man and you have reached your full growth and strength, seek out the white man who wronged you and kill him. But wait until you have your full growth and your full strength."

I always cry a little when I remember this story. The loss of a favorite horse, though, was nothing compared to what this evil man took from me. He filled me with fear of men. Oh! I'm not afraid of anyone, but to allow a man to get near me, after what happened, after the pain and the horror, fills me with fear. This man stole my husband and my children because, without his evil, I could have had those things. He stole my life. I am now full grown. I remember the Great Chief and his son, Quaskey, who also became a great chief. My father said we are descended from those great men. In my veins rushes the steaming blood of the Wapakonetan Shawnee, the Conoy, the Algonquin. It is time and he has returned to me.

He was a charming eighteen-year-old with a hot BMW, a year-old high school diploma and a good job at the quarry. I used to sit at the CCS and watch for him to drive past, stop for gasoline, maybe — buy a pack of cigarettes. He waved at me sometimes. I remember the thrill, now, with a sense of horror. One evening, late in the day, when he stopped to buy gasoline, he saw me sitting under the awning, watching him. He called me over to talk with him while he pumped his gasoline. He paid me compliments about my long dark hair, my fierce brown eyes. He was gorgeous, to my big, brown, twelve-year-old eyes.

"Hey, Kiddo. It's a full moon tonight, rising early. Why don't you hop in the car and we'll ride up to Chad's Knob and watch the moon rise? There's no view of it like that one!"

Nothing ever hurt like what he did to me. When he was finished, he put his hands on my throat and started to squeeze. I was really scared but not too scared to knee him in the crotch. As he writhed in pain, I grabbed my pants and ran, barefoot, straight into the woods, bleeding. My feet were bleeding. My crotch was bleeding. I had bruises on my throat, my arms, where held me down and my ass from the bumping I got on the rocks at Chad's Knob. I have never felt so betrayed! I loved him and he tried to kill me after forcing himself past my twelve-year-old hymen. I found a road, way down at the bottom of the mountain. I never told. Now I tell only, you, dear Diary. Tomorrow, I will start to make my special weapons.

Passers by, the next Saturday morning, wondered what the strange looking woman was looking for as she waded the shallows of the New River Gorge, not far north of the I-64 bridge. She had a small basket. Here and there, she would pause, reach into the water and pick up a small stone. Then she would throw it back and continue searching. When her basket was nearly half full of pieces of flint and quartz, she came back to shore and headed home.

Sherry was preparing for a ritual kill. She was making arrowheads after the manner of her people, chipping the pieces she had found with another stone until she achieved the shape she was after. She had not made arrows from scratch in many years, but she had not forgotten the skills. When she was quite young, her grandfather showed her how it was done and watched with satisfaction while his granddaughter struggled with the stone chips. Her determination to master the art overwhelmed her frustration at the nicked fingers and the broken pieces she had spent hours working on only to have them split when she was nearly finished. For the arrow's shaft, she chose native black cherry. For the bow itself, she chose white locust. Her bowstring would be composed of woven native hemp. It was doubtful that anyone would recognize the design and construction of the arrows as Shawnee or Conoy.

03 80

Way up north, Bill Parsons pulled his big rig into one of his favorite old truck stops just south of Oshkosh, Wisconsin. It was a Century Class Freightliner, pulling a fifty-three-foot box trailer loaded with huge roles of paper, 4,000 to 5,000 pounds each. The Planeview Travel Plaza, at the corner of Wisconsin Highway 26 and United States Highway 41, always had a parking spot for him if he got there early enough in the evening. They also always had cheese curds, unless he got there on Wednesday when they were always sold out. Cheese curds delivery comes Thursday. *Today is Friday. I haven't had a cheese curd in years.* His smile broadened as he walked into the restaurant. An image of a Piper Cub adorned the wall over the counter. The smell of fried food filled the air. The gift shop was still there and the cheese curds were stacked in one-pound packages on a table next to a "theater in the round" cash register station.

He took a seat at the counter and reached for the telephone on the counter that is usually available to the drivers. When Dan Maguire answered, he said, "Mr. Maguire, this is Bill Parsons. I'm in Oshkosh with a load going to Dallas. I'll be there the day after tomorrow. What's goin' on?"

"Oh, hi, Bill. We're makin' some progress, but it's not over yet. How do ya feel about bein' back in a big truck?"

"Much as I hate to admit it, it feels good. I'm in cheese curds country. I wish we could get that stuff in West Virginia."

"Well," Maguire chuckled, "we could import them, but by the time they got here, they wouldn't be squeaky anymore, like people like them."

"True. True. How's my little girl? I still haven't met her. You know, this is hard, what you asked me to do."

"I know, Bill and I'm sorry about that. This is for your protection. I don't think it'll be long. One of these days soon, your Qualcomm is going to go 'ping' and it'll be a message from me. You'll see. So, where ya goin' from Dallas? Do ya know yet?"

"Yup. I'm scheduled to drop and hook at the Bonnie View Road terminal. I'm gettin' a load of shredded paper goin' to Neenah."

As Bill headed west on Wisconsin Highway #26 toward Janeville, he munched on garlic and dill cheese curds and scowled at oncoming traffic. *What's 'at man have goin' on? Why's he have me in 'ese damned trucks? I paid my damned dues — twelve years in the freakin' slammer! I'd like some blood! But I don't know whose! Maybe Maguire knows!*

○ ◌

Billene hunkered back under her azalea bush in front of the Cleod cottage, watching Joe Cleod getting drunk on the front porch. *Maybe if he gits drunk enough, he'll fall down the porch steps and break his neck!* She visualized the image, then shook it off as too ugly. Besides, what could she do without him? He was her sole support and family. *Well... my real dad wrote that letter and said he's comin'. What's takin' him so long? It's been weeks since that letter came.*

Joe sneezed, wiped his nose on his sleeve. Then he held one nostril shut and blew the other one out on the porch floor, then the other nostril. *This man is truly disgusting,* Billene thought. *Another beer or two and he'll be lookin' fer me. I better git outta here.*

Joe heaved his empty out into the woods beside the house and went inside for another. Just then, Billene heard a car coming up the road. She waited, afraid to move for fear Joe would see the azalea bush moving and know she was there. The blue minivan turned into the driveway, such as it was — a dirt path leading from the dirt Goshen Trail to the Cleod cottage. The minivan parked behind Joe's white van. Bevin Hardy got out. Joe apparently heard the car door close and came rushing back onto the porch where he froze stock still. Mr. Hardy stood beside his car, smiling.

"Well. I'll be slap damned. My twin brother." Joe said half to himself. "Beaver Cleod. Where the hell you been? I thought you was dead."

Mr. Hardy started laughing as he approached the porch. "Ya got another beer?"

"Hell, yeah!" Joe headed back toward the kitchen and the refrigerator. "So where you been, Beaver?" he called over his shoulder.

Mr. Hardy took a seat on the top step of the porch and gazed out over what Joe Cleod called his front yard. Billene lowered her eyes, afraid he would somehow feel her looking at him, especially since he was looking in her direction. Joe returned shortly with the extra beer and the catching up began.

Hardy began. "First off, I changed my name. People kept callin' me 'cloud' instead of Cleod and I didn't much like it. Then there was that trouble Daddy got into years ago. People sometimes remembered and asked if I was related to him. What could I say? 'Uh huh'?"

"People don't 'member that much 'roun here," Joe slurred. "I juss work in the mine and keep my mouth shut, pretty much. What'd ya change yer name to?"

"Hardy. I have a wife, a step-daughter and a couple of college degrees since I last saw you." Bevin took a swig from the bottle Joe gave him. "I'm assistant principal at the school down the road. It was your stepdaughter that told me you live here. I guess you got married too, didja?"

"Yup. Shore did. I married Darla Parsons, but she was gittin' uppity. Had to get rid of her, but I kep' the daughter. She gotta be 'roun' here somewhere." He stood and looked around, calling out "BILLENE" in a loud voice. "WHERE YOU AT?"

Under her azalea bush, Billene remained quiet, eyes lowered, trying her best to stay invisible. *TWIN BROTHER! He lied. He said Joe was his half brother. Gawd! They were cut from the same cloth. I wonder if Hardy is as bad as Joe. Poor Angie! Well, she still has her mom, maybe she has some protection.*

Joe took a swig, blew his nose again and asked, "You still up to your old tricks?" He turned his gaze directly at his brother and a slow, evil grin formed on his lips.

"Oh. Every now and then I get the itch. You know what I mean."

Joe held the gaze and his grin faded slightly. "Was that one o' yours they found up on Chad's Knob about a month ago?"

Hardy took a long swig from the beer bottle and gazed out over Joe's small mountain of empties in the side yard. "You know we don't talk about stuff like that. You know what they used to say, 'loose lips sink ships.'"

Joe chuckled. "I shoulda known you was back. Nothin' like that's happened since you left. You better behave. They'll catch yer ass and when they do, they'll hang you high, after about thirty years in prison."

"Hush your mouth, brother. Beaver is careful. Maybe I oughta bring you along next time. Whadya say?"

"Well." Joe paused. "Sounds like it'd be fun, but it's jist too dangerous. I don't want to go to prison. Ain't no little girls in prison."

Billene listened in shocked disbelief. A rapist murderer was sitting on her front porch chatting with her stepfather about his crimes and they were talking about doing it together THE NEXT TIME! *I can't stay here.* She hugged her knees, bunched up in front of her. The horror and the danger she was in overwhelmed her. She just hoped they would not hear her sobs. *Where can I go?* She quivered with fear. *I can't go back in there. Ever!*

Chapter Nine

7:00 A.M.

Sally Colletti unlocked the door to the sheriff's office and seated herself at her desk. She turned on the computer and donned her headset, pulling out another sheaf of papers to rubber stamp with the sheriff's signature for the ongoing election campaign. She smoothed her short curly black hair away from the headset. The campaign was going badly. Deputy Joe Perry, who was running against Sheriff Rankin, had come up with some unexpected money and was running horrific television campaigns revealing unpleasant histories of Billy Rankin, anecdotes about his ineffectiveness in office and even attacking his personal appearance as unprofessional. *Doubt he's going to get re-elected. Hope I can keep my job.*

She picked up the rubber stamp and was about to begin when the front door of the building began creeping open. She stopped and watched. It was as though the door was too heavy for whoever was trying to get in. Sally rose from her desk, went to the door and gently pulled it open. There stood a little girl of about twelve years. Her long stringy red hair hung loose at her back. Her square face reflected light from the recent tears still wet on her cheeks. A nicely sculpted nose dripped slightly between pale blue eyes that looked almost wild with fear and darted all around as Sally opened the door. Scratches on her cheeks and legs led Sally to believe the girl must have been running through thorn thickets. Her tee-shirt was torn in spots. Her cut off shorts were mud stained and her bare feet left bloody footprints on the sidewalk.

"Come in," Sally invited, softly as she held the door open. "Here, have a seat."

The girl sat in the chair, shivering. "How about a cup of nice hot tea? I think we may have a couple of donuts around here, somewhere. Are you hungry?"

The girl wrapped her arms around herself and she nodded energetically. "Yes. Thank you."

As Sally moved around the office, heating up some water for tea and checking for donuts, she tried to chat — gaily, she hoped — to cheer up the little girl. After setting up a small portable table next to Billene's chair and concluding her cheerful chatter, she placed a cup of tea on the table with a paper plate bearing two donuts, one glazed and one covered with chocolate icing. "My name's Sally. What's yours?"

Billene looked up at Sally with doleful eyes that were tearing again. "If I tell you, you'll send me back. I can't go back."

"If you don't mind my asking," continued Sally, "Why did you come to the sheriff's office?"

Billene stared around the room fearfully. She glanced at the door, then back at Sally, still wearing her headset, with the plug-in wire stuck in a front shirt pocket. "My mama told me that the policeman is my friend. If I ever get in trouble to go the policeman and he will help me. I'm in trouble. Help me." She started sobbing again, her hands trying to cover her face, her shoulders hunched together, as though trying to embrace herself. Sally solved their problem and embraced Billene, holding her while she sobbed. This seemed to make her sob harder. Finally she began calming, then through the sobs she managed to say. "No one has hugged me since my mama died. It's almost two years."

At this moment, Sheriff Billy F. Rankin walked in the front door. He paused to survey the situation, put his hands on his hips and said, "What have we got here?"

By this time, Sally Colletti was in tears, crying almost as hard as Billene. She looked up at Rankin and said, "This little girl is in trouble. She says her mom, dead almost two years, told her the policeman is her friend and if she gets in trouble to ask the policeman for help and he will help her."

Rankin rolled his eyes, wiped his nose with the back of his hand and snorted, "Who is she?"

Sally was recovering her composure. She stood, her blouse smeared with blood stains from Billene's scratches, wet marks from both their tears; her headset's plug-in now dangled from her ear. "She's afraid to tell me. She's afraid we'll send her back and she says she can't go back."

"Why not?" Rankin demanded.

Billene started crying again and as she did so, she managed to get out, "Because if I go back, they'll kill me. I can't go back."

"What're you talkin' about child? The last thing I need today is something like this. I have the campaign to think of, there's still a child killer running around..." With that, he broke off and turned his attention more seriously to Billene. "How old are you, girl?"

"Twelve."

"Who do you think's gonna kill you?"

"If I tell you, he'll kill me for sure."

"Are you from Copperhead? Is this town where you live?"

"I can't go back!" Billene almost screamed. "I can't go back!"

Rankin poured himself a cup of hot water with a tea bag in it, looked around for some sugar and remarked, to Sally, "Why the hell didn't you make any coffee?" Then he turned back to Billene and said, "Ya gotta quiet down kid. Nobody's gonna hurt you. This is the sheriff's office and I'm the sheriff. I'm gonna make sure nobody hurts you." Rankin sat down in the chair beside Billene and continued. "Now, please tell me who you are and what happened that made you come here for help?"

Billene, calmer now, looked at Rankin and said, "If I tell you who I am, even if you don't send me back, you'll tell where I am. I need you to protect me, not tell or send me back."

Rankin took a sip of his tea, pulled the cup suddenly away from his lips because it was still too hot to drink. "Damn! I burned my lip. Sally..."

Sally was back on the computer, trying to look busy since the boss was right there. She stopped, took off her headset and said, "Yes sir?"

"It's almost eight o'clock. How 'bout call the school up the road there. I think summer sessions are going on. There's probably people there. Ask them to send someone over here who knows all the students. Let's see if we can identify this young lady."

About twenty minutes later, the office door opened and in walked Sherry Paulus. She took one look at Billene and rushed over to her. "Oh Lord, child, are you all right? What happened to you?"

Rankin came out of his office. "So you know her. Who is she?"

"Don't tell! Don't tell!" Billene started screaming.

Sherry stepped away from Billene and took the sheriff's gaze, eye-ball to eye-ball. "If she's afraid for me to do that, why should I? From the looks of her, she needs to be sent to a hospital and cared for, not kept sitting in a police station being questioned. Have you called Children's

Services in Beckley? She obviously needs help. Let's help her. My God! Look at her bloody feet, the scratches! Don't you people have any common sense at all!"

Billene watched and listened, wide-eyed. Sherry was a wonder — and a true friend. Within an hour, Billene was in the emergency room at the hospital in Beckley, West Virginia. Sherry took the day off from school to follow the deputy's cruiser in her own car, as Billene rode to the hospital.

Sally sat back down at her desk, put her headset back on her head and began working as though nothing had happened. *If Joe Perry gets wind of this, he'll make a major issue of it. I wonder where his money is coming from...* Sally eased her iPad from her purse, checked to see where Rankin was and what he was doing. He was in his office with the door closed. *Probably stuffing his face with donuts and reading* Field and Stream. Having booted the iPad, she clicked on "contacts," selected "Joe Perry" and began her message. "Be sure to check on the kid we sent to Beckley Hospital this morning. We need to find out who she is and what her injuries are all about. Thanks..." The second email was to Dan Maguire.

☙ ❧

Billene's curiosity and interest leaped as they entered the hospital. Her eyes never stopped moving. From the white clad personnel to the medical instruments she saw everywhere, something always waited just around the corner to fill her interest again. Sherry never left her side but she wore a bewildered expression on her face as she tried to answer Billene's questions.

"That's a stethoscope... Oh, that thing over there? That's a sphygmomanometer. No. I have no idea how to spell it.? What's it for? Taking blood pressures, I think. That thing, over there? I don't know. Maybe you can ask the doctor, when he gets here."

They kept Billene overnight and registered her as a 'Jane Doe.' Only Sherry knew who she was and Billene wanted to keep it that way. They pricked her and poked her. They looked at every inch of her body and as they did they shook their heads and murmured things Billene couldn't hear. They wrote things on clipboards and typed them into laptop computers. Other white-coated people came in and they shared what was written on the clipboards. Those seeing it for the first time would shake their heads and say things like "Good God!" and "that poor girl." Billene had begun to get over feeling sorry for herself, but with these people making these doleful comments, she began to think again about what had happened. *Thank God for Sherry! What a friend she is to hold my hand through all of this. ...and she knows me and she didn't tell!*

Sherry took a motel room for the night, to stay close in case she was needed again, and when she returned in the morning, there were two people with her, a man and a woman. The woman did most of the talking. She introduced herself to Billene. "Call me Amy. This is my sidekick for today." She referred to the man. "His name is Jeremiah. We're from Child Welfare of West Virginia and we're here to make sure you are okay and that you'll be safe. In fact we even have a safe place where you can come and live, for a while, until we find a better home for you."

∞ ∞

Two days later, the morning mail brought a medical report to the sheriff's office in Copperhead. It was Sally's job to open the mail. She spotted the return address of Beckley Hospital right away and opened the envelope. She skipped the intense medical language and went straight to the doctor's comments.

The patient Jane Doe has numerous lacerations of the face and upper body as well as the feet, obtained, apparently, in flight. The patient exhibits clear scarring and bruising resulting from repeated sexual abuse extending over a long period of time, complete with recently healed wounds and fresh abrasions and bruising in the vaginal area. She is suffering from syphilis for which she is receiving treatment. Recommend ongoing antibiotic treatment for the disease and psychological evaluation and counseling. Further recommend that she NOT be returned to her home, once that's identified, without an investigation as to the source of the sexual abuse. The Child Welfare Facility here in Beckley would be a far better choice, for the time being, for a domicile. Estimate the child's age to be between eleven and twelve years.

Sally photocopied the report, prepared an envelope to mail the copy to Dan Maguire and scrawled a note at the top of the page. *I believe this is the girl you're looking for, the daughter of Bill Parsons. She looks just like him.*

Chapter Ten

Sally Colletti, mind numb with boredom, continued stamping campaign letters for the sheriff. Her headset chattered all day. Seven speeding tickets filled out the daily log. An act of vandalism way down on the south side of town offered a slight variation from the routine. An angry boyfriend had scrawled the word "PIG" multiple times in white soap on his ex-girlfriend's black Toyota Corolla . When Deputy Joe Perry questioned him, he readily admitted it with intermittent ranting about why he did it. The boyfriend was now washing the soap off the car, under the supervision of Joe Perry. No charges were filed.

One interesting phone call broke the monotony of the day, from Sherry Paulus. *Why's she calling me? We were never friends! Maybe it's about the little girl...*

"Yeah, Sherry. How ya doin'? It was nice to see you the other day. It's been a long time. Any news on the Jane Doe?"

"You prob'ly got the report from the hospital. You prob'ly know more about it than me. Did you get the report?"

"Yes." Sally furrowed her brow at the thought. "Did you see it?"

"No. But I'm pretty sure I know what's in it. Did you forward it to the FBI?"

"No, Sherry. We don't report child abuse to the FBI. Murders and kidnappings, yes, but not child abuse. That's a local matter. What can I do for ya t'day?"

"I wanna talk to ya about something."

Sally put down her rubber stamp and closed the lid on the stamp pad. "So talk. Here I am."

"No. This is important. How about meet me at the CCS at 3:45. I'll buy you a sandwich and cup of coffee."

"Well, geez, Sherry. I have a husband and two kids to feed. I need to go home when I get out of here."

"This is important."

"Is this about that little girl that came in here the other day — the Jane Doe?"

"Indirectly. Yes. Maybe. You gotta be there by 3:45.

"Why?"

"If you get here on time, you'll see."

"Tell ya what, Sherry. Make it four sandwiches. Make them foot long, submarine sandwiches and I'll do it. If I think what you have to talk about it is worth it, I'll pay for three of the sandwiches. Deal?"

 C8   80

CCS customers tracked mud from the parking lot up the steps and all over the floor of the store. Not many people were shopping yet so early in the afternoon. Closer to 5:00 the store would become much busier. Sherry arrived early to make sure the four sandwiches were ready in time, so when Sally got there, Sherry was waiting for her on the bench in front of the store.

"We won't get splashed this far back from the gas pumps," Sherry greeted her. "And, oh. Thanks for coming."

"What's this all about, Sherry?" *She must have just got here from school.* "What time do you get out of the school at the end of the day?"

"About 3:30. I just got here a few minutes ago — in time to get these subs ready, so we don't miss the action."

"What action?" Sally demanded, wiping the rain off her face and shaking out her umbrella. This damned rain!"

"Sit down," Sherry ordered with a smile, handing Sally a cup of coffee in a Styrofoam cup with a tight plastic lid. "It's black. Here's some sugar packs and a couple of creamers if you want it. I even got you a little swizzle stick to stir it with."

"What do you think's gonna happen?"

"Nothing tonight," Sherry responded. "It's raining. But there's gonna be a full moon."

"So? We get one every month. What's special about this one?"

"Think back." Sherry took a deep breath like a long sigh. "What was the phase of the moon last month when they found that little girl from White Sulphur Springs?"

"It was a full moon. It was about a month ago."

"Twelve years ago, when they found that little Trudy Griffin, what was the phase of the moon that night?"

"I don't remember, Sherry. Was it a full moon?"

"Yes. Now think back a little further. When we were in sixth and seventh grades. Do you remember anyone getting raped back then — when we were kids?" Sherry had become very intense. Her eyes were darkened to almost black with her controlled passion. She wiped a wisp of wet hair out of her face and leaned a little close. "Do you remember?"

"There were rumors." Sally took a sip of the coffee. "It's hot." Just then, a blue minivan drove into the parking lot and pulled up to the pumps. Sally watched as the man got out of the car, pulled out his wallet to get a credit card, swiped it and turned to open his gas cap. She felt a slight chill run over her as the memories came back. She could feel Sherry watching her.

Sherry put a hand on Sally's wrist and said, "Do you remember?"

"My God! He's back. He was gone for a long time. I haven't seen Bevin Cleod in years. When did he come back?"

"Just about a month ago," Sherry answered, "in time to start summer sessions. He's our new assistant principal and his name isn't Cleod anymore. He changed it to Hardy somewhere along the line."

"He had a terrible reputation." Sally took another sip of coffee. "I always wondered if it was true — what the other girls said about him."

Sherry didn't answer immediately, then she muttered, "True enough."

Sally took the bag of sandwiches and opened her purse. "This is what you wanted me to see, isn't it?"

"Yup."

"You think it was him?"

Sherry turned her full gaze to Sally and replied, "Yup. That's what I think. He likes twelve year old girls. He likes to watch the full moon from up on Chad's Knob. He won't go there tonight. It's raining and cloudy. He won't be able to see it."

Sally turned her head to Sherry with a quizzical expression. "You been watchin' him for a while, haven't ya?"

"Yup."

Sally sat silently, sipping her coffee, watching Bevin Cleod pumping fuel into his car. He finished, collected the receipt from the pump, got in his car a drove off with only a glance at the two women. "So tell me, Sherry. When he left here, where did he go? Do you know?"

"Yes. He went to Indiana University of Pennsylvania. At least that's what the diploma hanging in his office says. He got a Bachelor's Degree in Education. Graduated in 1989. From there, he went to Penn State University where he got a Master's Degree in Public School Administration. That diploma says he graduated in 1993. From there he landed a job somewhere around Boston. That's all I got. Can you use it?"

"Yeah. How about find out where he worked near Boston. That would help too. How much did all this stuff cost?" Sally nodded to the sandwich bags as she fished in her purse for a wallet. "I'll pay for all the sandwiches. Does that answer your question?"

ରେ   ଛ

"Good morning," Sheriff Rankin smiled cheerfully as he entered the office.

"There's hot coffee, if you want it," Sally gestured at the Mr. Coffee on the table beside the sheriff's private office door. She went back to stamping campaign fliers. As the sheriff stirred some sugar into his coffee, Sally stopped, put down her stamp and took off her headset. "Sheriff, my I ask you a question?"

Sheriff Rankin turned to her and said, "Ask."

Sally shook her hair, brushed it back slightly and began. "I have an idea about those little girls that were raped and murdered. I don't want to make any accusations unless I'm pretty sure, but I'd like to do a little sleuthing on my own, if that's okay with you."

Rankin pulled up a chair beside Sally's desk, sat in it and leaned over slightly toward her.   Sally hated that because of the sheriff's constant cigarette breath. She leaned away from him and waited. "What, exactly, do you have in mind?" he asked.

"I want to request some statistical information from various places in your name and I don't want to do it without your permission."

"Be more specific," Rankin said.

"Sheriff," Sally parried. "If the search turns up anything interesting, I'll bring it to you and show it to you in an organized way, neatly laid out so you can go and arrest the guy. I don't want to stir up a lot of mud if I'm wrong. How about go along with me on this? Have I ever let you down?"

That afternoon, around 3:30, the front door opened and a man came in. Sally put down her rubber stamp and watched in amazement. *He looks just like Bevin Cleod, but he's not.* The man wore filthy work clothes, muddy boots, a gray flannel shirt with a dirty tee-shirt protruding at the top where three buttons to the flannel shirt were open. His long mustache hung slightly over his mouth and his head looked too narrow to contain the wide toothy grin he displayed when he greeted Sally. "My name is Joe Cleod. Is the sheriff around here somewheres?"

"He's not here, just now. What can I do for you Mr. Cleod?"

Joe wiped his nose on his sleeve and sniffed as he looked around the room. "Mind if I have a cup of coffee while we talk?"

"Help yourself." Sally slid her chair away from the coffee pot by the sheriff's door. *I'm not going to let this guy get behind me!*

Joe poured himself a cup of coffee then turned to Sally. "My step-daughter has run off an' I'm gittin' worried about her."

"What's her name?" Sally had a pen poised to start writing.

"Billene Cleod," Joe answered. "She been gone about three days. I figured she'd git hungry or cold 'er somethin', an' come home but she ain't come home."

"What does she look like?" Sally asked

As Joe described Billene, Sally became instantly aware that he was describing the little girl who had come to them about three days ago and was now in the custody of Child and Family Services in Beckley. She tried to hide that fact that she knew about Billene's condition as she eyed *this despicable son of a bitch.*

Joe didn't put up much of an argument when Sally explained that Billene was in Beckley and that she would probably be returned after Child and Family Services had completed their investigation.

"What investigation?" Joe demanded. "She jist up and run away. They oughta jist bring her back where she belongs."

"I'm sure," Sally tried to conceal her disgust, "they'll do the right thing by her and by you. Where can we find you when they're ready to bring her back?"

The rest of Sally's day was filled with campaign letters, answering the phone, updating arrest and traffic violations records and — thinking. When the sheriff left for the day, she put away the campaign letters — which were almost all stamped and most had been mailed. She pulled out four sheets of paper bearing the letterhead of the Sheriff of Copperhead County, West Virginia, and prepared four letters. Two went to the Registrar's offices at Indiana University of Pennsylvania and Penn State University. The other two went to the county sheriffs at Indiana County and Centre County in Pennsylvania. She mailed the letters on her way home that evening.

Chapter Eleven

The Child and Family Welfare (CFW) Facility reminded Billene of *just another school*, but more hostile. The floor consisted of square linoleum tiles laid out in an effort to please the eye with a sterile design of gray and yellow squares. Large yellow squares, four tiles on a side, contained boxes of smaller gray tiles, four in each box. The design filled the whole room. *B-O-R-I-N-G!* Billene tried to count the number of yellow squares, but she lost count several times because of tables and chairs on the other side of the room obscuring her view. Finally she gave up.

The windows, she thought, must have come from another century. They were way too tall, almost reaching the ceiling. The upper pane had a hook in the center, used to open and close the top pane. The bottom panes obviously could be just pushed open, sliding up a metal sash. Dr. Evelyn Grayson, sitting opposite her at the table crossed then uncrossed her legs. Billene could hear the swish of her nylons under her skirt as she moved, almost nervously. Billene glanced up at her in time to see her reach up and push her glasses back up to the top of the bridge of her nose. The horn-rimmed frames carried too much weight to stay up on their own. Billene half smiled at the ridiculousness of the scene. Her grilling this time had questions she had not been asked before. For the past week, since she had arrived, she had been poked and jabbed and questioned. Dr. Grayson's name pin said she was a psychologist.

"I guess that means you're a shrink. Doesn't it?" Billene challenged her on first reading it.

Dr. Grayson offered a smile that Billene thought looked practiced. *Talk about a phony grin!* "No," she said in tones of condolence. *Like she must think I'm four years old!* "A psychologist is someone who has studied how to help people work through things that trouble them. Sometimes people want to — not think — about these things because it upsets them. If they don't think about it and deal with the problems, the problems will always upset them. Sometimes, over time, the upset times get worse and worse. At the CFW, we just want to help you, so you don't have to go through that."

Billene squirmed in her chair and began studying the tiles on the floor again. *Four gray in the center, surrounded by a yellow border...* "Billene!" Evelyn Grayson interrupted her attempt at withdrawal.

"How do you know my name? I didn't tell anyone!" Billene started to get out of the chair, thought better of it and turned her gaze back to the tiles.

"We weren't sure. But we are now. Your stepfather went to the Copperhead County sheriff's office and reported you missing. He wants you to return home." Grayson watched Billene's face begin to grow pale, then she flushed, raised her eyes in wild anger and challenged Grayson again.

"I don't know who you are, Evelyn Psychologist, but you got damn nerve lockin' me up in this damn institution place and now threatenin' to send me back to be killed by that crazy man! I ain't goin' back an' that's a FACT!" Billene stood and slapped the table for emphasis on the word "fact." As she shouted at Dr. Grayson, children sitting at some of the other tables turned to watch. Some of them had adults with them. Two of the men rose from their seats in case Grayson need help. Billene could see this and quietly returned to her seat, but her demeanor remained fierce. "Just what do you plan to do to me?" She took satisfaction that Grayson seemed unsettled by the anger in Billene's eyes.

Grayson cleared her throat, opened her purse and pulled out a pack of Fishermen's Friend. "I'm sorry," she said as she popped one in her mouth. "The pollen sometimes gets to me this time of year." Billene leaned back in her chair, aware, on some level, that Grayson was doing a subject change to lighten the atmosphere. "There may be a favorable alternative," Grayson continued.

"What's that?" Billene demanded. "Stay here till I'm old and gray?"

Grayson smiled again. This time, Billene thought the smile seemed genuine. "Our people have been looking into your situation." Grayson put the pack of throat lozenges back into her purse and snapped it shut. "When your mother married Joe Cleod, you became Cleod's stepdaughter, but Joe Cleod never formally adopted you. When your mother died..."

"He killed her!" Billene interrupted. "He killed my mama! That son of a bitch killed my mama!" Billene started tearing up but gritted her teeth in determination to not completely break down and cry.

"Well!" Grayson crossed her legs again, then uncrossed them, *swish, swish.* "Maybe we'll look into that too. As I was saying there is an alternative. When your mother died, that left your legal custody in the hands of your real father."

"I don't know what that means," Billene snuffled. "What does it mean?"

"It means that your real father has the right to claim you as his own, raise you and take care of you." Billene's attention now fully focused on Grayson's smeared lipstick, but she didn't miss a word. It means that Joe Cleod, although he claims to be your stepfather, is not your real stepfather and he's certainly not your real father. That would be Bill Parsons."

"Yes," whispered Billene. "That's my real daddy's name. He wrote a letter that said he got out of prison, he was proved innocent of that awful crime and that he's coming. But he ain't showed up." Her voice was picking up strength. "Where is he?"

Grayson lowered her eyes, took a deep breath and said, "We don't know. If he's taken a job, it's too soon to track him through Social Security and so far as anyone knows, he did not come back to Copperhead. I was hoping maybe you would have some idea how to find him?"

"I donno where he is." Billene furrowed her brow, scratched her head, shuffled in her chair and said, "I know somebody who can find out. Ask Sherry Paulus. She knows everything and if she doesn't know something, she knows how to find out. Sherry is terrific. And she's my friend!" Billene couldn't hold back any longer. The tears came.

03   80

Sherry Paulus's eyebrows went straight up when she heard the name "Bill Parsons." The call interrupted her third period class. The message that an important phone call was waiting for her in the Principal's office came from Mr. Roddy, the janitor, who agreed to stay with the class until she came back. "I don't know where Bill Parsons is. I thought he was in jail."

Dr. Grayson's voice sounded strained. She was Billene's appointed case worker. "I now understand why you refused to identify her in the sheriff's office. I don't know how much of her case you're acquainted with but she certainly needed your protection at that time and you gave it without question, even taking the risk of being punished for withholding evidence. I respect what you did. Billene says you're her friend. I certainly believe that."

"I've known her ever since she started in our school system. I knew her when her mom married Joe Cleod and was with her sometimes after her mom's accident. Yeah. You could say we're friends. I always knew she was troubled. I've been suspicious of child abuse at home, but there was nothing I could do without making matters worse and I had no idea the degree of the abuse and certainly had no way of proving it."

"Billene says if anyone can find her real dad, you can. Any idea where to start?"

"I'm clueless. Any suggestions?"

"We know that when Parsons got out of prison, he came straight to Copperhead, went to the sheriff's office and was immediately arrested again. That was a big mistake for the sheriff. Parsons was released within hours and he's bringing litigation against the sheriff's office. They probably know where to find him. They refused to talk to me about it, but you live there. Maybe they'll talk to you, if you ask the right person in the right way. Will you try?"

"Of course."

Sherry was pleased to find Sally Colletti alone in the sheriff's office, headset on as usual, collating arrest reports and follow-up paper work for the State of West Virginia's archives. "Yeah! That was a mess," Sally remarked after Sherry reminded her of Bill Parson's recent arrest. "I don't know where he is now, though. His lawyer probably knows but I doubt the sheriff'll give you contact information for him."

"How can I find out?" Sherry was being meek, in full recognition that submissive body language stood a better chance of getting a boon from power than assuming power that she did not legally have.

Sally glanced at the sheriff's door to make sure it was closed. Then, in a lowered voice she said, "I suggest you ask Mr. Danny Maguire. I'd be surprised if he doesn't know."

ങ   ൠ

Sherry was surprised to get Maguire on the phone so easily. *I thought I'd have to talk to five secretaries.* She was further surprised that he agreed to an appointment so readily. *Doesn't he have anything else to do than talk about kids and stuff?*

Walking through Maguire's front door reminded Sherry of gangster movies, somehow. She couldn't quite put her finger on what it was. The surly young man who greeted her at the door certainly contributed. The secluded nature of the house's location sort of contributed. The faint smell of garlic made her think more of Italian restaurants than of gangsters. *It could be the reputation this guy has for owning everything and having his fingers in everything else. Of course, that his enemies sometimes mysteriously disappear doesn't help. I bet he is one interesting man!*

Maguire's laptop stood open on his favorite desk, the dining room table. He stood when she entered. With a charming smile he almost gave the appearance of slightly bowing, or was it just nodding his head in greeting that gave her that impression? Ms. Paulus," he greeted her. "I've heard so many nice things about you — horses, archery, Native American organizations, the school where you work... it's a pleasure to finally meet you. Let me offer you a glass of wine?"

Sherry took the seat next to him at the table as he indicated, raised one hand at the offer of the wine and with a smile that was almost a blush she said, "Thanks. Not just now."

"It's Fatascia Almanera Sicilia," he went on, pouring a small amount in a glass for himself. "A friend brought me a bottle from Sicily a few weeks ago. I liked it so much that I ordered a case, all the way from Castel Umberto. It just arrived this very morning. Are you sure you wouldn't like a taste?"

Sherry declined again, then said, "Well. How about just a taste?"

Maguire poured two fingers into a small glass and set it in front of her. Sherry took a light sip, and started smiling as she swallowed. "Cherry? Oh my God! This is good."

"I knew you'd like it. Now, tell me what's on your mind."

When Sherry finished, Maguire was sitting with his arms crossed, a deep frown on his face. "So. Parsons has legal custody, eh?"

"Yup. That's what they told me at Child and Family Welfare, but they've never met. Bill was in jail before she was born and he hasn't even seen pictures of her, so far as I know."

"That's true. But it won't be long now." Maguire picked up the phone, resting beside his laptop, dialed a number. When it answered Maguire said, "Heeey! DISpatch! This is ole Dan Maguire. How 'bout do me a favor, will ya? Yeah! I want ya ta Qualcomm Bill Parsons, driver #277850, and ask him to call me as soon as possible. Will ya do that? Thanks."

Sherry's amazement surprised even herself. *Maguire not only knows where he is, but a phone number, off the top of his head to where to find him, and his driver's number from memory! Parsons must be working for Maguire again. It looks like Maguire is protecting Parsons. If Parsons knew about Joe Cleod and what he did to Billene, he'd likely be here with murder on his mind. We find friends in the strangest of places and the strangest of people!*

Maguire put the receiver back in its cradle, picked up the wine bottle and poured some more wine into Sherry's glass. "I know you want to stay dry, but we're gonna both need another hit of this. Bill Parsons will be on the phone within five minutes. I'll put it on the speaker, so you can hear what he says."

Chapter Twelve

Camila Hardy gazed out the window of her classroom. Half an hour early for work left her time for grading papers, planning lessons and when she was finished with that, if she finished, window gazing. Beautiful summer days seemed to be a hallmark of West-by-Gawd. Nasty-chussets, as Bevin liked to call it, had beautiful summer days too, but Boston had more noise and fewer birds. Camila watched as two mockingbirds chased each other around the playground outside her window. *Are they two males, fighting for a female or a male and a female doing the mating dance? No species of bird can put on a show of aerial acrobatics like two mockingbirds having a disagreement or trying to procreate. Which is it?* She couldn't suppress the smile of enjoyment as the birds wheeled through the air, chasing each other. Suddenly the birds departed the scene, much to Camila's disappointment, as several of her about-to-be seventh graders came around a corner of the building, out of sight, or so they seemed to think.

One of the girls was Jeannie Hardwick, one of her students — the girl, she remembered, who had told her husband Bevin that she was going to marry him when she grew up. Two of the students sat down on the swings while the other leaned against the upright metal pole that supported the swing set. Waiting for 8:00 seemed to be the agenda, then she took a breath as her husband Bevin Hardy appeared. The scene took her back to a similar situation in Boston, just a year ago. There were three twelve year old girls, two on swings, one leaning against the pole pole when Bevin showed up. At the time, she was too distracted with family issues to pay it much attention, but this reminder...

Her memory of the situation renewed the pain she was feeling over her father's illness. The uncertainty had been wrenching. Daddy was dying, obviously, but he could still manage for himself, living alone in that two room apartment where he insisted on staying. "Was Bill Clinton ever President of the United States?" he asked her at least six times and with each "yes" answer he, would say, "Oh, good heavens."

Then it was, "Where are my pills? Do I have any Zyrtec?"

"Yes Dad, a whole pile of it on the table by the TV set."

Then "Was Bill Clinton ever president of the United States?"

Her memory of the two girls on the swing in Boston, then, was almost peripheral to the issues on her mind. *Should I put him in a nursing home? No, he'll be traumatized by being away from his belongings, away from familiar surroundings, surrounded by strangers. A nurse will tell him when to go to bed, when to wake up, when to eat, how to spend his time with inane crafts that he can't see well enough to do. He's losing his hearing, his vision. He can't even remember who is the president of the freaking United States. For chrissakes he's over ninety years old, still misses Mom ten years after her death and all he wants to do is go to sleep and never wake up. What can I do for him? Should I try to find a live-in companion, a part time caretaker to watch over him while I have to work? What...?*

As she now watched the playground scene from the window in Copperhead, West Virginia, Jeannie got off her swing, ran toward Bevin and leaped on him, wrapping her legs around him and giving him a big kiss on the cheek. Bevin seemed a little self-conscious about it. As he gently pushed her away, he glanced around to see if anyone had seen this display of affection, not noticing his wife in the window of the school, two floors up. Then, after a few comments that Camila couldn't hear, he turned and walked back toward the school. Jeannie went back to the swing and the girls started talking animatedly, as only twelve year old girls can.

Wow! Déjà vu! Camila returned to her memories of the time in Boston, but not without remembering that the same thing had happened on the playground in Boston, and that the little girl who leaped on her husband that day was the same one who turned up raped and strangled a few days later. She had ignored the coincidence — the déjà vu — for the moment, but it came back. She shook her head to clear it of the thoughts she was resisting and turned to her classroom. She was ready for the day but the issues from Boston kept coming back. That little girl who had been strangled and raped in Boston was named Terri

Sue Hildebrand. One of Camila's students, in those days, Terri had high grades and was a pleasure to have in class. Her horrific disappearance traumatized the whole school, including Camila herself. *Maybe I took it so hard because I was dealing with my dad's situation at the same time? He died soon after that.*

The Boston Police discovered Terri Sue's body near Park Circle Water Tower in Arlington on the north side of Boston, a relatively isolated area, on a low hill, overlooking the vast residential development all around it. Within a few days of the discovery, they came to the house. Bevin nicknamed one of them Joe Friday — ' 'juss the facks, Ma'am.' Interviewing Camila was their main interest. "Who were Terri's friends?" "Did she mention any adults she knew other than her family?" "Did she have any unusual habits?" "Was she precocious?" Bevin just sat there in the reclining chair reading the newspaper while they questioned her. Finally, they turned to Bevin.

"Mr. Hardy, did you know the deceased girl?"

"I knew her to see her. She was one of my wife's students. Cute kid. Too bad about what happened."

The police lieutenant continued. "As vice principal, were you aware of any suspicious characters hanging around the school in recent weeks?"

Bevin took off his reading glasses, laying them on an end table beside his chair, folded the newspaper and laid it beside his glasses. "The school is on a main street, what you guys call an 'urban collector.' We get lots of people passing the school all the time. They come by on bicycles, on foot. There are all kinds of people, including a number that appear to be homeless. I didn't notice anyone lingering and no one mentioned anything to me about anything like that."

"We think it was someone she knew," the policeman remarked. "She apparently had to enter some sort of vehicle to get so far as Arlington from here. We're trying to find someone who saw her entering a vehicle. If you hear of anything, please give me a call. Here's my card. By the way, you have a daughter, don't you?"

Camila answered. "My daughter, Angie, was one of Terri Sue's classmates. Would you like to talk with her? She's in her room, doing her homework."

Angie, obviously frightened, sat in the love seat, a few minutes later, in the living room with her mother, stepfather and the policeman. "Did you know Terri Sue Hildenbrand?"

"Yes." Angie fidgeted, arms clasped tightly around herself. "She was my friend. Everybody liked her." A tear was forming under Angie's right eye.

"Did you know anything about her private life, at home?"

"No."

"How about any friends she may have had outside of school?" The policeman had a notebook in one hand and a pen in the other and was obviously reading questions he had prepared before their visit. Bevin leaned back in his reclining chair, lifting the footrest and crossing his ankles on it. Camila was sitting on the edge of her chair, leaning forward, searching her heart for some way to comfort her daughter.

"None that I know of."

"Did she ever talk of any adults you know?" Angie squeezed herself tighter and the tear that had been forming under her right eye chose that time to fall, leaving a wet streak down her cheek.

"She had a crush on my stepdad." Angie nodded toward Bevin with a look of disgust. "She talked about him all the time."

The policeman wrote hurriedly then turned back to Bevin. "Did you know about this, Mr. Hardy?"

Bevin smiled, showing half a toothy grin. "No, I'm afraid not. These kids get some pretty strange ideas sometimes. She obviously knew I was married and way too old for her. No way of telling who a kid will have a crush on. I had a crush on my third grade teacher, Miss Berkeybile. I doubt that she knew it. Odd memory. I didn't even know her first name."

The policeman hesitated, then said, "So. If she had a crush on you, she would probably have been willing to get into your car if you asked her to."

"Now there's a thought," smirked Bevin. Then his face became more stern and he continued, "Maybe I could be the killer?"

The policeman hesitated again, put his pen in his shirt pocket, the notebook on the floor beside himself and he asked, "*Are* you the killer?"

Bevin lowered his footrest, raised the back of the chair where he had been half reclining, leaned forward in his seat and retorted, "Let's not get insulting, officer. I'm the vice principal of her school. I'm not a child predator. He then stood and said, "If that's all you have to ask us, maybe it's time for you to leave."

Camila jerked herself back from her memories of the past, back to present day Copperhead, West Virginia, back to her seventh grade summer school classroom and back to the scene with the twelve-year-old girls in the playground with two on swings. *Jeannie even looks a little bit like Terri Sue.*

The classroom door opened and children began entering the room for their first period class. Camila glanced out the window and saw that Jeannie and her two friends were no longer insight.

ભ ૪

Sally Colletti, headset in place, sat behind her desk in the office of Sheriff Billy Rankin, working slowly at updating the day's arrest and complaint logs. The day dragged on, quiet even for Copperhead, West Virginia, but there was always paperwork, endless paperwork. Mr. Coffee gurgled at making a fresh pot of the strong black stuff Sheriff Rankin so loved. A thick letter containing a CD caught her attention. Indiana University had responded more quickly than she anticipated to her request for the list of students registered at the school from 1985 to 1989. She would look at it when she completed her log updates. Another letter awaited her attention. This one came from the county sheriff of Indiana County in Pennsylvania and would inform her of rape/ murders from 1985 to 1995. She expected to see a surge between 1985 and 1989. *We'll just see.* No word had come, yet, from Centre County or Penn State. Next, she would write to the Boston Police Department and start inquiring about murder/rapes there and the possible presence of DNA samples, that is, if what she found out in Pennsylvania seemed to indicate any connections. I *love it when a plan comes together. We shall see. And then there's the need to inquire about DNA samples in Pennsylvania — maybe.*

Chapter Thirteen

Ping! Ping! *Damn! What's 'at thing want now?* Bill Parson's Qual-comm had started pinging as soon as he released the clutch to get back on I-44 West out of Joplin. *There's nothing on Earth like a late bar-beque lunch at the Big R BBQ in Joplin.* The truck was a sweet one; a condo-cab, a 2001, Century Class, Freightliner with all the bells and whistles, including XMRadio, a Galaxy 99 CB with a 250 watt signal kicker. *Hell! I can talk to China on that damn thing!* Ping! Ping!

The next rest stop waited thirty miles away. An exit was coming up in about five miles, but there was no truck parking. *I'll pull over on the next get-off ramp...*

The sun shone brightly, leaning low toward the west. The road dust, heavier than usual for that time of year, created a low cloud over the highway, not bad enough to impede visibility but enough that Bill kept his windows closed as he drove. Old Time Radio Classics was playing on the XM and he was unhappy, for the moment, to interrupt the cur-rent episode of "The Shadow." *No one knows what evil lurks in the hearts of men! The Shadow knows! Ha Ha Ha.* Ping! Ping! He crossed the Oklahoma state line. The next get-off ramp went to a state weigh station. *This isn't a very good place to park. I'm liable to get a DOT inspection. There's gotta be a rest comin' along soon.*

Ground pressure checked, truck eye-balled and x-rayed, he began gearing up, gathering momentum *and with a gross weight of 78,000 pounds, that ain't nothin' to sneeze at.* When he shifted into tenth, he switched off the radio and reached for the Qualcomm monitor. He laid it across his lap, glanced down and pressed the "read" button. All it said was "Call Dan" and a phone number. *Hell with the rest stop.* Bill slapped on the right turn signal, the third stage of his Jake and started easing on over toward the right shoulder. He was lucky. It was wide enough to get well off the highway and level enough that getting back up on the pavement wouldn't be too hard. *Thank God and Motorola for cell phones!*

"Hey Dan! What's new?"

"Whatcha all doin' there Bill? Where you at?"

"Listenin' to 'The Shadow' on XM Radio, about 5 miles west of the Missouri line, on the shoulder of I-44, west bound."

"Where ya'all headed, there, boy?"

"Laredo, via Dallas for the night. ETA the Bonnie View Road Terminal, around 10:00 Central Time, tonight."

"Bill? You ready to meet your little girl?"

Silence. After half a minute, Dan's voice came back. "Bill? You okay?"

"Dan! Yes and yes! What do I need to do?"

"Bill, whatchou haulin' right now?"

"Load a car parts goin' to Mexico."

"Anything assigned to you after that?"

"Not yet." Bill could feel himself sweating. His heart was pounding and a myriad of thoughts were racing through his head. His hands were even shaking a little bit. "They'll give me something out of Laredo, probably goin' back up north somewhere."

"Bill, I want you to drop the truck, trailer and all, in Dallas at the terminal, tomorrow. I'll have somebody else haul that load the rest of the way to Laredo. I'm going to have a car waiting for you at the yard in Dallas and I'm going to make a reservation for you at the Quality Inn in Beckley, West Virginia, for the day after tomorrow. I figure you can get there in two days, can't you?"

"Hell yeah! What's goin' on, Dan?"

"Your little girl, Billene, dumped her stepdaddy's ass and went to the sheriff's office in Copperhead. She's now at Child Protective Services in Beckley."

"What happened? Why'd she do that? And what about her mama, Darla? Didn't she have somethin' to say about that?"

"Bill. Darla's dead two years now. And there's somethin' else you need to know. Her stepdaddy never adopted her. YOU are her legal guardian! Howe 'bout them potatoes?"

"Damn! Are you tellin' me I have a daughter? I have family?"

"Now Bill! Don't you go doin' no marathon drive over here. You be safe. Get a motel room tomorrow night, wherever you are. Be safe. Get enough sleep! And Bill, I figure the first night on that run will land you in Memphis. You know better than to stay there without a truck, right?"

"I'll shoot for Jackson."

"Try not to get any damned tickets!"

Bill started laughing. "Just get me a car that's governed at sixty three miles per hour like these damned trucks and I'll be sure to not get any tickets." At that Maguire started laughing, too.

"There's one more thing I want to tell you, Bill. There's a young lady here who you owe a deep debt of gratitude. Her name's Sherry Paulus. You know her?"

At that, Sherry started squirming in her chair and clearing her throat. "Sherry Paulus? The name rings a bell. Is she the kid, about seven or eight years younger than me who kicked my ass at archery when she was in fourth grade and I was a senior in high school? I'm not likely to forget her name! What's she done now? Hell! I think she had a twenty pound bow and mine was a fifty. It was unbelievable!" Sherry started laughing.

"When you're good, you're just, well, good," she smirked.

"Hell Dan! Is she sittin' there right now?"

"Yup. She sure is, Bill. I want you to know that without Sherry, your daughter Billene just might be dead."

"Whadya mean, Dan? Geezus! What the hell's goin' on in Copperhead?"

"Well Bill, the shit's comin' down and the roosters are comin' home to roost. In the meantime, Billene is safe. She's going to be all right and she's yours, if you want her."

"Want her? I'll be at the Quality Inn in Beckley tomorrow night."

"No, Bill! The day AFTER tomorrow. Take the full two days to get there! I'll have some people there to fill you in, including Sherry Paulus, who you need to talk to."

ॐ ૭

When Bill got to the Dallas by-pass, he took it south and east, rounded the city of Dallas, for the most part, and took the Bonnie View Road exit. With a right off the ramp, past the Flying J, down the frontage road a couple of doors, Bill turned the big rig right, into the terminal. At the gate, the face level speaker requested his truck and driver number and when he gave them the voice said, "Are you Bill Parsons?"

"Yup."

"How the hell do you know Dan Maguire? I worked for this company for twenty five years and I never met him."

"Same home town. What can I say?"

"When you get your truck parked, come in to the desk, please."

"Forty Two!"

Bill liked the company's Dallas terminal. The cooks were Mexican and some of the food was Mexican as well. Bill liked Mexican food. The first time at the buffet he remembered ordering "dos huevos, salchichos, pan y mantiquilla, café negra Cubana." The cook answered, "Salchicho. No salchichos. Mira aqui." He pointed at the red sausages and Bill saw that they were not the small red sausages he called *salchichos* in South Florida. They were very large.

He answered, "Okay. Solamente, uno salchicho." Bill enjoyed the food, the quiet surroundings, the large company store and the Mexican food. *After today, I may never see this place again. I'll be sorry about that, but I can take Billene to Cotulla. That place has the best Mexican restaurant in the United States. How can I get her to agree to such a long trip? Oh. Maybe we can go to Amistad State Park for a nice trip and stop at Cotulla on the way.* His mind was going wild with fantasies and plans for what he could do with his new family! *College? Hell yes, and for me too.*

At the desk, he was told his car was already there but they had strict instructions to not give him the keys until morning, no earlier than five A.M. In the morning, he was told he could drop his trailer and bobtail to the car parking area to move his things from the truck, then re-hook the truck and he could go.

Bill didn't sleep well that last night in the truck. *What if she doesn't like me? What if I don't like her? What's all the secrecy about? Why is she in Children's Protective Custody? What happened to her? What is Maguire hiding from me? What's going on in Copperhead that he doesn't want me to know about — that he doesn't want me around? ... to be blamed for what?*

os   &o

Sherry Paulus, comfortable behind the wheel of her Dodge Dakota, motored west, toward Beckley. Her long black single braid rested over her right shoulder, consciously placed there so she wouldn't be sitting on it. She wore a deerskin vest over a plain white slip-over shirt embroidered by her grandmother with images of deer dancing in clover.

An advertisement for a sale on hay rolls gave her a second reason to head over there today. The other reason, though, was the big one. Bill Parsons had arrived at the Quality Inn and Dan Maguire had called Sherry to ask her to ease the first meeting. *That poor child!* Sherry pitied Billene *So many challenges she had had to face in her mere twelve years. The loss of her mother. The loss of her father. The loss of her virginity to a child molester. The loss of her home!* Sherry tried not to think about it. Every time she did, she would start tearing up. *None of that today. I have to be tough.* She gritted her teeth, furrowed her brow and drove on. *She's one tough kid, to stand up to Sheriff Rankin like she did.*

Sherry barely remembered Bill Parsons. Her recollection was bolstered by the picture in his high school yearbook. Copies, fortunately, were stored in the school library. She remembered him as a quiet sort of kid. *No football. No sports. No band.* She remembered seeing him and feeling curious because he was frequently present at the school's sporting events, but usually alone, quiet — *just a sort of a presence...*

I'll get the hay later, she decided, as she backed her Dakota into the parking space in front of Protective Child Welfare in Beckley. The receptionist directed her to the office of Dr. Evelyn Grayson who, she explained, was Billene's Social Worker. Grayson's office, a small cubicle, sported a window and its own movable walls, all institutional gray with framed college degrees and little else. The desk was clear except for the file labeled "Billene Parsons." Grayson herself was pleasant enough. *Pushing those glasses back up her nose over and over is a nervous habit,* Sherry thought, as she pushed her braid from her shoulder so it hung down behind her head, *like ME, fiddling with this damned braid. In school, they said, nervous habits like this are a sign of lack of self assurance. Well. We have something in common.*

"Hello, Dr. Grayson. I'm Sherry Paulus. I'm here..."

"Thanks for coming, Ms. Paulus. Billene certainly needs a friend she trusts today. I'm afraid she doesn't think a whole lot of me." Dr. Grayson smiled, pushed her heavy-rimmed glasses back up her nose again and continued. "She calls me 'Shrink Evelyn' ...and when she says it, she doesn't smile."

"She's been through a lot," Sherry offered.

"Yes. And it's not over. Do you know anything about this Bill Parsons who is supposed to be her real father?"

"Not much." Sherry straightened her vest and glanced toward the window. "I barely knew him when we were in school. When he was convicted of rape and murder, we were all shocked. No one ever thought he was capable of such a thing. I, myself, didn't believe it, but there was nothing I could do to help ... and maybe it was him, after-all, or so we thought."

"Who do you mean by 'we'?" Grayson queried.

Sherry turned her attention away from the window, looking Grayson directly in the eye, just in time to catch her pushing her glasses back up her nose. "I mean the other kids I went to school with back then. Kids that were in my grade — my friends.

"What's the game plan today? You're not going to just turn her over to Bill, are you? Shouldn't they have a little time to get to know each other a little more slowly?"

"Of course." Grayson opened the folder in front of her. "I think at least a week is in order, maybe even more time than that. They're total strangers to each other. Parsons may not even want her and if he does, if Billene isn't willing, that will be a major issue for us."

Chapter Fourteen

Dan Maguire's laptop, sitting on his favorite desk, stared back at him. A stack of papers littered the table and Dan had a phone stuck in his ear. Giuseppe "Chigger" Bartalucci could see him sitting there, through the windows on Maguire's rear garden entrance. Chigger left no track behind him. His concealment in the forest behind Maguire's house was complete. The two weeks in the forest, staking out Chad's Knob, had not been completely fruitless. His forest survival skills had returned, but he had grown weary of eating nuts and berries. He pulled out his untrackable cell phone and speed-dialed Maguire's number. He watched as Maguire jumped at the ring of the phone and smiled in amusement. When Maguire's voice answered the call, Chigger simply said, "I'm behind you." Then he disconnected.

Chigger smiled again as Maguire nearly knocked his chair over, getting up. Opening the back door, he stepped outside, gazed around, then took a seat in one of his garden chairs, glancing all around, trying to find Chigger. Chigger stood up and slowly began emerging from the forest so Maguire could see him.

"You're liable to get shot, sneakin' up on me like that," Maguire snapped.

"I didn't want to be seen approaching your house. Hard to say what people would think. I must look like hell. I've been living in the woods for two weeks. I want to fill you in on what I've learned and find out if anything's happening in town. I need a proper shower, some solid food and a soft bed for a few days. Any idea where I can get any of those things?"

Maguire softened his expression. "You do look like hell. How's your progress? Here. Sit down. How about a glass of Fatascia Almanera?"

"I thought you'd have that all drunk up by now."

"I ordered a case. I have plenty."

Chigger marveled that Maguire would go to the trouble to track down a source for the wine, then order so much. "Liked it, huh?"

Maguire went inside and came back out in a few minutes with two glasses, one of which he handed to Chigger, who smiled and took a tiny taste. "Ah yes. A reminder of home."

"So. You said you were pretty sure of one suspect and sort of sure of a second. Are there two of those perverts on that mountain?"

"I think so. I have pretty flimsy evidence, though — a tire track in the wrong place, but the best story is from the Keetowah."

"What the hell's a Keetowah?"

Chigger took another sip of the wine, savored the flavor, and took a deep breath. "It's sort of special breed of Cherokee Indian. This one lives alone, near Chad's Knob. He's been there for many years, living in secret. When I found him he was wearing a homemade Ghillie suit, of sorts, that was so well made that he was on top of me before I saw him and even then I wouldn't have seen him if he hadn't spoken. He could have killed me right then and there and I wouldn't have known what hit me."

"He snuck up on YOU? That's a trick I'd like to learn."

"Well, I snuck up on him too. He just saw me first. I wasn't actually trying to be invisible like he was."

"Did the Keetowah know anything? What did you learn from him?" Maguire rose from his chair and started pacing, pausing to shoot questions.

"Come on, Dan. Sit down. You're gonna make me nervous."

Maguire sat back down in his chair, leaned over, elbows on his knees and said, "I'm listening."

"He says there are two guys that show up there from time to time — always under a rising full moon."

"That usually means early in the evening," Maguire interjected.

"Yeah, they show up early in the evening when there's a full moon, just before dark. He says he's never seen them together. They always show up alone. He says he didn't know what they were up to and he didn't go out to the Knob to check after they left. He says he just glanced out from the forest's edge to see who was there. The one guy, he says used to come at every full moon but he quit coming for a long time, but he's been coming back, recently. The other guy — and this is odd. He says they look almost alike — he thought for a while that it was the same guy all the time — till the other guy started showing up again. The guy's almost a witness. He just didn't see exactly what was happening."

"Have you figured out who these two guys are?"

"I think so."

"Why aren't they dead?"

"They aren't dead because I'm not absolutely sure. I don't want to make any mistakes that I can't undo. I want to be there for the next full moon — in about three more weeks. That should do it. So. Is anything happening down below? Here in the valley? Any developments or clues?"

ଓଃ ଓଠ

Sally Colletti felt troubled. Ed and Jane, the kids were at summer camp, down near Fancy Gap — not that far away. *It's a nice church camp they have been attending for two to three weeks, every summer. It's right on the Blue Ridge Parkway ... safe, well chaperoned and well funded.* The problem was that Sally and her husband Jack had always taken that time away from the kids to do a trip somewhere. *Last year, Tombstone Arizona was a terrific trip. Yeah, we shoulda waited and brought the kids along, but hey, we can go back.* This year, Sally was so caught up in her murder investigation that she didn't want to go away. So Jack more or less went without her: he volunteered at the church camp where the kids went for three weeks and Sally was alone at home. *Bummer. But hey! If I can help nail that creep who killed those little girls, it's worth it.*

The outside office door opened and in came Sheriff Rankin, belly over the belt in front and shirt tail over the belt in back. *What a slime he is.* "Hi, Sally. What's the latest?"

Sally removed her headset, brushed her short, black hair back from her face with her hand and said, "I DO have a few things to show you. Can I have a few minutes?"

Rankin sat at his desk in the inner office with Sally hovering beside him, a pile of papers in front of him. "I found that my rapist suspect attended college at Indiana University of Pennsylvania from 1985 to 1989 and that he apparently changed his name midstream. Then he moved to State College, Pennsylvania, under the new name. He was there for three years. Then he moved to Boston, Massachusetts, for a job."

"Okay," Rankin was being sarcastic. "There's nothing damning about that. What else do you have?"

"From the sheriff's offices in Indiana County in Pennsylvania and Centre County, I got a list of murder-rapes of twelve year old girls complete with MOs. In Indiana County, there was a slight surge but if you include Cambria County and Westmoreland Counties, there was a substantial surge. In Cambria County, there had been no such killings since Harry Gossard murdered a little girl there in the early 1950s, but Harry's tastes ran to younger girls: six year olds. There were twelve killings in the four years my suspect was at school in Indiana, Pennsylvania. In none of those counties were any little girls killed before my suspect arrived. While he was in the area, there were twelve killings, in four years, then they stopped. But in Centre County, during the three years he was there, they had seven killings and when he moved to Boston, they stopped."

"Interesting," Rankin yawned. "But there must be over ten thousand students at Indiana University of Pennsylvania and State college has even more — at Penn State University. It could have been a freaking truck driver or a janitor or the bloody milkman for all we know. That our guy was there isn't even circumstantial. I'll need something better than this."

"I had a problem contacting the county sheriff in Middlesex County in Massachusetts. The county went broke and was abolished in 1997. I had to find out where the records went. They went to the Department of Public Safety and they still have a sheriff's office there for the county. I expect to hear from them soon."

"What do you expect to find? Another surge in killings? That won't damn your guy."

"It will if they have DNA evidence and it will if the DNA shows the same guy did the killings in Indiana, Pa., State College, Pa. and Arlington, Mass. To find that out, I have to contact the FBI. They have the DNA samplings, if there are any. I made some calls and wrote to *them*, too."

Rankin took off his hat, laid it gently on the desk, brushed off a fleck of dust with his handkerchief, then looked up at Sally, still hovering over his desk. "I'm afraid you're gonna stir up a mess. The FBI is a bit fussy about jurisdiction and they're gonna say we're steppin' on their toes."

"Que sera, sera," quoted Sally.

"What the hell does that mean," Rankin demanded.

Sally stepped back from the desk, swept a hand through her hair and replied, "That's Spanish for 'tough shit.' If they want to take charge, that's fine with me, but if they're going to take charge, they better be actually doing something. It's been twelve years since Trudy Griffin was murdered and that guy's been on a rampage in Pennsylvania and maybe Massachusetts and now he's back here! He's a serial murderer.

We need to stop him before he kills anybody else! If the FBI won't do it, I'll, by God, do it myself!"

"Simmer down, there, young lady. The FBI does a spectacular job on stuff like this. They have investigative tools we can't even dream about."

"It's been over twelve years, Sheriff. I'm not impressed!" Sally stomped out of the room and closed the door.

The next day, Sally found a letter in the mail from The Department of Protective Services, Sheriff's Office for Middlesex County in Massachusetts. It was a very polite one page missive, indicating that Sheriff Rankin's inquiry had been forwarded to the Federal Bureau of Investigation, who was handling all such cases for Massachusetts. Sally was furious. She immediately called the FBI offices in Clarksburg. She waded through five people before she found the right person to whom she proceeded to unload.

Finally, the beleaguered agent got through to her with placid and reassuring tones. "Please calm down, Ma'am. Let me ask you some questions."

The very next morning, as Mr. Coffee gurgled out the last of the latest new pot of strong black stuff, the front office door opened. Two very big men came in, wearing nearly formal business attire: a gray suit with a red tie, a navy blue suit with a gray tie. Their black leather dress shoes sparkled. Both apparently had had haircuts as recently as that very morning. They were crisply neat and very big. Sally didn't even pour herself a cup of coffee. She sat down at her desk and stared at them, eyes wide, mouth open.

"Good morning, miss. Is Sheriff Rankin in this morning?"

"He's not here yet, but he'll be here in about half an hour or so." Sally, not in the least intimidated, demanded, "Who are you two?"

The man who had spoken smiled as he reached into an inside pocket of his suit coat. As he pulled out a business card he said, "My name's Matthew Brown and this is my partner William Montgomery. We're with the Federal Bureau of Investigation. And who might you be, if you don't mind my asking?"

Sally suddenly wanted to crawl under her desk. Finally, she was beginning to feel humbled. She removed her headset, ran a hand through her hair and stood up. My name is Sally Colletti. I'm Sheriff Rankin's office manager. Can I help you?"

Chapter Fifteen

Amanda Hardwick absent-mindedly gazed out of the kitchen window as she rinsed and washed the breakfast dishes. Twelve year old Jeannie had just left for school. Jason, Jeannie's dad and Amanda's husband, was surely seated at his desk by now, at Hardwick and Hardwick Insurance and Bonding, down on South Main Street in Copperhead. Amanda would shower and dress when she finished the dishes. At least, that was the plan. Her medium length brown hair, although tied in back, allowed stringy locks to hang on both sides of her head and in her face. Her bathrobe mostly covered her pajamas and her nearly worn-out bedroom slippers were slightly wet from the dish washing exercise. *Can't seem to wash these damned things without getting water on the floor!*

The *Copperhead Observer* rested unopened on the kitchen table. *Damned thing always arrives on the porch, 'by air mail'* — she chuckled at the thought — *as Jason put it, as he is leaving. He never gets to read the morning paper until he gets home at night!*

When she finished the dishes, she took a seat at the table for the last cup of coffee in the pot before showering. The headline in the editorial section, when she got to it, snatched her attention:

Copperhead's Dead Children!

Brian James, the author of the article, was from Beckley and his work was often reprinted in the *Observer*, explaining why it took so long to hit the local paper. James continued...

"Two in twelve years ain't exactly littering the streets,"
was all Sheriff Rankin had to say when we called this morn-
ing. Sexual predation isn't exactly common in Copperhead,
with zero incidents like this until twelve years ago. But
now, there is a second! Just last week, the body of Amy Sue
Gardofsky, from White Sulphur Springs, was found in the
woods, just outside of Copperhead, raped and strangled.
Exactly how the child got from White Sulphur Springs to
Copperhead is not very clear, but it's obvious that the killer
abducted her near her home and transported her to Cop-
perhead before or after killing her. Not since Trudy Griffin's
twelve-year-old body turned up twelve years ago has there
been any hint of such a thing in Copperhead. Why the long
gap? Why twelve years between killings? Maybe the mon-
ster who did this left for a while. If he did, we now know,
he's back.

James went on to criticize law enforcement for not spending more time on the crimes. Bill Parsons name was mentioned and the fact that he had been exonerated of the Griffin slaying. Amanda continued reading without much retention. Her mind had immediately leaped to the safety of her own twelve year old, now a student at Copperhead Junior High School. She stopped reading and picked up the telephone. She dialed the number of the school office and when the secretary answered she interrupted the greeting with "This is Amanda Hardwick. I'm Jeannie's mother. She's in Mrs. Hardy's summer school class. Would you please check and see if she arrived yet?"

The five minutes Amanda had to wait for an answer seemed like days. She had risen and was pacing the kitchen floor when the answer came back, "Yes, ma'am. She's here, all right. Anything wrong?"

"No," Amanda answered. "I just got a little worried, especially with this editorial in the *Copperhead Observer* this morning. Would you please give Jeannie a note from her mom?"

"Of course, Mrs. Hardwick. What would you like me to tell her?"

Amanda was almost sobbing with relief. She sat back down at the table, pulled her coffee and the newspaper closer and said, "Please tell her I am going to pick her up after school today and *not* to walk home. To wait for me. Okay?"

"That'll be fine, Mrs. Hardwick. I'll tell her that. Mrs. Hardwick? What article are you referring to? I haven't seen the paper yet today."

"About the murder of those little girls. It's an editorial from Brian

James. Do you remember Trudy Griffin, about twelve years ago?"

"Yep. That was awful."

"I'm pretty sure you heard about the one last week, right?"

"Yeah. I sure did. That was that girl from White Sulphur Springs. I wonder how she got way over here."

"Me, too. James says the criminal is likely from around here some-where and that he was gone for a while and he's back. If that's true, none of our children are safe till they get him."

"What a horrible thought..."

C

Amanda showered, dressed, then read Brian James's editorial again. Later, on the way home from the grocery store, she stopped at Hardwick and Hardwick. Her husband looked up as she came in, smiled and hung up the phone.

"I know you're busy," Amanda greeted him. "I won't hang around. I just wanted to make sure you see this article." She plopped the newspaper on his desk, opened to the Brian James editorial.

She watched as he read the first few lines. His eyebrows shot up and he raised his eyes to her. "I'm going to start taking Jeannie to school in the car and picking her up after," she continued. "At least until we're satisfied that it's safe to let her walk. Do you agree?"

"Good idea." Jason eased his chair out from under the desk and ap-proached her. With a hug, he tried to reassure her. "Jeannie's probably fairly safe while she's at school. Not much could happen there. There are teachers and staff all over the place. But a ride to and from, for the time being, I think, is the right thing to do."

"Could someone from around here be doing something like that? This is a safe little community, or so I thought."

Jason shook his head. "Years ago, there was an incident but the girl got away. The guy went to jail and I think he died there. His name was Cloud or something like that. Do you remember hearing about it?"

"No." Amanda shook her head. "How long ago was it?"

"I don't remember. It's quite a ways back. So James thinks the guy is from around here, but he was gone for a while, then came back? I'll make some calls and see what I can find out. Maybe Brian James is right. I wonder who's new in town."

CR   80

Around three o'clock that afternoon, Amanda got in her car and headed out of the driveway. She made the left out the drive, stopped at the stop sign at State Road, then turned left toward the school and stopped. In the distance she could see Jeannie, walking up the road. She was alone, except for a blue minivan stopped beside her. Amanda could see the figure of the driver, leaning toward the passenger side window, talking to Jeannie. Amanda stepped on the gas. As she approached, the driver of the minivan evidently saw her coming, ended his conversation with Amanda's daughter and sped off. The minivan's smoked side windows prevented Amanda from getting a look at the driver. When she got to Jeannie, she stopped again, rolled down the window and said, with a tone of exasperation, "Get in."

"Who was that?" Amanda demanded after Jeannie got the car door closed.

"Oh that was just Mr. Hardy," Jeannie sort of giggled. "He's our new assistant principal at the school."

"Yeah? Where's he from?" Amanda began turning the car around to go back to the house.

"He's from Boston. He just started this summer. I have his wife for my teacher. Mrs. Hardy. She's nice."

"Why didn't you wait for me to come and get you like I asked?"

"Oh, Mom. I'm safe enough walking home from school. The sun's still high in the sky. It's not dark out. Why not walk home?"

"Because I asked you to wait for me. You did get the note from the secretary, didn't you?"

"Yeah. She brought it to me this morning. Well, Ma, I kinda forgot and there's no reason to not walk home."

"Yes there is, darlin'. You don't know who you might meet out here on the road. And you really don't know Mr. Hardy."

"Oh yes I do. He's our assistant principal. When I grow up, I'm going to marry him. He's nice to me."

"Seems to me, he has a wife. How you gonna marry him if he's already married?"

Jeannie seemed unconcerned. "Well, I don't know. We'll see."

"When you're old enough to get married, you'll probably have other ideas. He's too old for you, anyway."

"He's not."

Jason's car pulled into the driveway right behind them. Jeannie ran to her dad and gave a big hug and said, "You're home early," more of a question than a statement.

"Let's go in," he started toward the house. "We need to talk about some things."

Amanda related to him what she saw when she went to pick up Jeannie. "I know he's the assistant principal and she trusts him, but we don't know him. He's new in town. Jason! It could even be him."

Jason fingered his red checked tie, before loosening it. The *Copperhead Observer* rested on the table in front of him. "Jeannie. Please read this article."

Amanda put some coffee on, then joined them at the table, watching Jeannie read the words of Brian James. When she finished, she looked up at Jason, eyes wide. Then she looked at the concerned expression on Amanda's face and she said, "I'm twelve years old. That could be me."

"Exactly!" Amanda practically snapped. "We want to keep you safe. I'm going to drive you to school from now on, until this guy is caught. And I'm going to pick you up after school and bring you home. Is that understood?"

"Ah, Mom. I'm not in any danger. And that man today was Mr. Hardy. I KNOW him."

Jason interjected, "Most sexual predation comes from people the kid knows — or thinks she knows. I don't want you to talk to any men at all, if you're alone. If a man stops to talk to you, run away, no matter who he is or how well you think you know him. You don't know who this killer is and neither do we. The only way we can be sure you're safe is if you do what we tell you. Talk to no men *at all* if you're alone. Don't get into anyone's car except ours. I don't want you to walk to school anymore until we're sure this guy is off our streets. Will you obey me?"

"But Dad, Mr. Hardy is okay. He's nice. His wife is my teacher. What if she finds out I'm afraid of him? What's she gonna think?"

"I don't care what she thinks. And you can avoid him without being obvious about it."

CB ED

The next morning, Camila Hardy again stood watching through her office window over the school playground. The girls showed up again, the same ones she had seen before. One sat on the swing. Another leaned against the frame that supported the swings. Two others stood in the background toward the trees at the edge of the school property. The one on the swing was Jeannie Hardwick. One of the girls in the background produced a cigarette and offered some to the others. The one with her by the trees accepted. The others, including Jeannie, refused.

Typical kids, she mused. While she watched, a mockingbird swung by, grabbed a bug trying to make its way across the pavement, and flew back into a nearby tree, not altogether trusting the dietary habits of the young humans. *The mockingbirds never trust humans, no matter if we feed them, build houses for them — never trust us.* Then she noticed that the mockingbird had disappeared into a thicket not high off the ground and she mused again, *probably has a nest in there.*

Just then another figure showed up by the swings. He was a tall man, wearing a gray suit, starched white shirt, sporting a grin. Mr. Bevin Hardy couldn't forego saying hello to the girls. The cigarettes disappeared instantly and the two girls near the trees stepped closer to greet the new assistant principal, but Jeannie shocked her. Instead of gushing over her husband as she usually did, Jeannie rose from the wing and walked into the back door of the school and out of sight. She seemed almost sullen and glanced over her shoulder a couple of times before she disappeared. A few moments later, Jeannie walked into the door of Mrs. Hardy's classroom, took a seat at her desk and opened a book.

"Good morning Jeannie. How are you today?"

"I'm good, Mrs. Hardy. It's a beautiful morning isn't it?"

Chapter Sixteen

Camila liked the house on the Booleevard — Goshen Road, Copperhead, West-by-Gawd. She hadn't seen any snakes yet, and that was her chief fear in moving to such a place. She found the setting idyllic. The elms and oaks overhanging the back yard created a perfect place for deer to come to visit, to eat the apples and other fruit she put out for them. *It may be too far south for sassafras, or too low. Sassafras seems to like higher elevations.* She hadn't seen any — and she did look for it. Sassafras tea — *nothing like it to get your blood pressure up!* Not that she had any need for that, but Bevin liked it and remarked that he hadn't seen in the shops, around town or anywhere else, since they left Boston.

Camila rocked on the front porch, appreciating the screen Bevin repaired for them. The murders in the area hadn't concerned her much, until yesterday when the school secretary came in with the note from Jeannie Hardwick's mother. That evening, she asked Bevin what he thought about it.

"It's nothing to be worried about. That's my opinion. Angie's in no danger."

"How can you say that?" Camila's worry was eating at her. "Just up here at the end of the road, there have been two little girls, about Angie's age, found raped and murdered."

Bevin loosened his tie, took a seat in the living room and said, "The first one, ever, was twelve years ago. That's a long time ago. Whoever did that is long gone."

"But the last one was just a few weeks ago."

"Almost six weeks ago," he replied. She didn't understand his apparent irritation.

"Bevin," Camila practically paced the floor. She was wringing her hands and absent-mindedly tossing her hair out of her eyes. "I heard the little girl next door has disappeared — what's her name — you know, the girl that was here, visiting Angie — Billene? What could have happened to her?"

"I thought you knew. The sheriff's office has her. They sent her over to Beckley to Child Protective Services. I don't know what her problem is. She's apparently making wild accusations against my brother Joe. I called over there to find out what's going on and I couldn't get much out of them."

"What kind of accusations?" Camila more or less demanded. She noted that Bevin seemed uncomfortable with the questions. He was crossing and uncrossing his legs, wiping his mouth too often with one hand then the other. *He always does that when he's trying to be evasive.*

"There are allegations of child abuse. He may have some trouble over that."

"Well," Camila practically coughed out the word. "I think it's abusive to make a child live in such crude conditions. The man's obviously a drunk. There are beer bottles and beer cans all over the yard, all around the house. I drove past the house to look at it a few days ago. It's a hovel. I wonder if he even has heat in there for when it gets cold!"

"Have a little charity, for God's sake. The man's alone, trying to raise a precocious kid, working for a living, trying to cook, clean and keep after her to do her schoolwork. He's bound to have some problems along the way. What do you expect? I think he's practically a saint considering what he's done for her, and she's not even his real daughter."

"'Saint' my ass! Brother or not, the man's a pig!"

Bevin started showing some signs of annoyance. "You should talk nicer about my brother. He's had a hard time and he's my kin."

"Bevin, for all I know, it's him that's been killing these kids. Did you read the editorial in yesterday's *Observer*? I've been keeping poor Angie in the house. I'm afraid to let her go outside. No telling what could happen to her!"

Bevin rose from his chair, turning toward the bedroom to change clothes. Before he left the room he turned and nearly snarled, "My brother Joe ain't the killer. He don't have it in 'im."

Camila followed him toward the bedroom, unable to stop herself from thinking, *funny how his grammar falls apart when he gets annoyed.* "How do you know? You haven't seen him in twelve years. A lot can happen to a man in that time.

"You know, Bevin, the article pointed out that it could be someone who's been away for twelve years and now he's back. Sound familiar?"

Bevin turned toward her, an odd look in his eyes. A sudden calmness appeared in his voice, so unexpectedly that it took Camila back for a moment. "That murder twelve years ago happened a week after I left. I was in Pennsylvania when that happened."

"I know that. But others might get the wrong idea. The timing is too close."

"What the hell are you sayin', Camila? You think it's me? Get a grip! I'm your husband. I was out of state a week when that happened. Funny. You remember that Jeannie from your class, how she was all over me? Well now, it seems like she's afraid of me. I saw her this morning and she ran off like a scared rabbit. Maybe she thinks it was me, too."

"It might be the smart thing to do — not running away from you, exactly, but you're a stranger, more or less." Camila studied the floor, lost in thought for a moment. "I hope Angie is as afraid of strange men."

Just then, they could both hear the sound of an engine struggling up Goshen Road, past the house. Through the window they could see that it was a large SUV with a police light on top, not flashing, and the words "Copperhead County Sheriff" painted on the side of the vehicle. Bevin swore softly and turned to Camila. "The damned cops are goin' ta see my brother, I betcha. I gotta git over there and give him some moral support."

"I'm coming with you," Camila snapped.

CB   BO

Joe Cleod's cottage had two vehicles in the mud driveway, barely leaving room for Camila and Bevin to get the blue minivan in behind them. The police SUV had mud splattered on the sides from the crude road it had just traversed. Bevin snickered, "They come up here, they're gonna have to wash that thing. Look! He's already on the porch."

"Bevin!" Camila reached for the car door handle. "Is that Deputy Joe Perry? God! He's big."

"Yeah. That's Perry all right. Probably our next sheriff... and pretty soon too. Isn't the election just next month?"

Joe was at the door talking with the deputy when they arrived. As Camila and Bevin approached the porch, Perry stepped to one side, apparently so none of them would be behind him, and out of his line of sight. Bevin approached the steps first and began to mount them, wearing his best 'hail, fellow well met' demeanor, broad grin and all. "Good afternoon, Sheriff." Camila cringed at Bevin's shallow ingratiation, but Joe Perry smiled.

"I ain't the sheriff, yet," Joe guffawed. "But elections are coming. You gonna vote for me?"

Bevin's grin widened. "You betcha." Bevin nodded at Joe Cleod standing in the doorway. "I see you met my brother. Is he behavin'?"

Big Joe Perry took off his hat, scratched his shaggy blond hair and put his hat back on. He drew his lips into a thin line, took a deep breath and said, "I just dropped by to chat with ole Mr. Cleod here about a few personal things."

Joe Cleod opened the door a little wider. "Ya'll come on in, Sheriff." *Taking the lead from his brother,* Camila mused. "All ya'll come on in."

Deputy Perry objected immediately. "Mr. Cleod. What I have to chat with you about is personal. You might rather we be alone together for this."

"I got nothin' ta hide from m' brother Beaver, Sheriff. He's m' closest kin. If there's trouble, he oughta be here ta know about it."

"Well, I don't know," Perry began.

Bevin cut him off with, "Sheriff, I'm the assistant principal where my brother's daughter goes to school. My wife," and he gestured to Camila, still sitting in the car, "is one of her teachers. We may be able to help."

Perry's face took on a stern expression as he turned back to Bevin. "What makes you think I'm here to talk about Mr. Cleod's step-daughter?"

"Well," Bevin went on, "Billene's been missing. We know that she ran away from home just a few days ago. I'm assuming that local law enforcement has taken an interest in that. Am I right?"

"Right as rain," Deputy Perry murmured. "Still, I think it would be best if Mr. Cleod and I spoke privately."

"Oh, no such thing," Joe Cleod insisted as he exited the house and moved to take a seat on the front porch steps. "Have a seat in that there ole rockin' chair, Sheriff, an' let's git started. Beaver, have your wife come closer and join us. Ya know, Beaver, I don't think I met your wife yet. What's her name?"

As Camila climbed out of the car, Bevin made the introductions. "Joe, this is my wife Camila Hardy. Camila — my brother, Joe Cleod."

Joe Cleod pushed the dangling mustache out of his mouth. "Nice to meetcha, Mrs. Hardy. I'm glad to see my brother picked a pretty one."

Inwardly recoiling at the sight of him, Camila stifled a nasty response at this comment. She felt her eyes narrowing as she replied,

"The pleasure is all mine, Mr. Cleod."

"Ah, you can call me Joe. I AM your brother-in-law." The evil in his glance gave Camila such an itchy feeling, that she suddenly wanted to go home and shower to get the dirt of his look off of her.

"'Mr. Cleod', is good enough for now." She forced a smile.

Cleod turned his attention back to the policeman. "So what's this all about, Sheriff? What's up?"

Perry, now seated on the rocking chair by the door, leaned forward, elbows on his knees with all three of them in plain sight in front of him. *Not letting anybody get behind him,* Camila observed. "As you probably know," Perry began, "your step-daughter Billene showed up at the sheriff's office a few days ago, all scratched and bruised, apparently from running through the woods. She refused to tell us who she was or why she ran away. She was very frightened but we didn't know why. We had her transported to Family and Children Services over in Beckley. They put her in the hospital there and checked her out. What they found was very disturbing. Do you have anything to say about that before I go on?"

"What's to say, Sheriff? She run through the woods, she's likely to get bunged up a little bit. What's the fuss?"

Deputy Perry took a deep breath. "The fuss is, Mr. Cleod, they found she had been repeatedly sexually abused over a long period of time. That's the fuss, Mr. Cleod. Do you have anything to say about *that*?"

Everyone was silent for almost a full minute. Camila felt her eyes grow wide with the horror she was feeling. Her hands began trembling. *Is this the man? Is it my husband's brother who's been killing children? Oh my God!"*

Bevin's eyebrows rose slightly. He put his hands behind his back and clasped them together. His eyes shifted back and forth between the policeman and his brother. Deputy Perry, hands loose in his lap, held his fixed glare on Cleod.

Finally Joe Cleod broke the silence. "I don't know how that could be. They ain't no one round here but me an' her. She does wander off a lot, an' when she gets home before I do, I can't know what's goin' on. She never said nothin' to me about it. How could that be, Sheriff?"

Perry didn't move. "That's the very question the State Attorney's Office wants me to answer. That's why I'm here. It might also be of interest to you that Children's Welfare in Beckley is treating her for syphilis. Whoever has been doing this to her has given this child syphilis."

Camila watched Joe Cleod's eyes grow wide and his mouth drop open. His forehead wrinkled and he gasped, "Oh my God."

Bevin to the rescue. "Hell, Sheriff. She coulda caught that from a toilet seat. You know how that goes." Camila was horrified. Bevin caught her by the arm as she began to lunge forward to tear Joe Cleod limb from limb. She turned her attention back to her husband in shocked amazement.

"How can you defend him like that? You know..."

Bevin cut her off. "Get back in the car and shut up!"

Bevin caught her arm as she took a swing at him, nails ready to tear flesh. "Get back in the car, Mrs. Hardy, before someone gets hurt." Camila had never before heard her husband snarl in quite this way. The look in his eyes was murderous. Even with the policeman sitting right there, watching them, her fear of Bevin Hardy overrode her contempt for his brother Joe Cleod and the horrors she had just heard.

Near hysteria, Camila shouted at Joe Perry, "Are you going to arrest him? Are you going to arrest him? What are you going to do about this? Everyone seems awfully peaceful just now..."

Near hysteria, Camila shouted at Joe Perry, "Are you going to arrest him? Are you going to arrest him? What are you going to do about this? Everyone seems awfully peaceful just now!"

Perry rose from the rocking chair. "Calm down, Mrs. Hardy. We aren't going to press charges just yet, but I AM going to take him into custody for questioning and DNA sampling. Now, Mr. and Mrs. Hardy, get back into your vehicle and go away." Perry had his hand on the grip of his side arm, but had not drawn it. Camila shook Bevin's hand off her arm and returned to the blue mini-van. Bevin climbed in on the driver's side. As they backed out of Joe Cleod's dirt driveway, Camila watched as Joe Perry slipped the handcuffs on her neighbor, her husband's brother.

Chapter Seventeen

Sherry Paulus bided her time in the conference room adjacent to the office of Dr. Evelyn Grayson. The heavy wood chairs and the highly polished eight-foot-long mahogany conference table occupied the center of the old room. Heavily enameled white wainscoting covered the lower four or so feet of the off-white plaster walls. The dark-stained tongue-in-groove flooring was protected from the weight of the table in the form of a heavy area rug, which was long enough and wide enough to cover the entire area under the table, extending far enough from the table's sides to include the chairs.

Sherry was growing bored. *If I'm studying the furniture and the walls, I've been in here too long,* she thought — *about twenty minutes. ...tired of looking at this table ..must have cost the tax payers over five thousand dollars for this furniture.* The only thing Grayson had told Sherry in preparation was that Parsons had not been told about Billene's sexual abuse. "Let's just keep that personal item about the girl private for the time being. No need to stir up more trouble than necessary." Sherry could hear voices in the room next door — Grayson's office.

A moment later, the door opened. The big heavy wood door bore an opaque glass window displaying the words "Conference Room." Sherry was on pins and needles. Everything happening seemed to be happening in slow motion, including the door swinging open to the outside. Then everything sped up again, almost to a blur. Billene stood in the doorway with big eyes and a frightened look on her face. When she saw

Sherry, she ran to her. Sherry met her about half way with "Oh, honey! Are you okay? Come here and let me hug you."

Billene wiped a tear off her cheek. "Shrink Evelyn says my daddy's here — my real daddy. What if he doesn't like me?"

Sherry started chuckling. "Worse yet... What if you don't like HIM?"

Billene drew back, eyes big and round. "What's he like? Have you met him?"

"I knew him a long time ago." Sherry stood and pushed her chair back under the table. "Is he in Dr. Grayson's office now? She said he was right outside and I should wait with you. She said she met him yesterday. He was always a quiet sort of guy." Sherry's gazed was directed at the window but her vision was focused on the long ago. "He always seemed very nice, a hard worker. Kept to himself for the most part." Sherry turned her face back toward Billene with a smile. "Come to think of it, he sort of looked like you, back then. We're about to find out what he's like now."

Grayson appeared at the door. After clearing her throat and pushing her glasses back up her nose, she said, "Billene? I'd like you to meet Mr. Bill Parsons, your real father." She stepped into the room, out of the way, and Bill Parsons appeared in the doorway.

Sherry had not seen Bill Parsons since he graduated from high school, more than two decades in the past. He didn't look all that different to her now, a little heavier, frozen frown lines between his eyebrows battling laugh lines at the sides of his eyes. Billene had both hands over her mouth; it was one of the most emotionally tense moments of her life. Big tear drops hovered over each lower eye lid and dropped, forming straight wet streaks down her cheeks. Angrily, she brushed them aside. No more followed. Her eyes had become fierce but she remained silent, watching this myth-become-man standing right in front of her. "He's big!" she whispered to Sherry.

Sherry watched as Bill groped for something to say. He glanced out the window, then at Dr. Grayson, then back to Billene. He raised his right hand, as though about to take a vow, but it turned into a one stroke wave and he said, "Hi," and smiled broadly, lowering his hand. He walked slowly toward Billene and Sherry, pulled out a chair next to them and sat down. "Dr. Grayson says we should spend some time getting to know each other. How do you feel about that, kiddo?"

Sherry pulled Billene closer again with a light hug. "He's not so bad. Whadya think?" Billene turned away from Bill and threw both arms around Sherry's neck trying to hide the tears of fear. Sherry glanced up at Bill as she did so and gave a 'give it a few minutes' gesture with her hand. "Hey, Billene. Why not shake his hand? You can get the feel of a man by his handshake ... and tell him you're glad to meet him, finally." Billene squeezed her arms around Sherry's neck a little tighter, then gradually relaxed her embrace. She turned toward Bill with her head lowered as though she didn't know if she should fight or flee. With a glance back at Sherry, she took the one step required to get close enough to touch Bill's hand. Sherry admired him for sitting so still, giving Billene the chance to get used to his presence, saying nothing, just waiting. Sherry watched Bill's eyes softening and then beginning to tear up. "Come on, you two. We can't have both of you sobbing. Get a grip."

This time it was Bill who raised his left hand slightly in the 'give it a minute' signal. His right hand had been resting on his knee. He slowly turned it palm up and held it out slightly to Billene — a gesture of welcome and acceptance.

Sherry shuffled her feet, cleared her throat and said, "I don't know about you guys, but I'm just not into awkward silences. Let's do something. How about some ice cream? Bill, do you like ice cream? How about you, Billene? Let's go get some ice cream!"

Dr. Grayson, still standing in the background, stepped forward. "It may be a little too soon for an outing. We barely know Mr. Parsons, but we do have a file for you, Ms. Paulus. We know you are Billene's trusted friend and a teacher in her school. If we allow you to go for ice cream, you will be the guardian and you must commit to bringing Billene back in, say, three hours. Will that be acceptable to everyone?"

Sherry rose to her feet, returned Dr. Grayson's gaze and replied, "It's about ten o'clock right now. Let's say I'll have her back before your office hours close at five o'clock. How's that? The extra time will be a little less restrictive."

Dr. Grayson, lowered her head, took a deep breath and said, "That may be a little irregular, but I'll agree to it as long as you know that at five o'clock, the police will be called if you're not back."

"No need for the threats. We'll be back."

ભ ଔ

Alaska-Land in Beckley, West Virginia, opens at ten o'clock in the morning, every morning. "They have ice cream of every kind," Bill said to Sherry and Billene. "I discovered it yesterday, while I was waiting for our reunion, today. Beckley has grown since I was last here. It's been over twelve years," he added softly.

They chose a table big enough for four in the front of the store. The big display window overlooking the street practically burst with advertisements displaying the wares of Alaska-Land. Billene insisted on a seat facing the window. "I don't want to sit with my back to the window," was her only explanation.

"Suits me," her dad answered. "You afraid someone's going to sneak up on you?"

Billene lowered her eyes quickly. Sherry could see the fear and the body language answering distinctly, "Yes." Billene took her seat at the Formica-topped table and slid her chair in next to Sherry.

"So," Bill began, "who do you think is going to sneak up on you?" Sherry could see that his smile was intended to conceal the intensity of the question. So far, Billene had not told anyone why she ran away from home or of the overheard discussion between her stepfather and his twin brother, Bevin Hardy. Sherry knew about the evidence of molestation and she knew that Bill did not. Billene lowered her eyes again at the question and when prodded with, "You're safe here with me," she looked up again at Bill with big eyes, baleful with fight and fear. She remained fiercely silent.

"Enough already with the awkward silences," Sherry insisted. "I suggest we split a full-sized baked Alaska. Whadya think?"

"What's a baked Alaska?" Billene wanted to know. "I don't think I ever heard of that before."

"Me, either," Bill added.

"If you like ice cream, you'll like the baked Alaska. Anyway, if you never had one before, you should do it just for the sake of curiosity. baked Alaska is great!"

Billene, silent for a moment, looked to Sherry. "How can you bake ice cream? It would melt!"

"You'll just have to ask the waitress," Sherry answered.

The ice cream adventure went nicely. Neither Bill nor Sherry tried to play catch-up from their school days, but focused on getting Billene talking. "How do you like your teachers? What do you like to do after school? Any extra-curricular activities? What about girls' volleyball, swimming?" Their effort was successful. Billene was reluctant to talk at first but on discovering she had a willing and supportive audience, she began to open up. When the ice cream was gone, they continued talking while Bill and Sherry had some coffee. Sherry insisted on splitting the bill.

"It's too early to go back to Child Welfare," Sherry observed. "What can we do for a while in Beckley?"

"What're your druthers, Kiddo?" Bill asked Billene.

"I don't know," Billene answered. "I've never been to Beckley before."

Sherry stepped in with, "Let's go out to Stephens Lake and skip stones for a while. Bill, you ever been to Stephens Lake?"

"Sure," Bill said as he stood up and stretched. "Used to go fishing there now and then. A friend of mine had a boat and we'd go way upstream from the dam, into those little streams and fish for walleye and bass."

"Whadja catchem' on, Dad?" Billene asked.

Sherry beamed with delight. Bill's eyes started to tear up again and he quickly looked away, saying, "Worms. We'd go for nightcrawlers the night before. Always plenty o' nightcrawlers."

Dad! Dad! Billene tried the word on her lips to see how it felt, like the first time a lover says 'I love you.' *A test. A taste. How did it feel?* Billene watched her dad expectantly.

His eyes were dry when he looked back with a smile. "Ever go catchin' nightcrawlers?"

"Yup," Billene answered. "We got nightcrawlers on Goshen Lane. I guess they're everywhere."

Another admission! Sherry's thoughts were excited but she concealed it. *Since she ran away she hasn't admitted to anyone where she came from. I hope she doesn't tell him too much. Maybe it was just a slip.*

Sherry drove, since Bill had turned in his rental car. They squeezed together in Sherry's Dodge truck. The eight miles to Stephens Lake was covered with stories about catching nightcrawlers. A right turn off State Road #3 out of Beckley took them down Dam Road. Neither Bill nor Sherry made a joke of the name but Billene, when she saw the road sign started sniggering. "What a name for a street! Let's git on down the Dam Road." She giggled some more.

The road crossed the dam at the head of the lake and ended at a parking lot. At one end of the parking lot, a pickup truck was backing a boat down a short ramp into the water. Stephens Lake, a 300 acre cold water mountain lake, highlighted the foreground, framed in a setting of large trees rising from the hills surrounding the water. A large cluster of mountain laurel bloomed on the far bank. As they parked, the pickup truck pulled its empty boat trailer out of the water and parked in the center of the parking lot. The fisherman waved a friendly greeting as he headed toward the boat to join the lady who waited for him there. Sherry, hand in hand with Billene, who was hand in hand with Bill Parsons, walked out to the end of the short pier for a closer view of the water.

"Wow," from Billene. "One way you look at the water, it's dark. Another way you look at it and it's sort of dark blue. Then another way you look at it and you see a reflection of the sky. It's really pretty here."

"I wonder how fishin's been." Bill dropped Billene's hand and picked up a flat piece of stone. "How many times you think I can skip it before it sinks?"

Billene looked around and found a stone she liked, picked it up and said, "I'll say twice. Let's find out." It was a tone of challenge. Sherry stepped back and observed, very satisfied with how things were going. Billene and Bill were both relaxed and playful, competing for who could skip their stone the most times. Billene would win the contest and practically collapse with laughter. Bill would feign disappointment, then pick another rock and try again. Sherry watched, elated. *This is gonna work out.*

On the other side of the boat ramp, a small clearing provided a couple of benches where they sat later to just smell the air and listen to the birds. The fisherman and his lady had anchored their boat, or maybe they were drift-fishing, almost out of sight. Sherry watched the man draw back his arm and cast, then slowly retrieve his lure. His lady appeared to be bait fishing, worms probably. Billene broke the silence. "Where do you live, Dad?"

He seemed slightly taken aback. No one had asked him such a question in a long, long time. "Well, strange you should ask. I don't know, myself. I guess I'll have to pick a place sooner or later. You know I was in jail for a long time, don't you?"

"I read the letter you sent my mom."

"Oh Lord! I didn't know she was gone then."

"I know. I'm glad you're not in jail anymore."

"Me, too. It's a terrible place. Then I drove trucks for ole Mr. Maguire for a short time, waiting to find out how things were going with you. The lawyer says I have to get a regular address before Child Welfare will turn you over to me, if that's what you want, that is. You don't have to decide any time soon. There's plenty of time."

Billene didn't seem surprised at what he said. "Maybe." She looked up at him. Sherry was glad to see the fear that had been in her eyes was gone. "We gonna live in Copperhead?"

"Maybe we'll live in Copperhead for a while, but let's talk about that later. You ever been to Florida?"

Billene looked out over the lake. "No. They got alligators in Florida, and moccasins and mosquitoes."

Chapter Eighteen

Camila's classroom bustled with activity. Her seventh graders were working on a project detailing the local bird population. They had collected feathers they were trying to identify. Sketches of birds they had seen were taking shape and the three copies of Audubon's *Bird Book* were getting worn out. Two copies of *The Guide to Common Birds of West Virginia* by Norma Jean Venable were getting passed around. Of the some three hundred birds Venable listed, the students had identified only around thirty five. Mockingbirds were easy to find, but sightings and feathers from the ruby throated hummingbird were harder to achieve. Crows and jays were easy to find, but the tundra swan, the killdeer and others were elusive. Sally Abare complained, "I've never even heard of a lot of these. I bet the tundra swan is seasonal, if it ever comes around here at all."

Camila just smiled and said, "We just have to keep looking. Bird watching takes patience. It *is* summertime. This is when a lot of them come around. The least tern likes the seashore this time of year. That's when they breed and that's where they breed. The tundra swan probably passes through here on its way south when the winter winds start to blow, way up north."

Trouble at home distracts the most single-minded of us and Camila was no different. She was having a hard time being positive about this school project. She had never been interested in bird watching and now with the distraction of Bevin turning on her as he did, the discovery that her brother-in-law was a child molester — living almost right next door, no less — and with a twelve-year-old daughter who was not attending summer school with her, Camila found herself very distracted. *Joe Cleod was in jail for a few days, but Bevin went over to Beckley, this very morning, to make his bail. Joe's coming back, at least for a while!*

She found herself gazing out the window, leaning on the window sill. *How did I get over here, again?*

"Oh! Come to the window, kids. What are those two birds sitting on top of the swing set?"

Children crowded to the window. Camila smiled at the excitement. Half-finished sketches rested on desks. Hand drawings of birds of all kinds and descriptions, littered the walls, some of them nicely illustrated and in color. Jeannie Hardwick, squeezed among fellow students, called out, "Is that a goldfinch?"

Another of the children disagreed. "Looks a little bit like a nuthatch." It was Jimmy Bowen. Camila knew he was working on a sketch of a nuthatch. *Nice kids,* Camila mused. *Who'd have thought I could get them this interested in something as dry as bird watching?*

"I think that's a great crested fly catcher," twelve-year-old ruddy-faced Jake Norris interjected. He was one of the brightest of the boys. Camila knew his parents; his father was a devoted woodsman. Jake spent a lot of time in the forests around Copperhead with his father. *Not surprising he'd be the one to know.*

"Where's the bird book — *Audubon*, I mean. Let's look up fly catchers." Camila smiled again at the race for the three copies of *Audubon* that were scattered around the room.

Jeannie found it first. "It says they're members of the tyrant flycatcher family."

That set Camila off again. It only took the word "tyrant" to snatch her back to her worries. *"Shut up and get back in the car,"* indeed! *That son of a bitch!* The frown that formed on her face at the thought frightened Jake Norris who had just come to her with a copy of *Audubon* opened to the flycatcher images. She realized it immediately. "Oh! I'm sorry, Jake. Something else is on my mind. Good job — identifying that bird! I wonder if they'll leave us a feather or two." She wished her emotions didn't show so readily on her face.

She had bumped into Jim Gibbons, the school principal, that morning. He could see her eyes were red from crying and asked, "Are you okay?"

"Just a touch of hay fever," she called back to him as she scurried off toward her classroom. "It'll probably clear up pretty quickly."

"Well, the goldenrod is blooming. That makes a lot of people sneezy this time of year."

Camila was back at the window, this time watching some smaller birds and a couple of the ever-present mockingbirds. *Mr. Gibbons is no fool. He knows it's not hay fever. I wish I could hide my problems more easily!*

ᙯ ᙰ

After Joe Cleod was arrested, Camila and Bevin drove the short distance down Goshen Lane to their house in silence. Back in the house, she went directly to the kitchen and began cleaning. *A handy escape into daily necessities,* she rationalized. Camila was unaware that she was slamming things around in her anger until Bevin came into the kitchen. "Why you makin' so much noise? Here my brother's been arrested for something he sure never done, you're gettin' uppity right in front of everybody, especially my brother and that cop, and now you're acting like you're mad about somethin'. What the hell's the matter with you?"

Camila stopped. She had a broom in her hands, a small pile of dust and what-not on the floor that she had just swept up. She shook her hair back out of her face and looked up at Bevin with a glare she hoped would kill. "Just listen to you: the King of the Hill. You're brother's just been arrested for child molestation and you have the cheek to get indignant with *me*! Go back into the living room, *Beaver,* and find something to read. I need to think about all of this."

"You givin' *me* orders now? You're in West Virginia, now, darlin'. We don't take much shit from our women around here, so you best stop handin' it out."

It was only then that she noticed Angie peering through the door from the living room, cowering in a corner, eyes huge, watching her mother having an argument with her new stepfather. "Bevin!" Camila shouted, "quit while you're ahead." She pushed past him, put her arm around Angie and together they went off to Angie's room.

Safe, more or less, behind the closed door of Angie's small bedroom, she embraced her sobbing daughter. "It's okay, honey. Sometimes adults have disagreements and argue. It can sound uglier than it really is. No need to be upset. We'll get over it, probably."

"Mom! What did you mean — by child molester? Is Billene okay? It was Billene you were talking about, wasn't it?"

"Oh, she's okay. She ran off from old Joe Cleod. She's over in Beckley at Child Protective Services. I don't know if she's coming back or not."

"Mom! She's my only friend here in this God-forsaken place. She has to come back."

"Angie, she probably isn't coming back. And there's a possibility that Joe Cleod could go to jail. We'll find out, soon."

"Do you think it was Joe Cleod that killed that girl from White Sulphur Springs?" Horrified eyes, cheeks streaked with tears, turned up to Camila. "Mom, that was awful!"

"No, honey. Of course not. You're safe here in the house. Don't you worry."

"Wull, Mom, if it wasn't him then who? There could still be a kid-killer running around out there somewhere."

"I don't know, honey. We just need to be careful. Until he's caught, just stay in the house. Please don't go outside unless I'm with you."

℃ ℅

The opening of the classroom door was just enough distraction to bring her back to the present. Camila snapped herself out of the memory and back into her classroom. Principal Jim Gibbons stood in the doorway wearing his red bow tie, brown blazer and a look of alarmed concern on his face. His secretary, Ellen McCloskey, stood behind him. He beckoned to Camila and said in a voice low enough that only she could hear, "Ellen will watch over the kids for a minute. May I speak with you?"

"Of course, Mr. Gibbons." She stepped into the hallway as Ellen McCloskey moved into the classroom. The hallway was empty of people, and the acoustics again assaulted her senses. The high ceilings and masonry walls lined with lockers echoed her footsteps as she closed the classroom door behind her. "What's up?"

He ran a hand through his short dark brown hair. "I suppose this could wait, but I'm very concerned and I wanted to chat with you about this immediately. You know, of course, your husband took a personal day. He didn't say why. When I asked, all he said was, 'It's personal.'"

"Yes. I know." Camila was getting antsy. *He found out about Joe and he's putting two and two together.* "His brother, Joe Cleod, was arrested. He's in jail in Beckley. Bevin went over to bail him out. This is strictly confidential, of course."

"Well, we can pick our friends but not our family, eh?"

"Yes. Really." Camila could feel the tightness of her lips and hoped Gibbons wouldn't see how upset she was.

"I sort of found out," Gibbons went on, "that Billene Cleod disappeared a few days ago. Come to find out she's at Child Protective Services in Beckley. Her stepfather is being charged with child molestation. I suspect that's why she ran away. Joe Cleod denies any wrongdoing and the girl refuses to talk about it. The charges are still pending but he's being released on bail. They think since the little girl is no longer living with him that she's no longer in danger, if the charges are true, in any case."

"I'm acquainted with some of this," Camila answered. "My husband and I were there when Joe was arrested. The man is vile. I wouldn't be a bit surprised to learn the charges are true."

"The police think he may be the man who killed that little girl from White Sulphur Springs a few weeks ago, but they can't prove he was in White Sulphur Springs. He was at work that day. They took DNA samples, but it'll be a couple of weeks before they get the results. If the samples confirm it was him, he'll be back in the slammer pretty quickly. I just wanted to find out if you knew any more about it than I do." Gibbons gave a sigh of disappointment. "If you find out anything about Billene, will you let me know?"

Camila fought the denial she had smothered herself with about the recent killing. *That girl was killed the very day Bevin got back to town. He's trying to say he arrived a few days later, but I know that's not true. And he passed through White Sulphur Springs to get here, the day the girl went missing.* "If I learn anything else about it, I will tell you, Mr. Gibbons. If you hear anything more about Billene, please let me know. My daughter and I have been worried about her."

"Will do, Mrs. Hardy. I'll let you get back to your class."

Camila flitted from desk to desk, checking out the sketches and the notes each of her students had accumulated on the project. The kids looked at her sort of quizzically as she passed. It didn't take her long to realize she was being too positive, too up, covering what she was feeling or trying to, and the thoughts that made her reel in fear and apprehension. *It couldn't be him. I couldn't have made such a mistake. It's just impossible. But! Is he the one?*

Jeannie had been watching her roaming around the classroom. Suddenly Jeannie's hand went up and she said, "Mrs. Hardy?"

"Yes, Jeannie." Camila went to Jeannie's desk. Checking her sketch of the tyrant crested flycatcher, she said, "That's really nice. You do such good work."

"Mrs. Hardy. What's this really about? You don't want us to learn about birds, do you? How is that going to help me in life?"

Camila stepped back in surprise. She shook her hair and glanced down at Jeannie. "You're right, Jeannie. I don't care if you learn about birds. What I want you to learn is how to do research and profit by it. You'll probably remember some of what you learn today about birds, but the lesson I hope you remember best is how to do the research and how to organize your thoughts to do research. So when you want to or need to, you can be your own teacher, later in life, when you must be."

℃ℬ   ℬↄ

Sherry could see that Billene's happiness was growing. She was hand in hand with her real father, Bill Parsons, walking down the street in Beckley West Virginia on a sunny day with white puffy clouds floating in a blue sky. Her friend Sherry Paulus held her other hand as they approached a small, brick house with white shutters, a green lawn and a sidewalk in front of it. "Here it is, sweetheart." Bill Parsons had begun calling her 'Sweetheart,' and she obviously liked it. "If you like the house, I'll sign the lease and this is where we'll live for a while. Let's go inside."

This was their third day together. Dr. Grayson asked Sherry after their first visit, "How do you think this is going to work out? Are they going to be okay together?"

"Dr. Grayson," Sherry answered. "It's going swimmingly. They both seem happy with their prospects. Bill seems like a good man. Too bad about the lost time in prison, but as a result of the false imprisonment, he's loaded. He'll never have to work again, but I think he probably will. I can't imagine him idling away his time on a golf course or fishing every day."

"The house could be bigger," Sherry observed. "Only two bedrooms."

"There's only the two of us." Bill smiled at her. "At least for now."

Billene, only half listening, caught the innuendo and looked up at Sherry. That Sherry's wide eyed gaze threatened to drill a hole in the floor brought a chuckle out of Billene. Parsons was looking at Sherry but quickly broke the gaze and continued. "Of course, we're going to have to do some painting in here. Billene? You ever done any painting?"

Billene looked up at her dad with a big grin. "If you ever seen Joe Cleod's cottage, you'd know I never even seen painting bein' done. Maybe I'm about to learn." She glanced over at Sherry who was not quite finished reacting to Bill's earlier statement. "Sherry. You want to help us do some painting?"

Sherry could feel that her eyes were still unnaturally wide open. She took a deep breath and said, "We'll see." Then she glanced again at Bill, turned and walked out the door with "I'll see you guys outside."

Later, as they walked back to the car, down the street and around the corner, Billene suddenly stepped behind Bill, obviously hiding. Sherry saw the blue mini-van coming down the hill toward the nearby stoplight, but she did not at first realize that Joe Cleod was riding in the shotgun seat and Bevin Hardy was at the wheel. Billene practically screamed, "Don't let them see me!"

But it was too late. Joe was rolling down the window as the car slowed for the light with Bevin dramatically objecting. They were almost a comedy routine; a man sitting beside himself in the minivan — identical twins, one dressed in a coat and tie, the other in a dirty sweatshirt, in need of a haircut. His long moustache hung over his mouth as he called out to his brother, "Hey! That's Billene!" Sherry could hear his voice as they passed.

Billene cringed behind her father. "Oh my God! They know where I am!"

Chapter Nineteen

Tamarack! Sherry drove her Dodge Dakota into the spacious parking area reserved for merchants. She lifted a large box from the back of her truck and carried it to the Merchants' entrance of the huge circular building with the many gables. The gables were not true gables but gave support and structure for the many clerestory windows that brought light to the interior of the building in daytime. Just inside, in the main gallery, she turned and entered a mysterious-looking shop loaded with esoterica of the Native Americans. Blankets of the native peoples, made by Americans, hung neatly over display racks at one end of the room. Clothing made of natural materials including cotton and deer hide decorated another portion of the room. Sherry directed her steps toward the section of the small room that displayed bows and arrows. There she set down her box and turned to face the shopkeeper. He was talking with a woman who was quizzing him about the merchandise in the store.

"I bet all this stuff is made in China like everything else I find in stores today!" Her whining tones meshed perfectly with the stretched buttons on her blouse. Sherry wondered that the woman was not wearing suspenders to hold up her jeans since she had no waist at all. "How can you prove to me that this stuff is made by real Native Americans!"

The shopkeeper turned and beckoned to Sherry. Instead of opening her box, Sherry stood and approached him. "Hello, Hokolesqua." The man smiled, brushed his long hair out of his eyes and returned the greeting. His homespun cotton shirt overhung his deerskin trousers that mostly concealed his handmade moccasins. The Native American designs and stitching in his shirt blended with and complemented the bear-tooth necklace he always wore.

"Alsoomse. It is good to see you. Have you brought me arrows as you said?"

"Yes, Hokolesqua, and bows as well. I found hard stones in the river and shaped them. Then I found bird feathers to make the arrows fly straight. The bows are shaped from the white locust, the very best wood for bow-making. But I think you will find no warriors to use them, only women to hang them on their walls." Sherry turned her gaze to the fat whiner. "How would you use my bows and arrows?"

"I still think they're made in China," the woman retorted.

"For Chinese goods," Sherry answered without smiling, "you must go to Walmart."

The shopkeeper, obviously sensing Sherry's antagonism toward this skeptical customer suggested, "Alsoomse, please go ahead and stack the arrows among the other items. The bows are in your truck?"

"Yes," Sherry answered. "I'll get them in a minute."

"Well, go ahead and stack them for presentation and I'll get your invoice when you're ready. Let me take care of this fine lady. She may have more questions."

Two more people wandered into the shop, *a husband and wife team,* Sherry decided without giving it much thought. She was familiar with how the shopkeeper liked having his goods displayed and she set to work arranging her things accordingly. *Terry's in rare form today — calling me by my Native American name. I wonder if he'll even tell that fat thing what the names means — Hokolesqua — Corn Stalk — after the famous Shawnee Chief — or what my name means — Independent! I suppose I am, too.*

As she worked, her mind wandered to the last archery event where she competed for first prize. The white locust bow she used that day was shaped by her grandfather and the arrows she used, by her brothers. She smiled at the memory of her grandfather's words, when he introduced her as "Alsoomse. She can shoot a ring-necked pheasant in the eye at a hundred yards. Her skill with the bow will embarrass your best archers."

It was still very early in the morning. Not many people had arrived. The archery master's lips tightened into a thin line as he drew out a large piece of wrapping paper from behind his small counter. On it, he drew the life-sized outline of a ring-necked pheasant, making the eye as big as a quarter dollar. He paced off a hundred yards in the event field and pinned the target to a bale of hay. When he returned, he got out his bow, strung it and pulled an arrow from his quiver behind the counter. He drew the bow and released the arrow. It landed in the neck of the bird illustration, a hundred yards away, two inches behind the quarter-sized eye. Then he turned to Sherry and said, "Show me."

Sherry fetched her handmade white locust bow and one arrow from her grandfather's truck. She strung the bow and set the arrow to the string. She drew back, aiming for a few seconds, and released the arrow. It struck the drawing of the bird not only in the eye, but in the center of the eye.

Sherry chuckled at the memory. Terry the shopkeeper broke off his conversation with the fat lady. "What are you laughing about, Alsoomse?"

Sherry turned to the shopkeeper. "Nothing." Her smile broadened. "Just remembering a time when I shot a picture of a pheasant with one of my Chinese arrows."

"I was there." Terry joined in the wide grin. "Have you stayed in practice?"

Sherry's smile vanished. The last thing she wanted was anyone to remember was her prowess with the bow and arrow, not now. In fact, that was the reason she was selling arrows, so that there would be many of her handmade creations all over the state — all over the eastern United States. When one was found where it should not be, maybe no one would connect it to her.

"I was ten years old. It was a lucky shot. One in a thousand. No one is that good."

"You were. I watched you that day." Terry wouldn't give up.

Hokolesqua/Terry turned back to his customer. "She could hit a twenty five cent piece at a hundred yards. I saw her do it and with homemade arrows and a homemade bow." Sherry cringed and turned back to stacking arrows in Terry's display racks.

"That was a long time ago," Sherry reminded him over her shoulder. "I was ten years old. I'm a grown woman now. Women don't use the bow. We only cook what the men bring us. Sometimes, we make the bows and the arrows. Today they're just art work to be hung on someone's wall. If you want hunting equipment now, you go to a gun shop and buy machine balanced arrows with razor sharp hunting heads. These stone arrowheads guided by bird feathers are too unpredictable. They can go any which way."

Terry turned back to his customer. "She's modest too. Alsoomse is the best. Her arrows go where she wants them to go and nowhere else. I've known her all my life."

ᘓ   ᙏ

Sherry's next stop was a few miles north in Charleston. The shop called itself "The Wandering Buffalo." Their specialty was re-enactor supplies. They even had real deer sinew and real buffalo sinew. *Great stuff for bow strings, but it's not the real thing if you don't dry the sinews yourself.* From Charleston, she continued north on I-77 to Mineral Wells. The truck stops had agreed to stock her things. *The wider the audience, the better.*

When she got home that night, she found three messages on her answering machine; one from Dr. Evelyn Grayson, one from Sally Colletti and one from Bill Parsons. *What does HE want?*

Grayson questioned her about the developing relationship between Billene and her father.

"It sounds good to me," Grayson remarked, after hearing Sherry's description of the time they spent together. "But I think we should go slowly on this. That poor little girl has had a rough time. We want to make sure everything is going to be all right before we release her into the custody of a virtual stranger. We'd like to get to know him a little better. How do you feel about continuing to tag along with them for a while? We'll pay you, of course. It's not fair of us to ask you to take time from your own life for this."

"I have responsibilities to the school in Copperhead, too," Sherry reminded her. "I've already taken two days off work for this. They've been very understanding and patient about it but I don't want to push the envelope of that patience too far, if you get my drift."

"Of course," Grayson sympathized. "I'll give Mr. Hardy a call at the school office and discuss it with him. I'm sure he'll be agreeable."

Oddly, Sally Colletti also brought up Bevin Hardy. "I thought you'd like to know, I followed up on our discussion of a few weeks ago. I wrote letters all over the place asking for statistical stuff from the appropriate schools and counties where Beaver lived. It's weird that the county where he lived in Massachusetts went out of business as a county and they don't handle things like this anymore. They turn everything like this over to the FBI and guess who came calling shortly after I wrote to them!"

"Anything turning up to support what we think?"

"It's coming together," Sally told her. "We need some more pieces, then the FBI will be going to Hardy for DNA samples. That'll be the real clincher, if he's guilty."

"What's holding them up on that?"

"They said they don't want to make any big mistakes. If they're wrong it would just embarrass the guy, maybe ruin his career and maybe even his marriage. They don't want to ruin his life on a hunch."

"Well," Sherry answered, "I hope they don't drop the ball on this. It's gotta be a low priority investigation for them. Are you going to continue working on this on your own or leave it to the FBI?"

"I don't know what the FBI is doing or going to be doing. I don't have a whole lot of confidence in the federal government anymore, except to collect taxes and lose wars. Geez! Don't get me going on that. Anyway, The FBI is part of the federal government, so I guess I'll keep working on it on my own."

"Great!" Sherry was relieved. "If there's anything I can do to help, please ask."

Finally, Sherry picked up the phone to call Bill Parsons.

Sherry put the phone back on the cradle and went into her one-step kitchen where she put on a kettle of water for tea. *Why am I resisting calling him?* After studying the flower design in the ceramic finish of the tea pot as though she had never seen it before, she went back to the phone. She picked it up, put it back down again and said, "Damn!"

Back in the kitchen, she checked on the still-cold water in the tea kettle, then stomped onto the back porch muttering, "Damn him anyway!" Sherry had said many times that she did not like red-headed guys, but something about this one was needling her. *Is it the kid? What does he want, anyway?! Any involvement is too much involvement. But I'm already involved. Billene needs me.* She furrowed her brows and, with eyes flashing, pulled open the screened door and stomped back inside. *I don't want a man in my life! Why am I even thinking about this?* The spring on the screened door pulled the door shut with a BANG. Sherry jumped, startled, and said, "damn!" again. The water in the tea kettle was still not hot enough. She glared at it, as though glaring at it would make the water heat faster.

Nerves steeled, cup of tea on the table by the phone, her fiercest demeanor assumed, she dialed. It took him four rings to answer. She almost hung up. When he finally picked up the phone, she almost laughed at herself. The mixture of relief that he was there and the added annoyance that she actually called him back struck her as comedy of the absurd. Mixed emotions had never troubled her in the past. She always knew exactly what she wanted to do, but this was different. It was like jumping into the river for a swim for the first time in the late spring. She never knew if the water would be cold and take her breath away or if it would be just — cool. Making the decision to just jump in without testing the temperature was part of the adventure, she always thought. This time, she wanted to test the temperature and she really didn't want to jump in at all, or so she thought. *Then why did I call him back?*

"Hi Bill. It's Sherry Paulus. I'm returning your call."

"Oh. Thanks for calling me back, Sherry. I just wanted to thank you for your help with Billene. It was very kind of you to spend so much time with us. Child Welfare would never have let me take her out without you being there."

Sherry was disappointed that the call was just for a polite *thank you*. There was nothing to resist — no "come-on" no aggression. The fight she was feeling inside was disarmed. "No problem, Bill. Billene is a great kid. It's just awful that she would have to have such problems. How's it going with Child Welfare? Are they going to let you have her?"

"Well, I don't think they really have a lot of choice. I have legal custody since I'm her father and the other guy never adopted her. I'm going along with the slow transition because I agree with them that a sudden change might be too jarring for my daughter." He chuckled and added, "It might be a little jarring for me, too. Twelve years in prison and suddenly I have a routine domestic life raising a daughter... It's good that we're having a chance to get to know each other more slowly ...and you've been a big part of that."

So. He really has no interest in me, personally, at all and all my fussing has been for nothing, Sherry mused as she answered, "Well, Bill, like I said, it was no problem for me and I was glad I could help out. Are the two of you going to live in that little house you showed us in Beckley?"

"Yeah. For a little while. When you called, I was cleaning paint brushes out back. That's why it took so long for me to get to the phone. I'm putting a fresh coat of paint on the inside and replacing the carpet throughout. I want it to be nice for Billene when she gets here. She helped me pick out the carpet yesterday."

"I bet that was fun. Did she pick something you liked, too?"

"She did! You have to come and see it."

"I'd like that," Sherry was surprised at her own genuineness. She really did want to come and see the new carpet and the paint. The rest of what she was feeling she quietly repressed.

"If you want to," Bill began, "Billene and I are going to run up to Charleston this weekend. She's going to need a lot of clothes — she has nothing. We're going to check out the restaurants and maybe take in a movie. Come along, if you want to. We'd love to have you."

So! The specter raises its head again. I was right to be fearful... and now what am I going to do? I'm glad he can't hear my thoughts!

"Bill, I'd love to do that, but for the next couple of weekends, I have a business project I'm working on and I have some loose ends to tie up."

(The next full moon is in two weeks!) "Let's keep in touch and I'll get back to you. Maybe we can do something like that a little later. I'd love to come along and help Billene pick out clothes, but this close in, I can't get away. Sorry.

Chapter Twenty

The unexpected opening of the front door of the sheriff's office startled Sally Colletti enough that she made a typographical error in the traffic arrest logs she had been filling out on the office computer. Sally said, "shit," under her breath and repaired the typo. She removed the telephone headset from her head, ran her fingers through her curly black hair and smiled up from her seat at the two FBI agents she recognized from their last visit.

"Let's see," she muttered loud enough that they could hear her. "It's Matthew Brown and William Montgomery of the Federal Bureau of Investigation. Right?"

"Call me Mat, and this is Bill," the bigger one said. Both were wearing full suits, neckties. They were bareheaded, Mat with full, dark brown, business-cut hair. Bill was getting thin on top with his sandy wisps just long enough that the breeze outside had mussed it up. Mat removed his sunglasses and said, "You have a pretty good memory, Miss Colletti."

"It's Mrs. Colletti," Sally replied with a smile. "What can I help you guys out of today? Are you here to contribute to the sheriff's campaign?"

"If catching bad guys helps the sheriff's campaign, maybe we'll be able to help, but not just yet. Is Sheriff Rankin in?"

"He's out chasing bad guys who drive too fast," Sally lied, remembering that Rankin had gone to Beckley for a haircut, on the county's time. He'll be back in another hour or so. Is there anything I can do for you two fellas?"

"I suppose we should have called to tell the sheriff we were coming — make an appointment. Is he going to be here tomorrow?"

Sally pulled open her top desk drawer, pulled out a schedule book and said, "Let me just, uh, pencil you in and I'll make sure he's here tomorrow. When would you like to be here?"

"How about right after lunch," Mat suggested. "Like around one-ish?"

"That will be just fine," Sally offered as she scrawled the coming event into her book. "Can I tell Sheriff Rankin what this visit concerns?"

At this, William "Bill" Montgomery opened his mouth for the first time. Sally was amused that Montgomery's accent sounded like Wisconsin. *Why not Wisconsin — maybe Minnesoota. Then she smiled at her own secret joke and fine-tuned her listening.*

"We've done some of the background research our last visit suggested. What we are finding is that what you surmised about a certain suspect appears to be correct. He was in all of the cities where murder/rape incidents increased during his presence there. While this, in itself, is very circumstantial, we want to arrange for DNA testing and that's a slippery slope. We don't want to go to his place of business because if the testing proves fruitless, it will just embarrass him; even possibly provide him with grounds for litigation. We can't force him to give DNA samples without a warrant, which we don't have. This is just part of a fishing expedition. So, we have to gain his permission and cooperation. If he's guilty, he won't give it and then we might have enough circumstantial evidence to get a judge to provide a warrant for such a test. That's what we want to see the sheriff about."

At Mat's quizzical look at Bill for sharing so much, Bill continued. "The only reason I'm willing to tell you all this is that it was you who started the investigation of this suspect. That we were here and why is considered confidential, of course and you, I am sure, are aware that if you disclose the information inappropriately, there will be consequences."

Sally pulled her lips tight in an expression of frustrated disgust. "I'm aware of that. You don't mind if I tell Sheriff Rankin, do you?"

ఇ ఴ

An hour later, Sheriff Rankin walked through the door with his fresh haircut. The FBI was gone. As Sally related the visit to the sheriff, the office door opened again and who should walk in but the very subject of their conversation, Bevin Hardy, A.K.A. Beaver Cleod.

"Well, hello, Mr. Hardy," the sheriff began in his jocular tone. Sally's eyes grew big and she was relieved that the sheriff did not add "we were just talking about you." *It would be SO like him to do something that stupid!* "And what can I do for you on this fine day?"

Hardy was wearing the blazer he habitually wore to work. Summer school was in session and Sally was surprised that he was in the sheriff's office instead of at the school. *Abuses on every level of government!* Sally thought.

Hardy had a large sheet of printed paper in his hand that he did not hand to the sheriff until after he said, "I've been thinking about organizing a Neighborhood Watch Program for Copperhead. Lots of other communities have them and we certainly have reason to establish one here. What are your thoughts on the matter, Sheriff?"

Rankin was certainly no poker player. He eyes grew round and large and his eyebrows rose to their highest level as he turned to Sally to express the irony and surprise as he replied. "I think that's a wonderful idea. How about you, Sally?"

Sally could feel her eyebrows at their highest level as well as she replied, "Oh yes!" Her eyes slowly left the sheriff's as she turned them to Hardy. "I think it's a wonderful idea, too. Who will oversee it? You?"

Hardy's shoulders went back, head held high as he said, "Who better? I'm the assistant principal at the local middle school. The parents look to me and the principal for leadership in such matters, as well as to you, sir." Hardy indicated the sheriff. "With your blessing on the matter, I'll call a meeting after notifying key people concerned in the matter. We'll get this thing going."

Hardy only stayed long enough to get the sheriff's nod of approval and to drop off his pamphlet that read, in part, "Neighborhood Watch, Organizational Meeting — at Copperhead Junior High School, 7:00, Friday..."

After Hardy left, the sheriff started chuckling, non-stop. Sally had her headset back on and was answering phone calls, continuing to do her weekly updating of the arrest and disturbance log records. Finally, the sheriff stopped chuckling. Sally went to his open door and said, "Exactly what do you find so damned funny?"

Rankin started chuckling again and when he got control of it he managed to say, "The fox is trying to get in the henhouse, right past the farmer with his shotgun. Don't you find that funny? Where's that phone number for those FBI guys?"

ᎧᏃ ᏠᎧ

Amanda Hardwick, Jeannie's mom, eased the bottom round of beef out of the pot where it had roasted at low temperature for the last four hours, bathed in Carlo Rossi burgundy and Campbell's mushroom soup. She had been smelling it for the last two hours. The aroma filled the house and drifted onto the front porch through the open screened door. The potatoes in the pot were soft, as were the other vegetables she liked to roast with her beef stew. The broccoli was ready. The cabbage, the garlic, the carrots... everything was ready. She carefully moved the large piece of dripping, falling-apart meat out of its pot and onto a large cutting board and began pulling it into tiny bite-sized pieces when she heard the knock on her screened porch door. It was Bevin Hardy! Jason was at work. Jeannie was at school and here she was home, alone with Bevin Hardy at the door!

"Why, Mr. Hardy! It's a surprise to see you here. Are you here on school business? I'd invite you in but I'm alone and I don't think that would be a good thing. What can I do for you?"

Hardy was not put off. "What's that wonderful smell out here? You must be cookin' somethin' good."

"Dinner for tonight. My husband will be home shortly. I hope he likes it. It will be beef stew over curried rice. I'll give your wife the recipe if you want. My mother used to like this recipe. Now my family likes it as much as I did when I was a little one...and what brings you to my door during school hours?"

"Ma'am, I'm starting a Neighborhood Watch Program for our little town of Copperhead, West-by-Gawd. I think we could certainly use one. Don't you?"

Amanda checked to make sure the door was hooked, trying to not look obvious about it. It was. "Yes, Mr. Hardy. I do believe that's a good idea. How will we get such a thing started?"

"We're having a meeting at the school tomorrow night. I'm going to ask for volunteers to watch their particular corner of the town and I was hoping to ask you and your husband to take part. Is that something you think you two might be willing to think about to help our little community?"

"I'll talk to Jason when he gets home." Amanda was wringing her hands absent-mindedly, nervous about this man, more or less a stranger, at the door.

"I'll just leave this paper on the chair, here on your porch. There's a meeting at the school tomorrow night at 7:00. I hope you can join us. I'll tell you and your husband all about it then. Okay?"

CB ED

The last bell of the day finally rang. Sherry Paulus walked out of her classroom thinking about how many more arrows she needed to make to sell in various places so that her arrows would be commonplace and not conspicuous when a certain arrow showed up in the wrong place. Her bow was ready for bending. *Tonight is the night for shaping the bow.*

White locust is a tough wood. She smiled as the memories of her grandfather bending wood for bows over an open fire returned to her. Sherry had found a way to do it with a steam kettle and a piece of PVC — much easier than over an open fire and much less likely to burn her hands.

Before heading for her Dakota, she swung past the principal's office to check out the bulletin board. Too often, she had ignored it and missed something important. This time she found something of definite interest.

Neighborhood Watch Program
Organizational Meeting
7:00 P.M., Friday
Copperhead Junior High School Auditorium
Come and help us organize to protect our home,
Copperhead, West Virginia

Beneath the headlines was a re-hashing of the sexual predation that had taken place in Copperhead twelve years ago and two weeks ago. Beneath that was a clipping of the Brian James article. The signature was that of Bevin Hardy, Assistant Principal.

What is that son of a bitch up to now? You bet I'll be there!

ೞ ഔ

Camila went straight home after school, without checking the bulletin board. On the car radio, she tuned into the local news station out of Beckley. The newscaster, Ray Peck, was just starting with, "Big news tonight out of Copperhead! Mr. Bevin Hardy, the new assistant principal at Copperhead Junior High School, is organizing a Neighborhood Watch Program. It seems that Copperhead has had more than its share of problems. While none of the area anywhere around Beckley ever had child predator problems, Copperhead has had one recently and some think it's connected with a killing that took place there twelve years ago.

Just a few weeks ago, twelve-year-old Amy Sue Gandolfsky of White Sulphur Springs was found up on top of Chad's Knob, raped and murdered. No clue how she got there. No clue who did it. When Vice Principal Hardy called in the news today he said, 'We're going to put a stop to this craziness.' Well, folks, the meeting is at the junior high school Friday night, that's tomorrow night. If you want to help protect the people and especially the children of Copperhead, ya'll come on over to the school and pitch in..."

When Camila heard her husband's name mentioned, she pulled over to the side of the road and stopped so she could listen without distraction. Her first thought, unbidden, sprang from her deepest fears. *Exactly what is that son of a bitch up to now?* She repressed it as quickly as it came to her, dropped the car into gear and proceeded toward the left turn onto Goshen Road.

ᘓ   ᘔ

Bill Parsons, paint brush in hand, carefully applied fresh paint to the door frame on the inside of the front door of the house in Beckley where he and Billene had taken up residence. The local radio station had been playing all afternoon as he repainted the trim on the inside of the house. He had decided on off-white walls with a darker tan trim. Billene liked it, too. She had picked out the colors with a little nudging on his part and even took up a paint brush and painted almost half of the trim in the living room herself. The country music on the radio became part of the game. They played at singing along, trying to remember all the words to the songs, at least the older ones. Then came the news by Ray Peck.

Billene immediately stopped painting. Bill watched her eyes grow wide and the fear appear on her face. "Billene," her father said to her. "You're safe here with me. No one can hurt you."

Billene looked at her dad and said, "That man is evil. His brother, Joe Cleod is evil. They are the Devil."

"Hardy is trying to do something good for the town," Bill answered. "Copperhead needs a Neighborhood Watch program. If they can get something like that started, maybe there won't be any more trouble."

Billene had not told her father of the conversation she had overheard between Joe Cleod and his brother Bevin Hardy, so Bill Parsons had no clue what she was talking about. "He's the assistant principal of your old school. He's the logical one to take control of organizing something like this. Why do you think he's evil?"

"He just is."

Chapter Twenty-One

The gymnasium seemed the logical place for the Neighborhood Watch organizational meeting, since it denoted action. Principal Jim Gibbons decided the auditorium would be too comfortable, that the hard seats of the bleachers overlooking the basketball court were uncomfortable enough to match up with the occasion. Camila noted that the crowd filling the room brought the temperature up quickly. Eighty two degrees outside and growing humidity didn't contribute to anyone's comfort. She watched with relief as Gibbons unlocked the cover over the thermostat and increased the power to the air conditioner. He then continued to the entrance to greet people coming in the door. Sherry Paulus arrived in jeans and sweatshirt, hair tied back. *Looks like she came right over here after feeding the horses.* Camila smiled inwardly. She liked Sherry. *The kids like her too. Oh, she could be iron handed, but with velvet gloves.*

Amanda and Jason Hardwick followed with Jeannie between them. Amanda, slightly wild eyed, surveyed the room as Jason picked seats for them near the door. It amused Camila, for no reason she could ascertain, that he had *spoofed down* for the meeting: dress slacks, fresh shave, long-sleeved shirt but no blazer and no tie. *Maybe this is one night he won't be trying to sell anybody insurance — well, maybe life insurance?* Her smile faded toward grim at the thought. She watched Bevin Hardy coming through the door, arms loaded with a coil of wire and a couple of microphones. He busied himself arranging the electronic equipment on a table in the middle of the room. Mr. Roddy, the janitor, followed a few minutes later with a cart loaded with folding chairs to place near the table. Camila still argued with herself that her apparently well-meaning husband *could not possibly ... but he was in the right place at the right time. We know of no one else who had been away from Copperhead for twelve years who appeared just in time to be here when the last murder took place.*

Sally Colletti walked into the room, followed by Sheriff Rankin with Deputy Joe Perry right behind him. This reminded Camila that the election would be coming up shortly. She had decided more than a week ago to vote for Joe Perry for sheriff and wondered idly who would win. *I wonder what Rankin will do if he finds himself out of a job. Maybe Perry will keep him on as a deputy?*

Although Camila was new to Copperhead, it was such a small town that she thought she knew just about everyone, but when Special Agents Matthew Brown and William Montgomery walked in, she watched curiously when they seated themselves next to Rankin in the bleachers. She did not know them and she did not know the FBI was investigating.

At the direction of some of the teachers who volunteered for the job, everyone was instructed to sit on one side of the gymnasium. "We don't want theater in the round," Bevin had explained in advance. But the room filled so much that some people could only stand in the sidelines and in the aisles. Camila was surprised that so many of the parents brought their teenaged daughters with them. *Afraid to leave them home alone, I suppose. Can't blame them.*

Finally, Bevin rose, picked up one of the microphones and began with the standard greetings, thanking everyone for coming and the interest shown by the community to support the Neighborhood Watch for Copperhead. As he did, Camila noticed a man enter the room alone; he looked very familiar but she was quite sure she had never seen him before. She watched him look for a seat, and finding none, take up a stance beside the door as some of the others had done. Then she realized she HAD seen him before — but this time he was somewhat cleaned up. She was staring at Joe Cleod, Bevin's brother. *What's HE doing here?*

Bevin explained how the town had been apportioned, and who would be watching and where for each area. He pointed out that they might not be looking for a stranger, that the perpetrator could be anyone, and very likely "someone we all know. That is, after all, the only way he could slip among us and not stand out as a stranger."

Camila noticed that Sherry sat with crossed arms, defensive and angry looking, her lips drawn into a tight thin line as she glared at Bevin. Camila grew aware that Sherry was not the only one glaring at her husband. Sally Colletti of the sheriff's office wore a fierce expression, as did Amanda Hardwick and several others. *Well, it's a grim situation,* Camila rationalized. For a moment, her eyes rested on the face of Sheriff Rankin. His look of boredom contrasted with the intensity of the two men beside him, whom Camila still did not know were FBI agents. They watched Bevin with guarded interest, almost as though they would pounce at any time. *Why do they look so intense?* Principal Gibbons remained seated, taking notes in a lined school tablet. Many of the parents watched with concern evident on their faces but no apparent rancor.

Bevin concluded the meeting by introducing the people who had volunteered from the various sections of the community and suggesting a self-imposed curfew: "Make sure the kids are in before it gets dark."

As the meeting broke up and people headed for the doors, Camila made a beeline for Sherry, catching her just before she got to the door. When she stopped her, the glance she got from Sherry startled her. The look of pity left Camila with food for thought that would last quite a while. *Does Sherry know something I don't know?*

"Hi, Sherry. Don't mean to hold you up. What do you make of all this?"

Sherry grimaced and released a loud huff of breath, almost like a snort. "This is awful."

"You've lived here all your life haven't you?"

"Yes," Sherry snorted again. *Like one of her horses,* Camila couldn't help thinking.

"You must have some idea who could be responsible for these murders. Do you?"

Sherry's brow furrowed deeply, she snorted again and glanced back into the gymnasium where Bevin was coiling the microphone wire to be put away. "Camila. What's happened here in Copperhead is unthinkable. What's happening is unthinkable. We're going to put a stop to it, once and for all."

Camila pulled Sherry out of earshot of the crowd and tried to press a little harder. "Do you think it's Joe Cleod, my husband's brother?"

Joe had already left but Camila scanned the departing crowd for a moment, looking for him. Sherry looked at her again, a quick glance, but what Camila saw in her eyes sank in. "No." Sherry almost snapped it out. "I don't think it's Joe Cleod. Gotta go, honey. See ya in school."

Camila watched Sherry's quick departure with surprise. *She DOES know! ...and she doesn't want to talk about it. Was that a brush-off?*

Angie, who had been seated with some friends, came up to her. "Mom, I'm scared. Do you think that killer is still around here somewhere; that it's like Bevin said, it's someone everyone knows and wouldn't suspect?"

"Please quit using his first name. It would make him feel much better if you could call him 'Dad.' Even if he's not really. He tries."

"Mom. Changing the subject isn't going to make me forget the question." Angie's eyebrows were up. She was waiting.

"Angie, there is evil in the world. We never know where we're going to find it. That's why we send you to school, so you can learn what to be afraid of, what to fight for and how to live a successful, fulfilling life..."

"Mom, you're beating around the bush." Angie interrupted. "Is there a killer in the town?"

Camila recognized that she wasn't going to be able to guide her daughter's attention away from this so easily. *She's growing up!* For a fleeting moment, she felt proud, but the pride was edged away by the fear that filled the air that night, making a Neighborhood Watch program a necessity. "It appears to be so. What do you think of that?"

Angie crossed her arms. *Almost like she's hugging herself,* the thought came to Camila unbidden. Then one arm snaked out and around Camila's waist, the half hug evolving into a full hug. "This is scary."

The gymnasium was nearly empty except for the sheriff, who was talking with Principal Gibbons and Camila's husband Bevin. The two strangers remained, participating in a discussion she couldn't hear. Sally Colletti seemed to be contributing, but as Camila and Angie approached them, the conversation went lite. *It's as though they don't want me to hear what they're talking about.* It was then that her husband introduced Matthew Brown and William Montgomery. "Call me Bill," Montgomery insisted.

Camila looked from face to face. "I'm glad the FBI is on this. Are you making any progress?"

Brown answered, "Some. Yes. But we really can't talk about it. We may be ready to make an arrest in another week or two."

At that, Bevin's eyebrows shot up. "So, you have a suspect?"

"Indeed we do, Mr. Hardy. But the evidence is still circumstantial. We aren't ready to make any statements about it and we won't until the time is right."

"When will that be?" Principal Gibbons wanted to know.

"That will be," Montgomery interjected, "after we make the arrest."

The expression on Bevin's face was priceless, thought Camila, but so were the looks of excited anticipation on the faces of Sally Colletti and Sheriff Rankin. The FBI guys remained opaque. Principal Gibbons glanced around at them in what Camila decided was a sort of quiet amusement. "I get the idea that there's a lot going on behind the scenes, right now. Am I right?"

Special Agent Brown took the lead. "This isn't open for discussion, but it will be eventually."

Camila looked from face to face, settling on Agent Brown. "Are you looking at someone locally, then or is it someone from outside of the community?"

"Ma'am," Montgomery spoke up. "It's a closed investigation — closed means closed."

Chapter Twenty-Two

Amanda Hardwick turned into the CCS. *I think I'll make pulled pork again for tonight.* To add to the pork, she bought potatoes, onions, garlic and some Sweet Baby Ray's Barbecue Sauce. *Mmm Mmm!* At the counter, she had to wait behind one other customer. The man was alone, dressed as though he were homeless, except, Amanda noticed, for the very well maintained shiny black Army boots he was wearing. When Amanda noticed the boots, she began looking him over more carefully. His shaggy coat, torn pants and faded full brim canvas hat were oddly in contrast with his fresh haircut, manicured finger nails and new-looking boots.

As he paid for eight boxes of twelve-gauge shotgun shells and four bottles of Hoppe's gun powder solvent, gun cleaning patches and four bottles of gun oil, she noted another oddity: his exceptionally long, delicate fingers. He paid in cash and quietly loaded the merchandise into a canvas backpack. When he turned to leave, Amanda saw his face for the first time. His pristine shave shocked her. The fifty-year-old tanned face radiated health. The laugh lines stretched from the back corners of his eyes, almost reaching his ears. Bushy black eyebrows framed his most startling feature: fierce black eyes, which, when he caught her looking at him, softened into a devilish twinkle, highlighted by a toothy grin with excellent teeth. He shouldered his pack, muttered, "Buon giorno," smiled even wider then headed for the door.

Amanda watched him walk away before approaching the counter to pay for her groceries. The young woman at the cash register who had greeted Amanda weeks before had also greeted Bill Parsons when he had first arrived from Morgantown on the bus. Her sandy hair, gathered behind her, swayed as she moved her head. Her Mumford and Sons T-shirt looked new and she was sporting a fresh tattoo on the left side of her neck, featuring a red and blue fire-breathing dragon and an armored knight with a sword; she had since added body piercing to her lips and forehead. These additions were new to Amanda and she stopped herself from staring by glancing into her purse, looking for her wallet. "Hi, Jen. Who was that man? Ever seen him before?"

The cashier paused in ringing up the groceries. "Nope. I'm pretty sure I'd remember him if I ever did. What did he say to you?"

Amanda counted out the amount of money she thought she owed, looked up and said, "I don't know; it sounded Italian, but I don't think it was. I wonder what he's going to do with all those bullets and gun-cleaning stuff."

Jen finished ringing up Amanda's purchases. "I didn't see a shotgun, and I think he was on foot — no car. Whatever he's going to do with that stuff, he's going to have to carry the weight of it in his pack."

"He looked like he could manage — somewhat muscular."

Jen smirked. "I noticed that too. I bet he has some interesting stories to tell!"

That afternoon Amanda's house smelled of freshly cooked pulled pork. She set the food aside. Time to go pick Jeannie up after school.

She parked in the school driveway in plain sight of the front entry. Summer School for many of the children meant an opportunity to pick up courses that were not available during the school year. They offered foreign languages, cooking, marksmanship. They even had a small class of young boys who wanted to get airman's licenses eventually. Sometimes they would go to the airport at Beckley to study certain aspects of the airplanes there. They even got to go flying with an experienced pilot a few times.

Amanda waited. Finally, no more children exited the school. She left the car and went inside, looking for Jeannie. There she bumped into Camila Hardy, heading for her own car. "Well, hello, Mrs. Hardwick. Jeannie wasn't in school today. Are you here to pick her up?"

"She wasn't in school? I dropped her off here this morning in time for her classes. Have you not seen her at all?" Amanda could feel sweat forming on her forehead. Her heart was pounding. Her voice was more elevated than she intended when she said, "Where could she be? Oh my God! I hope she's all right!"

Camila gave the required conciliatory response, "I'm sure everything's all right. I bet she's at home waiting for you, forgot — again — that she isn't walking to school and home anymore." Amanda could see the concern on her face. Camila knew as well as everyone else that a killer of twelve year old girls was running around Copperhead somewhere.

"Good God!" Amanda was practically shaking with fear and apprehension. "We tried to explain to her about the danger but she shrugs it off saying, 'It's daylight. It's safe. I'll be okay.' She doesn't understand the danger she could be in. She doesn't even know what rape is and that someone she doesn't know from a faraway town like White Sulphur Springs was found way up on Chad's Knob has little meaning for her. I need to see the sheriff."

When Amanda burst through the door of the sheriff's office, she could feel the tears burning her cheeks. Sally Colletti was behind her desk in the reception room, in her uniform of headset, sweatshirt and jeans. She rose immediately, tearing off the headset, and rushed to Amanda. Hugging her, she said, "Oh, Amanda. What's wrong?" Amanda was so choked up she had a hard time talking.

Rankin was at the federal building in Beckley with the FBI guys, but Sally knew what to do. In a flash she was on the radio to Joe Perry. "Joe, I need ya ta run up ta Chad's Knob real quick and make sure nothin's goin' on up there. We got another twelve-year-old girl missing — Jeannie Hardwick. We gotta find her. Her mama's goin' crazy with worry." Next, Sally called Copperhead's two other deputies, Harry Miller and Larry Ober. She sent Harry down to the river landing ramp, behind the boat rental to see if Jeannie was down at the river. "Sometimes when the kids play hooky," she explained to Amanda, "That's where they go. It's out of sight. Then they get involved in having a good time and forget to come home before they're missed. I bet that's where she is."

Jason Hardwick was next to burst through the door. His black suit with the white pinstripes had splashes of mud on the trouser leg. His tie was pulled loose but still hung sloppily around his neck. The gold pen in his shirt pocket told Amanda he had been pitching group health insurance today. "Exactly what the hell is going on?" His uncontrolled tones were unfamiliar to Amanda. She had never before seen him in all-out, terrified rage. "Is Rankin here?"

"He's over in Beckley," Sally explained again. I got Joe Perry on it, and Harry Miller and Larry Ober. The whole Copperhead police force is turned out, focused solely on finding your daughter. So calm yourself. Sit down..." Amanda was surprised at the force coming out of petite Sally Colletti. "...and have a cup of coffee. We'll hear from our officers soon. You can depend on it!"

ca   &

Giuseppe "Chigger" Bartalucci slapped a mosquito that landed on his left cheek. *Or was it one of those damned gnats?* Nearly to the top, on his way to Chad's Knob, he heard the roar of Joe Perry's engine racing up the rocky, rut-ridden dirt road. Ever so quietly, he slipped between branches and bushes, like a deer, disappearing into the trees, careful to not bend the smallest branch or loosen a leaf from a bush. He knew his heavy army boots left tracks, but he mitigated the effect by walking on the hardest ground — no mud — keeping to the rocks as much as he could. When he tired of tip-toeing up the road, he stepped into the trees where he felt he could walk less guardedly. He remembered the moccasins of Spook, the Keetowah. Smooth-bottomed, perfumed with rabbit dung and deer urine so as to not leave a trail dogs would follow. *Smart idea. I should be using something like that right now, myself.*

As Joe Perry sped by, Chigger watched from behind a stand of elderberry, ragweed and chicory. *I wonder what he's doing up here now. Full moon isn't for a while, yet. Maybe he doesn't know to come at the rise of the full moon. But that's good. By the time he gets here, I'll be long gone.*

Perry had apparently parked at the top and was walking around. It wasn't that far and Chigger knew that if all Perry was doing was driving up for a quick scan of the area, he'd be back in a few minutes, but he stayed more than thirty minutes. Then Perry came flying down the road as fast as he had ascended it. *If that cop wants to live to retirement, he better start driving better. I bet he doesn't know how to use his turn signals and cruises in the passing lane on high speed highways. I'll never understand cops in this country!*

After Perry left the scene, Chigger waited a few minutes until he couldn't hear the engine of the police car any longer. Then he waited another fifteen minutes to see if anything interesting happened. When the gray squirrels came out of hiding, he felt it was safe to continue. He had not forgotten the spot where he had found "Spook sign" before. He found the bushes undisturbed this time, but he remembered where they were. Quietly, he slipped into the trees again. Inching his way into the forest, he watched for the mockingbird that had given him away the last time. *Mockingbird's gone. Babies grown.* In spite of that, he decided to give Spook a "heads-up" and gave the kiss sound of the birds. He waited. Nothing stirred that he noticed. Chigger waited and watched.

His considerable forest wisdom hadserved him well in the past but he knew the Keetowah to be a master of woodcraft who deserved studying. Shortly, he felt a prod from a hard object in his back. *The shot-*

gun! He smiled because he knew the Keetowah had no ammunition, but Chigger offered no disrespect. He said, simply, "Hello, my friend."

A voice, gravelly from lack of use, answered, "You would call a man friend who holds a shotgun to your back?"

Chigger tried to conceal his amusement. "A man with an empty shotgun held to my back must be a friend who trusts me very much since my gun is NOT empty. Would it offend you if I turn to face you as I speak?"

The Keetowah was not wearing a ghillie suit this time. His deeply lined face and the fear in his eyes betrayed his bravado. "You were here before."

"Yes," Chigger answered softly. "You asked me to bring you gun oil and shells for your twelve-gauge. Have you forgotten?"

"I have no friends. I am alone on this mountain. No one comes here to see me but for other reasons. What are your reasons?"

"What you say is true, Keetowah. I have other reasons to be here, but made use of the trip to bring you what you asked me to bring you."

The Keetowah's brow furrowed. The corners of his mouth turned down — an anti-smile. "No one brings me things. Show me." The shotgun had been lowered and was replaced with a stone knife that Chigger believed would have been as lethal as a carbon steel one.

"As you can see, I have a pack on my back. Please permit me to lower the pack and reach into it."

The Keetowah glowered even more fiercely. "Lower the pack. *I* will reach into it."

Chigger heaved the pack off one shoulder and allowed it to slide to the ground. "I fail to see why you are so suspicious of me. I was here before. We spoke as comrades of the forest. I brought you no ill. What is different now?"

The Keetowah reached into Chigger's pack. "The front pocket," Chigger guided him. The Keetowah removed his hand from the main pouch and reached into the front pocket. In a moment, his hand came out of the pocket holding a box of twelve gauge shotgun shells.

"Well. I'll be damned. What else did you bring me?"

Chigger relaxed a bit. "I brought you eight boxes of those, Hoppe's gunpowder solvent, gun cleaning patches and gun oil, as you request- ed. Now you can not only fire your gun, but care for it as well. Would you like me to bring you a new shotgun, next time, maybe? If that one hasn't been cleaned or cared for in a long time, it may not even fire. And if it does, it may not give you the performance you would prefer, to be gentle in my meaning."

The Keetowah frowned again and turned away. "You come bringing gifts and offering more. I have nothing to offer in return. No gifts. But I have food. Are you hungry?"

"When I was here before, we spoke of what happens here during the full moon, sometimes. Do you remember?"

The Keetowah's frown returned. "I remember. He has not come here since we last spoke."

"There will be a full moon soon."

The Keetowah raised his eyes to the heavens and said, "I know this. I prayed to the Moon for shotgun shells. The Moon sent you. You brought me more than shotgun shells. The Moon be praised."

Chigger understood the primitive faith being expressed. He neither respected nor disrespected what faith can do, however it is directed. "When the moon is full again, it is my belief that the man will come again. I will wait on the top of this mountain until he comes."

"Is it your intention to kill him?"

"Perhaps." Chigger's rifle, disassembled and stashed in his coat, could drive nails at three hundred yards, but he didn't expect to have so much distance to be concerned about; maybe only fifty yards, if that. "If he brings a child to kill, I will take his life. That is why I am here. I am here to kill a killer of children. Will you tolerate me being on the mountain with you for a few days, until the full moon?"

The Keetowah grew silent. His eyes scanned the heavens through the heavy, leafy cover of trees above. Chigger watched his countenance harden. He spat to one side and said, "I may even take your kill away from you. Such a kill would be honorable."

ᘓ ᘔ

Amanda Hardwick sensed that Sally wasn't telling everything she knew about the child killer. There were subtle body language signs, or so she thought. Jason was finally sipping coffee; Amanda had refused it. They waited in the sheriff's office reception room half an hour before the radio finally came to life; a male voice calling for Sally.

"Colletti here. Whata ya have?"

"We got 'em — the girls that is. I'll have them there in ten minutes."

Amanda started crying. Jason wrapped an arm around her saying, "She's okay. It's like Sally said, they played a little hooky and lost track of the time. That's all it was."

The girls were ushered into the sheriff's office by Deputy Larry Ober. Amanda lit into Jeannie like a one person hornets' nest. Jason stood back for only a moment before stepping in. "Amanda, take a breath. Jeannie, your mom is going off like the Fourth of July but you have no idea the pain you caused her. She isn't angry so much as relieved that you're safe. We need to have a long talk about the situation in our town right now, about playing hooky from school. We're paying, by the way, a lot of money so you can take these summer courses. The least you can do is respect that enough to attend school faithfully."

"Dad, it was just one day. Julie and me went down to the river and went swimming."

"Julie and *I*," Amanda corrected her. If you can't learn to speak English correctly, you'll be playing hooky all your life. You won't be able to get any job better than that and the boys will think you're stupid. So you won't be able to get a decent husband, either."

"Dad," with long drawn out tones, "didn't you ever play hooky?"

"No."

Chapter Twenty-Three

Billene Cleod. Billene Parsons. What's in a name? "Dad? Do you think we could change my first name to Wilhelmina? You could still call me Billene for short."

Their yard on Tupping Court needed fertilizer, according to Bill. She still wondered why her dad snorted at the name of the street, "Tupping Court." When she asked him why, his reply was even more puzzling. He said, "It's the home of the beast with two backs." Then he laughed again and added, "When you read *Othello*, you'll probably understand." Bill had a small bucket beside him, filled with a sort of cement and a flat-sided tool in his hand that he called a trowel. His chore for the day, as he put it, was repointing the brickwork along the bottom of the outside of their house. While he did this, Billene took it upon herself to pull weeds from their sparse and long neglected lawn.

Since Billene saw Bevin Hardy and his brother in the blue minivan, she never left Bill's side. He was of, course, aware of this. His gentle prodding to tell him what happened only tightened her lips. She didn't miss the ramshackle cottage on Goshen Road, but she did miss the huge trees and the rich vegetation of her mountain. There was no wild chicory to be picked here. The place had no elderberry bushes to pluck stems from to be hollowed out for peashooters when the chokecherries were ripe and, for that matter, no chokecherries. On the other hand, Bill Parsons was not a drunk like Joe Cleod and so far as she knew, he had no twin brother who liked to kill children. The thought brought on an angry shiver that her dad noticed.

"You're safe here with me, Kiddo." He liked to call her "Kiddo." They were still visiting the hospital twice each week, where they sometimes drew blood from her, for what, she had no idea. Each time, they gave her another shot and that hurt. "You caught a disease in that other place, Kiddo. They're treating it and soon there will be no trace of it left. I know the shots hurt. It has to be done."

"What disease, Dad?" How old would she have to be to understand that her stepfather had given her syphilis?

"Oh, just a nasty disease that people catch sometimes. If you behave yourself, you'll probably never get it again."

"How does behaving myself have anything to do with catching a disease?"

Bill took a deep breath and raised his eyebrows slightly as he looked at her, considering his answer. "Right now, it would be sort of hard for you to understand, but when you're older, I'll explain it to you. But not now. Deal?"

As she watched her dad carefully clean out loose mortar from the brickwork and replace it with fresh, the memory of hiding under the azalea bush returned again. Every now and then, she would see a Daddy Longlegs spider here, making its way up the side of the house, or trying to hide under a bush at the side of the yard. It reminded her of the safe haven under the bush where she could listen and watch unseen. Every time the memory returned, in her mind's eye she would see the blue minivan coming up their dirt driveway with Bevin Hardy at the wheel. He looked very spiffy in his coat and tie, but underneath, she knew, he was just as coarse as his brother, or worse. At the memory of their conversation, instead of sneaking into the nearby forest and spending the night running barefoot through the woods to the sheriff's office, she jumped up and ran closer to her dad. She plopped down beside him now and hugged herself, trembling. Bill put down his trowel, wrapped a big arm around her shoulders and said, "You're safe here, Kiddo."

She wrapped both arms around his sweaty neck, held him tight, whispering through an onrush of tears, "I know, Dad."

"Billene, I know you have a lot of hurt connected with what you've been through, and a lot of fear. Sometimes when a person is hurting, if they talk about it, some of the hurt goes away; not all of it. Sometimes things that hurt us never completely go away, but talking about it can help."

She tightened her grip around his neck and whispered, "I can't. Maybe later."

"Maybe when I finish this, we can hop in the car and take a ride over through Copperhead — with the doors locked. You'll be safe with me. Maybe seeing it again will soften the memories a little bit. It's just another town, after all, like any other. There are good people there. Right now, they're having a real flap. The assistant principal, Bevin Hardy, has organized a Neighborhood Watch Program to try to protect the children of the area. They have people out every evening, watching for strangers, trying to make sure this stuff never happens again in their town."

She drew back from him, lips drawn tight in anger. "Bevin Hardy organized the Neighborhood Watch Program? That's a laugh." She drew away, picked up the plastic grocery bag she had been stuffing weeds into and angrily resumed pulling wild plantains and dandelions.

Bill watched her in amazement, then picked up the trowel, took a dip of cement from his bucket, and said, "It's a laugh that Hardy started a Neighborhood Watch Program? You don't like him very much do you...?"

She straightened up to her full height of about five feet, threw the grocery bag full of weeds on the ground where some of them scattered and shouted, *"No!"* She could see by Bill's look of surprise that her fierceness about Bevin Hardy was a revelation.

She furrowed her brows even more deeply, gritted her teeth, picked up her grocery bag and snapped, "He's the one they're looking for!" Then she picked up the weeds that she had scattered and resumed weeding. Bill sat there on the ground, trowel in hand, stunned.

She could feel him watching her. *He's a real father. He doesn't push. He just waits. He's patient.* The afternoon grew warmer. Billene was sweating, like her dad. He had made her wear garden gloves so she wouldn't "get any spider bites," as he put it, or nick her skin on a sharp twig or something.

Bill started back working with the mortar. She could hear the sound of his trowel against the side of the house. It was comforting to know he was close and that she was safe. She walked to the foot of the porch steps and placed her bag there to put in the garbage later. Then she walked over to Bill Parsons who was still seated on the ground, nearly finished with his repointing job on that section of the house. She sat down on the ground beside him.

"Dad." He stopped his work for a second and glanced over at her. Then he continued his mortaring.

"Yeah, Kiddo?"

"In front of Joe Cleod's house, there is a big azalea bush where I used to hide, to get away from him. It's a beautiful bush. In the spring, it gets covered with flowers. But the flowers don't have any smell. Mr. Hardy came over one day while I was under the bush. He didn't see me. I heard them talking. Mr. Hardy killed those girls. Joe knew. Mr. Hardy invited him to come along next time." Billene felt his arms encircle her, gentle, reassuring, but she couldn't talk anymore for crying, except to say through the tears, "It's why I ran away. Next time it might be me."

Bill sat perfectly still, a frown deepening on his face. "What's he like, this Mr. Hardy? I've never met him."

Billene let go of her dad's neck and slid away a little bit. "He looks just like Joe Cleod. They're twin brothers, except Mr. Hardy is much cleaner and no mustache."

"So. Bevin Hardy, the organizer of the Neighborhood Watch and the assistant principal at your school is the man who killed that girl from White Sulphur Springs?"

"Yup. ...and the girl you went to jail for killing twelve years ago."

"Good job to get for a child molester, assistant principal of a junior high school. It gives him immediate access to a wide selection. And if he organizes and takes charge of the Neighborhood Watch program, it means he'll be in control of where people watch."

Bill put down his trowel, although he had a few more feet to cover. He took the bucket, now nearly empty of its cement mortar, and held it under a hose bib to thoroughly dilute it before dumping it on the ground. He set the bucket down near the hose bib and went back to Billene, taking a seat on the grass beside her. "Does anybody else know about this?"

"No. I didn't tell anybody."

"Let's go inside and have some ice cream. After working out here in the hot sun, that seems like a good idea to me. You game?"

Billene followed her dad up the porch steps into the house, wiping the tears from her cheeks. During the period of time Dr. Grayson was considering releasing Billene into her father's custody, Bill had furnished the house — "making it fit for people," as he put it. Since Bill enjoyed cooking, the kitchen stood fully equipped. For ice cream dishes he chose a white background decorated with blue chicory blossoms.

"I like the dishes, Dad. It reminds me of the flowers on Goshen Road."

After the ice cream, Bill poured himself a cup of coffee. As he sipped his coffee, they chatted about other things that needed to be done to the house, to make it more "people friendly." They settled on throw rugs and some wall hangings to be chosen later. "Ya know, Kiddo. I need to make a phone call." His stern expression signaled Billene that the phone call would be about what she had told him.

"Daddy, please don't tell the sheriff. Joe will come after me. Mr.

Hardy might come after me...and I'm twelve years old and a girl."

Bill picked up the dishes from table, carried them to the kitchen sink. He returned to the table and sat down beside his daughter. "Billene? Do you trust me?"

"Yes, Dad."

He took both of her hands in his and said, "Then trust me now. I'm going to make sure that man not only does not come after you but he won't go after anybody else, ever again."

He dialed the phone, waited a moment and then said, "This is Bill parsons. I need to speak with Mr. Maguire. Would you please ask him to call me?" After hanging up, he poured himself another cup of coffee and took a seat beside Billene, still at the table. Within minutes, the phone rang.

"Yeah, this is Bill." Pause. "Hello Mr. Maguire. Thanks for calling back so quick." Pause. "I just wanted to tell you, Billene finally told me what happened and why she ran away, and there's something else I learned that I think you might be interested in." Pause. "Yes." Pause. "Okay. We'll be here." He hung up the phone.

"Billene, my old friend and boss Dan Maguire is coming over here for a visit. He's as good a man as there is and he knows right from wrong. He said he'd be here in about twenty minutes. He's a man you can trust. I think you'll like him. I do."

They soon heard Maguire climbing the porch steps. Before he reached the door, it was opened by Bill Parsons, smiling, hand out to shake; Billene, feeling fearful, was right behind him. Billene had seen Maguire before but she hadn't known who he was. He had always looked scary to her with his flannel shirt, graying hair, a little too much belly and a growth of hair on his chin and cheeks that gave the impression that he might be homeless. "Great to see you, Bill; and this must be the famous Billene?"

After brief greetings, small talk and Maguire praising Billene, Maguire finally cleared his throat. Although Billene had never met him before, even she recognized that was the signal that it was time to talk business. "Let's take a seat at your desk," Maguire said, indicating the kitchen table. "I feel more comfortable talking about business when I have somewhere to prop up my elbows." He smiled at Billene's look of inquisitiveness as they headed to the kitchen table, where Bill poured coffee for himself and Maguire.

"So," Maguire opened, looking at Billene with as friendly a smile as Billene thought he could muster. Despite herself, she felt comfortable with him. "Bill tells me you think you know who our bad guy is. Do you?" His smile was gentle.

Billene was still a bit shy about this subject. She furrowed her brow, lowered her eyes and nodded her head. "Yes."

Billene repeated the story that she told her father earlier, with some detail added. Maguire leaned back in his chair, elbows off the table. He lowered his eyes, evidently in deep thought. "Billene, what you just told me I already suspected. I've been doing some digging on my own. I know it was hard for you to share this with your dad and with me and I want to thank you.

"Bill," Maguire continued, "how about another cup of that coffee." After taking a sip of the very hot liquid, Maguire continued. "Billene? You ever been to Disney World?"

Billene looked up at him with a smile and said, "No. Have you?"

Maguire sort of chortled and said, "Yes. Yes. It's a wonderful place. Maybe you can go there sometime soon." Maguire turned to Bill and said, "Bill, I know you're a free man and I'm no longer your boss. But for your own good this is what I want you to do."

"What is it, Boss?" Bill's smile was to that of a friend, not an employer.

"It's about time Billene had a break from West Virginia, a little time to blow out some of the cobwebs. I want you to get in your car tomorrow morning very early and take Billene to Disney World in Orlando, Florida. Plan the trip for two weeks. On the way, stop in St. Augustine. That's on the east coast, about 655 miles from here. Make it a leisurely trip. At St. Augustine, my recommendation is the Silvan Inn. Make a reservation. They fill up pretty quick. It's right on the beach, too. Billene? You ever been to the beach?"

Billene was getting excited. She looked directly at Maguire and answered, "No."

"The Sylvan and some of the other beach hotels have a bus that picks up there, free, to take you into town. The beach bus driver in the morning is John. Say hello to him for me. In St. Augustine, take the tour of the city on Old Town Trolleys. Ask for Friar Bob. He'll give you a good tour. While you're in St. Augustine, register for at least one night at one of the local motels if not the Sylvan Inn and while you're there, make sure you get an ATM withdrawal from one of the banks where there is a security camera. I want the security camera to document that you were there. Make sure Billene is standing right beside you when you do this, where she can see the camera, so she'll be in the picture, too.

"From there, go on down to Orlando and register in a motel. While you're in Orlando, go to another bank that has a security camera and make another ATM withdrawal to document you were in Orlando and when. Every two days, get another ATM withdrawal from the same bank. Can you do that for me? — Hell — for yourself..."

Bill turned to his daughter. "How do you feel about that, Kiddo?"

"Disney World? The beach? Can we go to Universal Studios and Sea World too?"

Bill turned back to Maguire and said, "Thanks, Boss. We'll do that."

ᚳ ᚣ

Giuseppe Bartalucci leaned against a towering oak, blanket under him, dozing. His cell phone buzzing woke him. The text message said, "1, 2, confirmed. $1 + 1 - 2 = 0$." Later that afternoon, Chigger climbed through the woods to the edge of the clearing at the top of Chad's Knob to watch the moonrise. *He might come early. He might not come at all. If not, I know where he lives.*

Chigger texted back, "1 + 1 confirmed. 228." *Eight is the symbol for infinity, standing on its side. Maguire's code is perfect. I will send 2 into infinity.*

Chapter Twenty-Four

On this day Principal Gibbons appointed Camila Hardy and Sherry Paulus to be two of the lifeguards/chaperons to watch over the girl's swim team practice. They arrived at the women's locker room at the same time. Camila and Sherry had both had lifeguard training in college but neither was currently certified. That argument did not relieve them of the duty of backing up Coach Bernice Jackowski. *She's not from around here, I'd think,* Camila thought. *Sounds Polish... or Russian...*

Ms. Jackowski arrived just after Sherry and Camila. *That bitch!* Camila's smile did not betray her thoughts. *Perfect body... What's she... 23?* "So nice to meet you, Ms. Jackowski. You must not be from these parts. I haven't heard any Russian names in Copperhead until today."

"It's Polish. Not Russian. But I forgive you. My grandmother up in Pittsburgh pronounces it with a 'Y', like 'Yackowski,' but we tell her, 'Bubba, we're in America now.' People think it's pronounced with a 'J' and that's all right with me."

"Bubba?"

"'Bubba' is old country for old woman or grandmother. We call grandma Bubba. Everybody calls their grandmother that, don't they?"

Camila chuckled at the thought of Bubba Manussi who she knew in Boston. He was from down south somewhere. In Boston he ran a fishing charter service off Stellwagen Bank and Mass Bay. The only thing more prominent than his redneck swagger was his belly that always showed a little bit under his Jaguars' T-Shirt. "Bubba huh? I'll have to remember that. So how do you like Copperhead West Virginia?"

Just then Sherry came in, just in time to catch Camila's question. Ms. Jackowski smiled as she pulled on her swimsuit. "Not long ago, I would have said the air is sure cleaner than the smoky Old Town, but they cleaned up the air by closing the mills. Now we have low air pollution and high unemployment. The New River is nice and easier to get to than the Allegheny or the Monongahela, but it's harder to go boating because it's so shallow and there's no Gateway Clipper running out of Copperhead."

"What's a Gateway Clipper?" Camila wanted to know.

"Dinner-dancing cruise on the river. It's wonderful."

"Here come the kids," Sherry observed. Sherry had her swimsuit on under her clothing so all she had to do was undress a little bit and she was ready for the pool.

"I can't do that," Camila observed. "It's just too warm to wear all those clothes all at the same time."

"You just haven't acclimatized from Boston, yet," Sherry quipped. "It's so much cooler there."

"Oh," Bernice Jackowski interjected. "Are you from Boston? I just *love* Boston... unless I have to drive in the city, of course." Boston's gnarled streets instantly came to Camila's mind, forcing another laugh out of her.

"Well, you have a point there, but we have dinner-dancing cruises in Boston!"

To get to the swimming pool they had to climb some stairs, squeezing past a group of girls who were headed downstairs to the locker room. *This Olympic-sized pool must have cost Copperhead County a bundle.* Camila gazed around in wonder at the quality of the construction, the ceramic tile with the school's insignia on the bottom of the pool, and foam-core lifesaver rings, easily removable from wall mounts. "Quite a swimming pool," she remarked to Ms. Jackowski.

"It's almost new, too. Everything works. It's even heated so when it gets cold in the winter, the kids don't have to shiver for the rest of the day after being in here."

"If you don't mind," Camila continued. "I'll just perch myself in one of those observation chairs over there and take in the action."

"That's fine," Jackowski answered. "Make yourself comfortable."

"I think I'll join her." Sherry said as she headed for the sidelines with Camila.

The chairs were not comfortable. Canvas straps cross-woven over an aluminum frame did not make for luxury. *But that's not why we're here,* Camila kept her grousing to herself. She was surprised to see Jeanie Hardwick come waltzing in. Her one-piece, low-cut swimsuit was not the regulation two-piece that the other girls wore. When Jackowski pointed that out, Jeannie said, "I joined the team at the last minute and didn't have time to get the other suit."

The first line for free-style assembled at the deep end of the pool. Jackowski called out, "Swim caps!" The girls started groaning and complaining, but they all placed the swim caps on their heads, strapped the chin strap in place and were about to dive in for their first run at a practice record when Bevin Hardy came through the door.

"Well, guess who's here," Sherry muttered.

Camila was shocked at the disguised acid in Sherry's voice and glanced at her quickly. "You don't like him much, do you?"

Sherry smiled deceptively, wiped her hand across the back of her neck and said, "What's not to like? I just do my job and try to stay out of trouble." She slouched in her chair and crossed her legs.

Bevin hadn't seen Sherry and Camila yet, in the corner of the room under the observation balcony. Camila was surprised at how openly he admired the young body of the swim team coach, but his attention shifted quickly to the girls lined up, ready for the flat racing dive. Camila deliberately stilled her thoughts but she could feel her lips tightening and she involuntarily crossed her arms and legs.

Sherry shifted in her seat and softly asked, "How's the Neighborhood Watch thingy going? I haven't been involved in it — too busy."

Camila took a quick glance at Sherry as she answered, but her eyes went straight back to watching Bevin and his interactions with Jackowski and the swim team. "He's been working very hard at it. He has the whole town covered. The Hardwicks agreed to keep an eye on their stretch of State Road. The Farrels and the Burkhardts at the south end of town are watching people coming into and leaving, looking for strange vehicles coming or going and town people who are going back and forth for no apparent reason. We're watching Goshen Road, the path up to Chad's Knob and Bevin's brother Joe agreed to help us with that. He spends most evenings on his porch anyway." *Drinking beer and stinking for the most part,* but Camila didn't share that thought with Sherry. "Have you heard anything?"

Sherry shifted again in her chair, obviously as uncomfortable as Camila. "That little Jeannie Hardwick gave us quite a scare the other day. I wonder why nobody missed Julie Biederman who was with her. Julie must play hooky often and not come home at any regular time. The Hardwicks were frantic and for good reason. We have no idea who this guy is who is killing children and we don't know when he'll strike next, if he's even going to strike again. For all we know the guy lives in Pittsburgh or Morgantown or Fairmont or Charleston. We're totally shooting in the dark."

Jackowski suddenly shouted, "Bang!" pretending to be the starter gun. Ten girls flat-dived into the water and began stroking toward the other end. "My God!" Camila spurted. "Ten belly floppers! I bet that hurt!"

Sherry chuckled. "It's called a racing dive. It's flat so they don't sink into the water and lose time. It's a faster way to enter the water. Not graceful, particularly, but faster."

Camila watched as the girls energetically clawed their way through the water. Jackowski had a finger on the button of her stop watch and observed intently as they approached the far side of the pool. "This is apparently over and back."

"Nah. This one is six laps," Sherry explained. "Part of the training is how to quickly change directions. Watch. They're coming to the first return."

Camila was surprised to see how fast that change of direction took place. Some of the girls did a sort of somersault while others just turned and started back."

"Sherry, we think the killer lives here in Copperhead. It would be hard for someone from out of town to find his way to Chad's Knob. It's not exactly on the map. When I first met him, I thought it might be Bevin's brother Joe but now I don't think he's organized enough to do something like that and he wasn't in White Sulphur Springs. He was at work that day."

"Any other suspects come to mind?"

"None. But I don't know the area and I'm just beginning to get to know some of the people who live here. You've been here all your life. You grew up here in Copperhead. If anyone would have a meaningful hunch it would be you. Do you have any suspects?"

Sherry turned her full gaze on Camila, looking straight at her. Her fierce black eyes frightened Camila, who involuntarily drew back a little. Sherry tightened her lips and then through clenched teeth she said, "One thing I learned, living in this small town is that gossip is dangerous. We have a tendency to take care of our own in this place. As roused as the people here are, I'll be surprised if the situation isn't resolved soon. As for me? I just do my job and try to stay out of trouble." Sherry turned back to watch the swimmers. The subject was obviously, closed.

The swimmers were on their third lap. Some of them were now swimming in opposite directions from each other. *I suppose the lead girls are more than a lap ahead of the slower ones. I wonder how Jackowski keeps track of who's supposed to be where.* Finally some of the girls started getting out of the pool back at the starting point and Jackowski started clicking her stop watch. Bevin was still there. *To greet the winners, I suppose. I'm surprised he's not in a swimsuit and in the pool with them.* Unbeknownst to Camila, Sherry had been watching her face instead of the swimmers. Camila's tightening lips and furrowing brow, every time she laid eyes on Bevin, made an impression.

"Doesn't look like you much like him either." Sherry's statement shocked Camila.

"He's my husband!"

"Just sayin'."

೦ヌ   ೮つ

At first, the Neighborhood Watch turned out to be more interesting than Camila thought it would be. She rode with Bevin that evening as he made rounds, checking on the watchers. They left the house after a quick snack and drove to the south end of town where they found Allen Burkhardt and his wife Mary sitting on the porch with a digital camera and a pair of binoculars. Next to his rotund wife, Allen's thinness made him look even thinner than he was. Camila took their joking lightly in view of the paraphernalia they had stacked beside them on the porch, including the binoculars. "We won't both sit out here all evening," Mary told them. "We take turns on the beer runs and snacks."

Allen chimed in with "Even if we don't see nothin' this gives us an excuse to sit out here and watch the sunset, maybe talk a little bit."

A little closer to town, Dave Farrell and his wife Donna told much the same story, although Donna thought she had seen a strange car drive through town a little while ago. "But we only seen 'em once," Dave contributed. "They was just passin' through. They ain't nobody."

This is accomplishing nothing. These people are using this as an excuse to sit outside on pleasant evenings and they are going to find nothing. "I guess what this is doing is providing eyewitness stuff to keep the kids safe as they have to walk through these sections of town. Is that your take on it, Bevin?" Camila was already bored and they had only visited two watching posts.

"You're probably right, Cam. One thing it does is to make everyone feel a little safer, however false that feeling may be. It could also create an atmosphere where someone up to no good will stay out of the area because of the increased likelihood of being observed." His driving was conservative, as though he were doing some watching of his own.

"You always drive so slowly?"

Bevin smiled at her quickly, then turned his attention back to the road. "With all the crap coming down on this little town, Jeannie gone missing — what, yesterday? — the place is crawling with the three cops Copperhead has on the force. They want action and they might not hesitate to try to get some brownie points from the sheriff by giving the assistant principal a speeding ticket."

"You think he's going to get re-elected?"

"I don't know about that. Perry is coming up with some pretty strong advertising. The real thing he has in his favor, it would seem, from a public point of view, is that Perry is better looking. They usually vote for the best looking one. Whatever his background and record says about him doesn't seem to matter."

"Perry has a good record. Rankin has made some mistakes that have cost the county some money." Camila was thinking of Bill Parsons' arrest and subsequent litigation. "Bill Parsons will never have to work again, unless he wants to."

Bevin responded by changing the subject. "Next stop is the Hardwick residence. I don't think we need to go see my brother. Do you?"

"No."

The Hardwicks were also sitting on their porch. Jeannie sat in the corner chair where she could watch the birds and the rabbits in the yard as well as seeing the road. When she saw Bevin and Camila drive up, she jumped out of her chair and ran down the steps to the car. "Mr. Hardy!" Then she noticed Camila in the shotgun seat and said, "Hi, Mrs. Hardy. So nice to see you."

Camila knew the score here. Jeannie had a crush on her husband; not a good thing, and she heard the disappointment in Jeannie's voice when she saw her. Camila smiled as she rolled down her window and said, "Hi, Jeannie. Beautiful evening isn't it?"

Jason and Amanda were not so jovial as the Burkhardts and the Farrells. "No one ever comes up this road at night," Jason told them. "If they do, like as not, they're lost. Have any of the others seen anything?"

"Not really," Bevin answered. "Mrs. Burkhardt said they saw a stranger pass through but Allen thinks they were doing just that — passing through."

"Who could it be that we're looking for, Mr. Hardy? Our town's people are good people. We don't have anybody living around here who has that kind of evil in him. It's got to be someone from out of town."

"I hope you're right, Mrs. Hardwick. It would be awful to discover that someone we know and respect is guilty of the kinds of crimes that have taken place here in Copperhead. Sooner or later, we'll all know."

Camila took it all in without a word. Sherry's fiercenss earlier led her to believe that Sherry DID know who it was. That gave her chills every time she thought of it. It's someone Sherry knows. If Sherry knows him, I probably know him as well. On Bevin's last statement, she looked at him and said, "You're right, Mr. Hardy. Sooner or later, we'll all know."

Chapter Twenty-Five

Seated on the bench outside the sheriff's office, Sally Colletti lit a cigarette. Pressure and stress often made her want to smoke. Sally's last cigarette butt probably still floated in the New River, somewhere way down stream, cast there with a curse seven years ago. Sally hated herself for starting again, but just for a moment... As soon as she got home, her husband would smell it on her and exclaim, "Oh, shit! Not again!"

Just then she saw the blue mini-van coming up the hill. As it passed the sheriff's office, the right side window came down and Bevin Hardy waived at her with a grin. A chill swept up her spine. What a charade! Most of the answers to her requests for information lay in a drawer in her desk. Rankin had reviewed it and the FBI had copies, yet here she sat, smoking a cigarette, and there drove Bevin Hardy, up the hill toward Goshen Road, still free. Rankin said the FBI would be back, and soon, with a warrant to get DNA samples from him, but where were they?

Another car, coming the other way, pulled over to the curb. Amanda Hardwick got out. She took one look at Sally and exclaimed, "Oh no! I thought you gave up coffin nails!"

"Seven years!" Sally hung her head in mock shame. Then she lifted her head and took another drag. "There's too much going on around here right now. I need an outlet and booze doesn't work for me. How's Jeannie?"

"We made her stay inside for a couple of days. She doesn't much like that. After that episode of swimming in the river — skinny dipping, no less! — we had to do something. Now when I take her to school, I personally hand her off to the teacher, Mrs. Hardy — Camila. She seems like a nice sort of person. I trust her."

Amanda ran her fingers through her hair, almost like scratching her head, as she added, "This neighborhood watch thing seems pointless. We never see anyone on our road in the evening. Hardly anybody lives up our way and the road dead-ends in just a few miles, so no one will be coming the other way."

Sally dropped some ash in a butt bucket beside the bench. "It may seem that way. We think it's a good thing, though. It gives people something to do to let them feel like they're helping, like they're doing something. And you never know what you might see out there." *Maybe I should tell her to watch out for blue minivans?*

Amanda took a seat beside Sally on the bench. "This is a nice shady spot and that breeze feels good. I AM upwind of you so you don't have to lean away." Amanda chuckled. "I quit some time ago too. So did Jason. We didn't want to be a bad influence on Jeannie, but I still miss it."

"Maybe I'll quit again next week." Sally shook her head in light frustration. "...or the week after..."

Amanda took a deep breath and said, "Any news about your investigation?"

Sally was aware of the danger of gossip and that anything she said, could and probably would be repeated. "Can't really talk about it. But I would certainly like to. Don't let the fact that everything seems very quiet fool you into thinking that nothing is happening."

Sally stubbed out her cigarette in the butt bucket and turned to look directly at Amanda, eyebrows raised, "I heard the girl's swim team has some new stars this year. Jeannie's on the team this year, right?"

Amanda shook her hair back, glanced at the puffy white clouds floating by high in the sky and said, "Yes. And you are changing the subject."

"Yeah." Sally rose to return inside to work. "...to something I CAN talk about."

Amanda rose, too. She made a swipe with her hands in an attempt to brush off dust from the bench and said, "Just wait a minute, please. Can you give me any hope at all that this is going to be over sometime soon?"

Sally stopped with the office door half open and said over her shoulder, "Amanda, the investigation is ongoing. We seem to be making progress but whether anything's going to come of it or not, it's too soon to say. If I could tell you, I would. Geez, I need another cigarette."

Instead of another cigarette, Sally poured her fourth cup of coffee for the morning, took a seat at her desk and pulled open the drawer containing the correspondence she had received about Bevin Hardy from virtually all over the eastern U. S., at least that's how she thought of it. In frustration, she thumbed through the papers again, just as the front door opened to admit Sheriff Rankin and Deputy Joe Perry.

"There's fresh coffee if you want it." Sally indicated the coffee pot. As the sheriff poured coffee for himself and his current political opponent, Joe Perry, Sally continued, "Sheriff, I showed you all this stuff that came back on the investigation. Don't we have enough evidence for an arrest? Boston reports elevated rape/murder activity of twelve-year-old girls all the time he was there. When he left, it ended. Penn State says the same thing. Indiana County in Pennsylvania says the same thing. It stopped in Copperhead when he left and as soon as he came back we got another one, from a town he had to pass through on the way to get here."

Perry took a seat in front of Sally's desk. Rankin leaned against the wall next to the coffee pot stand. He took a sip from his cup and jerked it from his lips, spilling a little on his hand and nearly dropping the cup. "Damn! That's hot!"

Sally waited. Joe Perry broke the silence. "We want him off the streets the same as you, Sally, but we already talked about this. That Boston hasn't had any more rapes of kids since the suspect left there isn't a big deal since he's only been gone a little over a month. So we can't use that as a significant factor. That things were happening in towns where he was living doesn't pin anything on him. People move in and out of those places all the time. It's interesting that rape rates were higher when he lived in those towns but what makes that interesting is how small our town is and that nothing happened while he was away and that didn't change till right after he got back. It's even more interesting that the girl we found here is from a place he had to pass through to get here and she disappeared at the same time he was passing through. What we have is a pile of information that looks interesting, but the real deal is going to be when the FBI gets its DNA testing done."

Sally stood behind her desk, shaking all the papers in her hand into a neatly lined up pile which she placed on the desk in front of her. "But we know he's the guy."

Rankin, recovered from burning himself with his coffee, interrupted. "No we don't know he's the guy. We just want this to be over and it looks like he might be the guy."

"If he is," Perry contributed. "It's sure cagey to put himself at the head of a Neighborhood Watch program that's supposed to be protecting us from him."

"You're dead on," remarked Rankin. "On the other hand, he's doing what we would expect any other man to do in his position. He's enlisting the town's folk to do what they should be doing anyway. He's giving them the feeling that they can help, and something substantial to do to actually provide that help."

"Yeah," Sally interjected. "He created a setup so he knows where everyone is watching, so he can avoid them, if he decides to do it again."

"Hardy seems like a smart man," Rankin began. "The guy who did this isn't very smart. If he had any brains at all, he wouldn't have left DNA evidence. Our perpetrator DID leave evidence."

Rankin took his coffee, went inside his private office and closed the door. Perry finished his coffee in one gulp and walked out the front door with, "It's almost lunch time and prime time to watch for speeders and red light runners. See ya later."

Sally reached into her purse, slid another cigarette out of its pack, pulled her cell phone out of its case and walked out the front door. She lit the cigarette and dialed a number on the phone. Finally a voice answered with "Hi, Sally. This is Maguire. What's the latest?"

After Sally told him, Maguire responded with, "Well. Sounds like good news all around. Maybe I should mention that Bill Parsons and his daughter are headed for Florida. By tonight they oughta be in St. Augustine and then tomorrow or the next day, Disney World. That little girl's pretty excited."

"I wish I was going." Sally exhaled a cloud of white smoke. "Any revelations at your end that we should know about?"

Maguire was silent for a few seconds. Then he answered, "Nothin' that's gonna change anything."

Sally snuffed out her cigarette and went back inside. The sheriff was standing by her desk. "Where you been?"

Sally headed for her desk, cell phone concealed in a pocket. "Just smelling the air. It's getting pretty intense in here."

Rankin headed for the coffee pot again and poured another. "If the bad guy is who you think it is, then we still have a perp running around the town and the kids may be in danger. If it's not him and we arrest him, there will be hell to pay and we're already payin' hell — to Bill Parsons — to be exact. We don't need to make any more expensive mistakes like that, especially right before the election."

Sally started smiling but stifled it. "Anybody can make a mistake, Sheriff, and that was a logical one to make."

CR &O

Joe Perry. Six feet two inches tall, broad shouldered, narrow at the hip, a lean and mean ex-Navy Seal, he decided to not look for speeders and stoplight runners. He headed his cruiser up the mountain on State Road, turned left on Goshen and crept up the road slowly. *While Rankin hides in his office, maybe I can scare out a rabbit ... or a snake.* As he passed the Hardy household, he noticed that the blue minivan was not in the driveway. *Nice job Hardy did of fixing up that old hovel. The old lady that lived there must have been born in that place and all the years she and her family lived there, never learned of the existence of paint brushes.* A little further up the road he passed the cottage of Joe Cleod with no white van in the driveway.

As scruffy as that guy always looks, he still holds a job. What's he, a coal miner?

Joe stopped periodically and got out of the patrol car to look for tracks in the soft dirt of the road — any kind of tracks. *What's up here?* About half way up, he discovered a clear boot track, but only one. *Either this guy just stepped out of the sky, and only once, or he's being very careful about not leaving any tracks.* Joe pulled the patrol car to one side of the road in case other traffic wanted to get past. *Unlikely, but let's be considerate.* He shut off the engine, locked the car and proceeded on foot, one slow step at a time. With each step, he inspected every leaf of every bush up to the height of a man, looking for a bent twig, a torn leaf. He didn't expect to find footprints, but every now and then he'd spot a partial of the boot track he had seen earlier. *These tracks look to be about a day old ... and there are none coming back ... at least that I've seen so far.*

Painstakingly, Deputy Perry crept up the mountain road on full alert, listening, inspecting, watching. There were no more boot tracks, indicating that the walker entered the forest somewhere, but where, Joe did not notice. *Probably a fisherman, headed for the trout waters of that creek below.* He continued the climb, seeing nothing out of place or unusual. A copperhead's tail disappeared into the bushes on the side of the road ahead of him, to the accompaniment of several loudly scolding squirrels. As the snake disappeared from their view, the scolding diminished but didn't stop for quite a while. *Hell! Maybe those squirrels are chattering because I'm here, not the snake at all ... or there could be some other reason why they're chattering like that.* He stopped to look into the trees. He wanted to find some of the noisy squirrels to see which way they were looking. *Give me a clue about what's disturbing them ... or at least where it is.*

After a few minutes of that, he gave up in frustration. Every time he saw a squirrel, it would only be in sight for a few seconds then it would dash up or down the tree or out onto a limb. *It's why they call those damned things squirrels, I guess — they're squirrelly.*

As Joe approached the top of the mountain, Chad's Knob, he began to experience an eerie feeling — a sort of prickling on the back of his neck. It reminded him of a hill he had climbed in Bosnia. The tree cover had been thick, just like this. Little animals rustled the leaves, just out of sight. Everything was quiet except for the birds and squirrels. With him were four other Seals, all clad in helmets, utility laden belts, rifles — and this eerie feeling. Not all at once, but gradually, the birds stopped singing. *Even the squirrels seem quieter.* Those squirrels in Bosnia were different, he remembered, sort of reddish, devilish color but as large as the American gray squirrels that he saw near Chad's Knob. Then, adding to his feeling of being watched, Joe noticed that the birds on Chad's Knob had indeed become relatively silent. The squirrels were no longer scolding, but there were some mockingbirds in the trees around him, hissing their warning hiss.

Maybe it's the ghosts of those little girls that were killed up here that I'm feeling? On the other hand... Nah. There are no Serbian soldiers on this mountain laying in ambush like those in Bosnia. Joe had been wounded in that ambush. Two of his companions were killed. He and Paul Kelly were the only two of the four who survived.

Joe thought he heard the click of a rifle being cocked. *It's gotta be my imagination. There's no one up here but me.* Then the memory of the army boot track came back to his consciousness. *Too spooky up here for me.* Joe Perry turned and retreated at a brisk pace.

Chapter Twenty-Six

Well, Sally Colletti considered quietly as she sipped a cup of her favorite Maxwell House Dark Roast, *maybe it's going to be a peaceful day... until the FBI shows up ... if they're going to...* There was no ringing of the phone yet today. The sheriff was in his office writing a letter on his computer. Joe Perry had a speed trap going, on the edge of town — south side. *Harry Miller is off today, probably chipping away at another piece of white marble. The guy loves sculpting — what a waste of time. I bet Larry Ober is in a boat on the New River trying out some of the flies he tied last week. It'll be a peaceful day...*

Maybe this would be a good time to consider redecorating the office. She gazed, probably for the thousandth time, at an enlarged photograph of the New River Gorge Bridge. The valley was full of clouds as it often was early in the morning. Robby Solana took the picture from his Cessna 152 that he so loved. *Sold that thing all over town. I wonder what Robby's doing these days?*

The thought was interrupted as the door opened — a little too quickly. *So much for a peaceful day...* Sally sipped her coffee, mentally assessing the guy in the doorway. His grimace looked dangerous. The solid white long sleeved shirt, dress jeans and gray suede oxford shoes clearly indicated to Sally *this man is not from around here.* She estimated he was five feet nine inches of anger. Business cut hair, clean shaved chin, clear skin and eyes... *This guy isn't very big, but he's in shape.*

"Good morning, sir. How can I help you?" The man paused for a moment as his eyes adjusted to the dimmer light inside. *Wow! Thought Sally ... clenched fists. This guy's hot about something...*

The man closed the door behind him, walked a few steps closer to Sally's desk and said, "Is Sheriff Rankin available this morning? I'd like to speak to him."

"Well," Sally began the dance. "He's here, but he's quite busy. May I ask who you are and what this is about?"

The man's fists clenched even tighter. Moderately alarmed, Sally said, "Just a moment, sir." She picked up the radio microphone and called Joe Perry. "Hey Joe, The coffee's ready, if ya want some." The code that he was needed at the office immediately was not ambiguous. He would be there in minutes; no siren. "Coffee and donuts" was the code for siren — emergency.

Joe responded with, "10-4. Thank you."

Sally looked back to the man in front of her desk. "I'm sorry sir. You were saying?"

Through clenched teeth and tight lips, the man said, "My name is John H. Hildebrandt. I am from Arlington, Massachusetts, and I need to speak to your sheriff. Do I need to make an appointment?"

Sally ran her fingers through her short dark hair, eyebrows up half in fear and half in frustration. "Let me check."

In a moment, Sheriff Rankin's girth appeared in the doorway of his office. "Please step into my office."

As they disappeared, Sally opened the drawer with her "Hardy records," as she thought of them. *Hildebrandt ... Hildebrandt — Familiar name. Who is he?* Then she found it. John H. Hildebrandt and Tammy Hildebrandt were the names of the parents of the little girl found killed and raped in Arlington, Massachusetts, just before Hardy returned to Copperhead from the Boston area. *Oh my God! What's he doing here?*

Sally could hear raised voices coming from Rankin's office. Hildebrandt was obviously raising hell. She could only make out bits and pieces of what Hildebrandt said. "It's him!" and "Why isn't he in jail?" She could hear nothing of the sheriff's replies. For a brief moment, Sally felt sorry for Rankin, having to field the barrage of just and angry sentiment from the father of one of Hardy's victims. ...and yes! Hardy worked, even now, as the assistant principal in Copperhead's Middle School ... a perfect place for a predator who liked girls of that age. *He isn't in jail because the evidence is still too circumstantial for a conviction, but when they get the DNA samples, I think this will be all over.*

Hildebrandt burst through the door of Rankin's office and nearly collided with Joe Perry as he entered. When Hildebrandt saw how big

Joe was, he stepped back a second, then started for the door again with an "Excuse me," on his still tightly drawn lips.

"Jusss hold on a sec, here," Joe stopped Hildebrandt by not stepping out his way at the door. At that moment, Sheriff Rankin appeared at his inner off doorway. "Is everything all right, here, Sheriff?"

Hildebrandt tried for the door again, almost pushing Joe out of his way, but Perry put one big hand on Hildebrandt's arm to hold him. "Just hold on here, buddy," Joe said. "We need to figure out what's going on. Sheriff?"

Sheriff Rankin cleared his throat. Sally wondered briefly if it was in imitation of Dan Maguire's famous gesture and half smiled at the thought. She looked with anxious interest from Joe Perry to John Hildebrandt to Sheriff Rankin and was relieved when Rankin took control of the conversation. "Mr. Hildebrandt, this is Deputy Joe Perry. Joe just came to us a few years ago, fresh out of the Navy. He grew up here in Copperhead and we're glad to have him, except he's running against me in the current election. Joe, this is John H. Hildebrandt, from Arlington Massachusetts. He's the father of a little girl who was victimized there just a few months ago and he thinks that the killer is here in Copperhead."

"Victimized hell!" Hildebrandt sputtered. "She was raped and murdered! And the killer is here!"

"Who do you think it is?" Joe Perry still stood at the door, now with raised eyebrows, wrinkled forehead and a quizzical look in his eyes. *He couldn't resist asking that!* Sally almost chuckled. *This isn't funny, but...*

"It's Bevin Hardy. He's now assistant principal at your school. Great place for a sexual predator!"

Joe refused to move from blocking the exit. "That's a pretty tall accusation, Mr. Hildebrandt. If you have any evidence we can use in court, I'll be happy to go and arrest him right now. We've had some killings here, too, and we'd like to put a stop to it." Sally found herself amused again, this time at Joe's stern demeanor, as though he was offended that the assistant principal at the local middle school could be accused of such an atrocity — when Joe knew very well that Hardy was the one and only suspect.

Rankin interjected himself again. "Mr. Hildebrandt, we are in the midst of an ongoing investigation. We think we've made good progress. We don't want our investigation muddied up by loud and reckless accusations. If the suspect we have in mind is alerted to the fact that he's under investigation, he could get away. I think the best thing you can do right now is get back in your car and go back to Boston."

Hildebrandt was not about to be put off so easily. "I came all the way down here to get this settled and I'm not going home till it's over."

Rankin answered, "You can stay as long as you like, of course, but there isn't much to do in Copperhead and the only motel is the Slipped Dysk. I doubt you'll like it. They don't have a restaurant and there is no swimming pool and the noises you hear at night might well keep you awake. The biggest problem you'll face, though, is getting locked up in jail for hindering an ongoing investigation. If you don't get in your car and go home, that's likely to happen."

Hildebrandt looked from face to face and sighed in apparent resignation. "Okay. Will you please let me out, Deputy Perry?" Joe stepped aside and Hildebrandt left. Joe took a seat by Sally's desk after pouring a cup of coffee. Rankin took the seat beside him. Sally took a sip from her coffee and said, "Do you think he'll go home or is he going to cause trouble?"

Rankin stood again and said, "Joe, maybe we better keep an eye on him. Would you mind?"

With an "okay, boss," Joe headed out the door.

cß ℞

Angie Hardy sat in the back room of their newly air conditioned cottage on Goshen Road overlooking the small garden in back. Her mom and Bevin had planted tomatoes back there. Some butternut squash sprouted right beside the tomatoes with romaine lettuce beyond that. Her mom liked playing with string beans so she had a few posts in the ground that she planned to tie the beans to when they came up. *This is the most boring freaking summer of my life. I'm trapped in the house while Mom plays teacher and Bevin plays principal.* She frowned at the book in her lap, *A Tale of Two Cities* by Charles Dickens. *Why am I trapped in this place for the summer of my twelfth year, reading freaking Charles Dickens?*

Camila had made herself very clear. "It's a classic that you'll have to read someday anyway. You may as well use the time to get a jump on some of this stuff. And it's a wonderful book."

"Okay, Mom. I'll try, but Dickens even *sounds* boring." Angie was surprised to discover that it was really a pretty good book. She was half way through it and reluctant to put it down, even to moan and groan about how bored she felt and how imposed upon she was, shut up in the house in this gorgeous weather. Her only friend Billene was gone. She hardly knew her but now, Angie knew, she never would. *Bummer*!

That thought was interrupted by the sound of footsteps coming up to the porch. *Geez,* she muttered, looking at her wristwatch. *It's too early for anyone to coming home yet. Who could that be?* She slipped quietly over to the window overlooking the porch and saw a strange man climbing the steps, carrying a shotgun. His white dress shirt had a smudge on one sleeve. Angie didn't recognize that it was from gun oil.

As he reached the porch landing, a police car came up the driveway, parking right behind the yellow Volkswagen the man was apparently driving. The police car would have screeched to a halt if their driveway had been concrete instead of dirt. The man on the porch paused and turned to watch the police car. Big Joe Perry hopped out of the car, drew his nine millimeter Glock and called out, "Hold it right there, Hildebrandt. Lay the shotgun on the porch and come down the steps with your hands behind your head."

The man seemed uncertain what to do. He obviously didn't want to comply with Perry's order but was afraid to continue to the door for fear that Perry would shoot him. "Do it NOW!" Perry shouted at him. The man bent over slowly, placed the shotgun on the porch deck and began descending the stairs. The man protested loudly as Perry handcuffed him and locked him in the back of the patrol car. Then Perry ascended the steps and picked up the shotgun. After pumping all the shells out of it and collecting them in his pockets, he rang the doorbell.

"You okay, Angie?" Perry wanted to know.

"Yes." But Angie was frightened. "Who is he?"

"Just a man who is making some big mistakes and screwing up his life. I figured he was headed up here so I followed him to make sure everything was all right. I'm going to take him off to the jail. If you have any more problems, please call me right away, okay?" Perry handed her his card.

"I sure will. What did he want? Do you know?"

Perry swiped a hand across his brow and around the back of his neck. He drew his lips tight and said, "Just a man making some mistakes. Don't you trouble yourself with it, okay?"

The first thing Angie did after Perry left was to call the school and get her mother on the line. Camila managed to get Sherry Paulus to combine her class with Camila's so she could get away and go home. After Angie explained what had happened, Camila called Rankin's office. "Exactly what the hell happened at my house this afternoon?" She demanded that Sally, who had the misfortune of answering the phone, provide an explanation. Sally deferred the call to Sheriff Rankin who was as evasive with Camila as Perry had been with Angie.

"The man made a mistake. We have him in the lock-up."

"Sheriff Rankin," Camila was not to be redirected. "I think you owe me an explanation. A man came to our door with a shotgun while our daughter was home alone. There was a police officer right behind him as though in pursuit. The officer arrested the man right there in front of our daughter and confiscated the shotgun. Now you tell me exactly what happened! Who is that man? Why was he at our house?"

Rankin, not easily intimidated, listened quietly to Camila's demands. "That man is from out of town," he replied. "He is here under a misunderstanding that we intend to get cleared up. Right now, he's cooling his jets in a jail cell. We haven't decided yet whether we're going to charge him but if we do it will be for interfering with a police investigation. He had no business coming to your house and frightening your daughter. I'm very sorry that he did that. He was clearly wrong and maybe even a bit crazed. He won't be back. You have my guarantee."

os so

Sally Colletti was privately disappointed when Perry showed up with John Hildebrandt in handcuffs. *What a shame. That poor man! If my daughter had been raped and murdered, I'd feel exactly the same way and if the law didn't appear to be doing its job, I'd get a shotgun, too, and come after the bastard that did it. Anyone would!*

Perry ushered Hildebrandt through the side door into the section of the building that contained jail cells. No one was there at present; Hildebrandt would be all by himself. A few minutes later, Sally was summoned by Rankin and Perry to record and take notes as they questioned him.

Hildebrand appeared very subdued by his arrest. "You know," Rankin couldn't restrain himself from saying, "If you managed to kill that man, even if he's guilty of what you say, you would spend the rest of your life in prison and your life might not be all that long. We have capital punishment in West Virginia."

Without much prompting, Hildebrandt explained. "After our daughter was killed, the police would only say there is an ongoing investigation. But it went nowhere. They said they had a suspect but there wasn't enough evidence to get a warrant for DNA testing. They like to use the words 'probable cause.' Eventually it came out that another girl had been assaulted by this man, but she got away before anything bad happened to her. Her accusation was hushed up, but in time the truth comes out. We heard about it. It seems to us that nothing like that happened before he came to Arlington, but after he got there, things started happening. He's the guy, Sheriff."

Chapter Twenty-Seven

The skies of West Virginia converged this day to clean the streets, wash away fallen leaves *and rinse the damned dust off my dirty car.* Sally Colletti daydreamed happily under her headset at the sheriff's office. The campaign for the office of sheriff was just about over. There would be no more public money spent on campaign leaflets, no mad flurry of trying to get radio and TV interviews for the sheriff. Joe Perry led in public opinion, so far as Sally could tell. Unknown to Sally, it was Bill Parsons' money that buried Rankin with "Joe Perry for Sheriff" television advertising all over the county and probably several counties beyond. In another few weeks the former Sheriff Billy Rankin would be standing in the unemployment lines over at Beckley.

Sally smiled at the thought. *Tonight, I'll open that olive oil...* For her birthday Sally's cousin Joyce had sent a bottle of the family's product from Caltabellota in Sicily, home of the world's best olive oil. Tonight she would pour some of that nectar over a Megan Salad for herself. Her family, still in Fancy Gap, Virginia, would be home in two more weeks. She drooled at the thought of the olive oil, slightly sorry that she would be enjoying it all alone.

Sally started in surprise at the interruption of her daydream, as the outer door to the sheriff's office opened suddenly. *I'm going to have to put a bell or something outside to warn me when people are approaching the door. It always startles me!*

Bill Montgomery entered first, followed by his partner, Matthew

Brown. "Good morning, *Mrs.* Colletti. Nice to see you again." Montgomery held the door for his partner, entering behind him.

"Good morning, yourself." Sally felt that her answer sounded too much like a retort and tried to soften it with, "Here to catch the bad guy, today?" She felt that wasn't enough, so she added a smile. *After all, they ARE the FBI.*

Brown closed the door behind him more gently than they opened it. "The Federal Judge in Charleston thinks we have enough circumstantial evidence to warrant a warrant."

"Oh, stop that," Montgomery cut in. "That's the kind of joke that's only funny once."

Brown continued, still snickering. "A warrant for DNA tests, that is. Any idea where we can find a guy by the name of Joe Cleod? ... and there's another one. We think they're related, Bevin Cleod, A.K.A. Bevin Hardy. From what we've been able to gather, he's also known as Beaver Cleod or Beaver Hardy."

Sally picked up the phone and buzzed the sheriff's intercom. "Could you please come out here?"

Rankin's door opened and he appeared, with part of his shirttail hanging out and a doughnut crumb on his chin. "How can I help you guys?"

After posing the same questions to the sheriff, Montgomery and Brown stood silently waiting while Rankin swallowed his last bite of doughnut. "I didn't know Bevin Hardy had all these aliases. He's the assistant principal at the local middle school. He's probably there right now. Joe Cleod lives on Goshen Road. That's not too far from here, but I believe he's a coal miner and he's probably at work right now. We might have to wait for him to get home."

Montgomery shifted on his feet and, with a glance at the coffee machine in the corner, said, "We should probably go over to the school and get this over with. We're not going to arrest him or anything like that. We just need to collect some DNA samples."

Sally caught Montgomery's glance at the coffee machine and suggested, "The sheriff is sort of busy catching up reports and other paper work. Joe Perry should be here in just a few minutes. Why not have a cup of coffee and a doughnut and wait for Joe to get here? Hardy isn't going anywhere. He'll be there when you get there."

Sally also didn't miss Brown's smirking glance at the crumb still on Sheriff Rankin's chin. He answered for the two of them. "Sounds good to me. Breakfast was a long time ago, way up in Charleston. You hungry at all, Bill?"

ᘓ   ᘒ

Joe Perry saw the "FBI mobile," as he thought of it, as he approached the sheriff's office. His routine of watching for speeders coming into town from the south and leaving by the same route usually had him showing up at the office around 10:00 A.M. No one watched the road to the north because there was none. Copperhead's only road came from the south, toward Hinton and Sandstone. He seldom caught many speeders because they all knew he was there, every morning. He enjoyed the time, watching the New River in its slow movement to the north.

Copperhead took its birth from that river in the days when river boatmen poled the *bateaux*, loaded with lumber and pelts one direction, then back again with supplies of tobacco, gunpowder and whatnot, for the small settlements in the other direction. They used Copperhead for a stopover. There was an active saloon there in those days.

But Joe's attention was drawn now to the FBI mobile. *What do they want now?*

It didn't take him long to find out, and as he rode in the back seat of the FBI mobile, headed to the school nearby with a DNA kit beside him, he frowned at the thought. *This going to create a real stir!*

The school, like the other government buildings in the area, showed excellent care. The landscaping was "just so." The sign in front that said, "Copperhead Middle School," Joe knew, had a fresh coat of paint every other year — and how old was the school? *About three years old. With the cutbacks in the mines, the reduced railroad traffic and the slowing economy, only government stuff is in really good condition.* Most of the homes the FBI mobile passed on the way to the school were built prior to 1970 and the vast majority before 1950. *Times change. Might not be all that long before we see the* bateaux *on the river again.*

As they approached the school, Joe noticed a face in a second floor window that vanished almost as soon as he saw it. Montgomery picked a parking spot near the door in front of the building. As they exited the car, Perry said, "Why don't one of you guys hang out here while the other of ya and me walk around back. I have a hunch."

The direction Joe chose around the building followed the path of the driveway to Teacher parking. The hot pavement enjoyed no cooling breeze and no shade. Joe and Montgomery were sweating before they rounded the front corner of the school.

His hunch proved right. As they rounded that corner, a blue minivan headed their way from the rear parking lot. "That's Hardy," Perry said to Montgomery. "You gonna let him get away?"

"Help me block the driveway," Montgomery ordered. They placed themselves in the driveway in such a way that Bevin could only leave if he ran over one of them.

Instead, he stopped, put on his most charming toothy grin and said, "Good mornin' fellas'. What brings you out here on this rainy morning?"

Joe answered, "The rain's stopped now. The sun's out and it looks like it's going to be a gorgeous day. We're here to see you, Mr. Hardy. Do you mind if we all just step inside for a few minutes?"

Hardy put his minivan in "Park" and got out. "I was just headed over to Beckley on some school business. Do you think this can wait a day or two? I'll come over to your office and we can chat."

Montgomery took over. "Mr. Bevin Hardy?"

"That's me," Hardy grinned from the mouth only.

"Please give Officer Perry your car keys. He'll park it for you, right over there." Montgomery pointed to a nearby parking spot. "We need to see you right now."

"What's this all about, Bub?" Joe admired Hardy's *chutzpa*. *Grinning innocence all the way to the chair.*

Montgomery continued. "I have a warrant here from a Federal Judge in Charleston empowering me to collect DNA samples from you, with or without your permission or cooperation. It would be far easier, simpler and cause you far less embarrassment if you cooperate. We can do this inside your office behind closed doors or here in the parking lot with you on the ground in handcuffs. What's your pleasure?"

At this point, Matthew Brown appeared, apparently having seen them talking with the man from the blue car. "Need any help, guys?"

Montgomery glanced at Brown, turned to Bevin Hardy and said, "How should I answer him?"

Hardy reached into his pocket and took out the car keys, but not before Montgomery had his hand on the butt of a semi-automatic Glock, hidden under his coat.

Hardy, clearly shaken, blurted, "No need for violence, fellas. My office is on the second floor in front of the building." As Hardy pointed, Joe realized that the office windows Hardy indicated were the very windows where he had seen the face briefly as they had approached the building.

Curious faces turned to watch as Hardy led the way up the stairs, through the school building and into his office. He closed the office door, eyeing the small case Brown had in his hand. "Why are you collecting DNA from ME?" Hardy wanted to know. "Is this in connection with that little girl that was killed up on Chad's Knob some time ago?

You probably know I started a Neighborhood Watch program here in Copperhead. I'm doing everything I can to help you guys protect our town. I don't see any reason why you'd choose me for this."

"It's a routine investigation," Brown lied. "You're not the only one we're getting samples from. You can trust me on that. You should be glad we're doing this. It'll prove you're innocent of all suspicion. You want that, don't you?"

Hardy sat down at his desk, leaned back in the plush desk chair and eyed each of them closely, if briefly. "Yes. I do want that. Thank you for being so thorough."

Joe almost rolled his eyes. *This guy is either very, very cheeky or he's innocent.* Joe didn't like the defiance he saw on Hardy's face as they exited the office. Montgomery paused as he left the room. Turning back for a moment, he said to Hardy, "By the way, Mr. Hardy, this will take a little time to analyze. I'm going to have to ask you to not leave the county until we get back to you and give you a clean bill of health, so to speak."

Joe had never before seen a man so close to sputtering when Hardy answered, "Of course," following it with the forced smile from the mouth only. *His eyes look like bloody murder. I'm going to have keep an eye on this one.*

Hardy's secretary, Roseanne Barrett, watched as they passed through her reception area on the way to the exit. Her eyes were wide, her mouth half open. She knew Joe Perry but she did not know the FBI agents. "Hey Joe," she queried. "Who are these guys?"

Joe paused to answer. "Just a couple of guys I asked to come along to help me with something. Nothing to worry about, Roseanne."

Outside the school, Perry called the sheriff's office on his cell phone. When Sally answered he said, "We need to get Harry or Larry out here to sit outside the school with a patrol car and make sure if Hardy leaves we know where he's going."

"Sure, Joe. No problem. Do you think he'll make a run for it?"

"I don't know, Sally. But I think we ought to make sure."

The trip up State Road to Goshen Road drew comments from the FBI guys about the natural beauty of the area. Montgomery, an Iowa native, exclaimed, "State Road is like a tunnel of green. Look at how big those trees are!"

Brown agreed. "Look there! Is that a Monkey Puzzle Tree?"

Perry glanced in the direction Brown indicated and said, "Yup. Sure is. We don't have many of those. They seem to like colder weather than we get, but we do have a few. I saw one in Inverness, Scotland, once, and there's one in Raphine, Virginia, there at the truck stop. It was just little but it was a Monkey Puzzle Tree, nevertheless."

Goshen Road brought out comments as well. Montgomery brought the car to a stop before entering the road. "Perry? Are we going to need a four wheel drive to get up this road?"

"Nah. It's okay. Just keep the wheels out of the deeper ruts, so the car won't scrape bottom. I was up here just a few days ago. The road's rough, but it's passable. Hardy lives up here, ya know."

"We were up here a while back, too," Brown added. "But we were in a taller vehicle and it looks like the rain may have made these ruts deeper."

"Love this thick foliage," Montgomery remarked. "Where I come from we don't have many places anything like this. There are flowers everywhere, trees hanging over the road. What a great place to live!"

"Yeah," Perry grimaced. "Come by in February and maybe you'll think differently."

"I don't think so," Montgomery argued. "It gets colder in Iowa than it gets here and we get more snow than West Virginia."

"Maybe so." Perry found himself growing weary of the small talk as the car bounced up Goshen Road. "There's Hardy's place." He pointed as they went past.

"How much farther is it to Cleod's?"

"He's just up here around the corner," Perry answered. "If you go all the way to the top, Cleod's is the last place you can see from the road."

"You mean other people live up here?" Brown was pretending incredulity and Perry knew it.

"We think there are others but no one knows how to find them." He thought of his visit a few days before and remembered the uneasy feeling of being watched. *At least I'm not alone this time.*

As the car labored around the next bend, where Billene used to hide behind the elderberry bush, Perry pointed and said, "That ramshackle cottage coming up on the right is Joe Cleod's place. And his white van is in the driveway. He's home. Probably sitting on the porch, half drunk or better."

Montgomery turned the car up Cleod's dirt lane, bushes so close to the car on either side that they scraped the sides as they pulled in behind the van. Perry was right. Joe Cleod was sitting on the top step to the porch, beer bottle in hand. As the three exited the car, Cleod challenged them. "Who the hell are you and what are you doing on my property? Do I need to get my shotgun?"

Perry smirked inwardly. *Smart-assing it off the top when visited by three law enforcement officials is not the best way to start a conversation.* "Hello, Mr. Cleod. Beautiful day, ain't it?"

"Beautiful hell, Perry! It rained like hell up here just a little bit ago. Who are these guys with you?"

Perry introduced Montgomery and Brown. Brown told Cleod why they were there and Cleod responded, "Sure. I'll give you DNA samples. I didn't do none of that stuff. You'll find out."

Montgomery took over. "You live up here, Mr. Cleod. Do you have any idea who killed that little girl a few weeks ago up here at the top of the hill?"

Cleod swiped the back of his neck with his hand, lowered his head for a second then looked up and said, "Nope."

Chapter Twenty-Eight

Amanda Hardwick had never liked Sheriff Joe Rankin. *It seems like he has a fundamental assumption that he was born knowing everything. It's how he got in so much trouble with that Bill Parsons. Arrested too fast...too many assumptions.* Amanda stewed for quite a while over her chance encounter with Giuseppe Bartalucci at the CCS. Her trip to Rankin's office, accompanied by the steady beat of her windshield wipers, resulted from her paranoia, however justified. She found Sally Colletti inside at her desk, headset on, typing away. "Hi, Sally."

"Amanda?" Sally looked up from her computer monitor, smiled, removed her headset. "What brings you to my cave? Want some coffee?"

Settled in the over-stuffed chair in front of Sally's desk, small talk over, coffee in hand, Amanda began. She described Giuseppe Bartalucci as well as she could remember him and the strange remark on leaving, "'Buon giorno.' What could that mean?"

Sally smiled, shaking her head. "I don't know. Sounds Italian. We haven't had any other reports of the guy, misbehaving or otherwise. He's probably just some homeless guy passing through."

Amanda took a sip of her coffee. "That's what puzzles me. He was dressed like a homeless person, but he had a fresh haircut, manicured nails and new shoes. I don't think he was just passing through. It's hard to just pass through Copperhead. There's only one road in and the same way out...and it's not all that good a road. No one comes here that doesn't mean to."

"Maybe a train dropped him off. The trains roll through here all the time."

"But they don't stop here anymore," Amanda insisted. "The Greyhound comes in here. Maybe he got off by mistake?"

"That's possible," Sally said, trying to be supportive. "The CCS IS a bus stop."

Rankin, passing through from the outside door to his inner office, paused for Sally to update him about their conversation. "Just some vagrant," he remarked. "If he causes trouble we'll soon have him here in lockup."

"He was buying shotgun shells, Sheriff." Amanda was not about to be comforted; she was quite sure Giuseppe Bartalucci was going to be trouble in some way.

"Maybe he wants to shoot some clay pigeons. Nothing else is in season right now. Want me to call Wildlife Control?"

"Well," Amanda remarked as the sheriff disappeared into his office, chuckling, "he certainly looked like wildlife." Just as she finished, the sheriff re-appeared from his office.

"If it makes you feel any better, Mrs. Hardwick, I'll let the deputies know about him and have him picked up for questioning. At least we can find out who he is and why he's in Copperhead. How's that?"

As the sheriff disappeared back inside his office, the outer door opened again and Sherry Paulus hurried in. "Sally!" Sherry was slightly out of breath. "Bill Parsons and Billene have disappeared. I've been trying to call them and all I get is the answering machine. I went over there and the house is all closed up, shades down and no one in sight anywhere. Isn't he supposed to stay in the area for a certain period of time so Child Services can learn to trust him?"

Sally put down her coffee cup. "Well that *is* odd. We thought he was supposed to stay in the area, too. I wonder where they went."

After Amanda and Sherry had left the office, Sally got out her iPad. She tapped on "Contacts," selected Dan Maguire, and began pecking away feverishly. *The sheriff's too close for me to make a personal phone call. This will have to do.* Of the things Sally told Maguire in this email was the recent contact from the phone company, reporting to the sheriff's office that occasional text messages had been detected from somewhere in Copperhead to somewhere on the mountain, near Chad's Knob; they appeared to be code of some sort. *I wonder what that is! Maguire will want to know.*

ଔ ଚ

Giuseppe Bartalucci didn't much like being stuck outside in the rain, especially on the top of some strange mountain, isolated from the world — his wife, children, brothers and sisters. Some hot pasta and Fatascia Almanera would suit him just fine right now. A little cayenne in the tomato sauce with just a touch of garlic and a nice antipasto salad would make good background for the rapid-fire, multi-leveled conversation of family.

I'm not going to do this anymore. This is the last time. From now on, it's retirement, fishing, golf and lazing on the porch, overlooking the olive groves and fields of capers with Mount Etna in the distance.

His protection from the rain consisted of a plastic camouflage rain coat, not too heavy. The full-brimmed hat kept the rain out of his eyes. He frowned at the high polish on his boots, now covered with rain and mud. His waterproof pack kept his things dry but his rifle, ever ready for action, dripped with fresh water. He would oil it again when the rain stopped and make sure all the water was out of it.

On this trip up the mountain he had only shouldered the rifle once, to use the scope, not to fire it. A visitor had wandered up long steep Goshen Road. He used the telescopic lense of the rifle to keep a watch on the intruder. It was a policeman. Chigger didn't recognize him and wondered, as he watched, if the Keetowah also saw the man and what his thoughts were of receiving such a guest. *Not too pleased to see him, I'll bet.*

The biggest problem Chigger had with long stakeouts like this was the boredom. *I eat too much and don't get enough exercise.* The Kindle in his pack proved helpful. The battery was good for at least a week, so long as he didn't try to use the 3G utility and download more books. He had enough books to last him much longer than the battery, anyhow.

His visits to this mountain had acquainted him with the wildlife and he enjoyed watching the creatures around him, even the occasional copperhead snake that slithered past from time to time. *They want no more of me than I want of them. I leave them alone and they leave me alone.* The squirrels were getting used to him, reluctantly, but gradually. They no longer scolded loudly every time he moved, but stayed warily away from him. *That's okay with me,* Chigger smiled to himself. *The damned things bite if they get too close.* It was on that thought that he felt his cell phone buzzing against his chest. *Here's something else that has a battery that lasts a week or better if I don't use it,* he reflected, as he reached inside his rain slicker to pull it out. Another text message: "*!"

Chigger found this message puzzling. The asterisk meant *radio silence.* An exclamation point meant *turn off your phone.* Chigger knew Maguire's phone would be off already but that it would be back on tomorrow, just after noon — the day of the next full moon. He frowned as he turned his phone off. There would be no contact until tomorrow night. He was on his own — no support — no matter what.

He considered wrapping the phone in aluminum foil just in case the rumor was true, that the phone company could remotely activate such devises. *That's bullshit!* He hoped. *These phones have no GPS device. How could they locate it?* He remembered his conversation about that very subject with Maguire when Maguire first handed it to him. *But if they want to, they can still triangulate the position of the phone from its broadcasts. I've only made two broadcasts, how could they pinpoint me so fast? Well, maybe they haven't, otherwise someone could be up here looking for me, but there's no reason to do that yet.*

Chigger began very slowly and quietly to move from his temporary camp to a spot about fifty yards from the clearing at the top of Chad's Knob. His chosen place gave him a clear view of the clearing in a position that would not require him to fire his rifle in the direction of the road or in the direction where he expected the Keetowah to be hiding. *If I have to fire this big rifle, I don't want to hurt anyone I don't mean to hurt.* He liked this spot because he was completely out of sight of the clearing and had an unimpeded view through his rifle scope. The spot, fifty yards from the center of the clearing, was exactly what the scope was sighted in for, and he knew that at that range, he could put the bullet through the center of a penny, every shot — if it was pennies he was shooting at... He would wait in that spot until at least midnight tomorrow night, when the full moon reached its zenith. *If he's not here by then, I'll go to his house. I hope I don't have to do that.*

CΩ ℬ

Camila Hardy stared out the window of her classroom while her students completed a brief writing assignment she had given them. She saw Sherry arrive and back her Dodge Dakota into a parking slot right beside Camila's car. *I wonder where she goes on her free period. Must not be far; there isn't that much time. I wonder why she always backs into her space instead of driving in frontwards like everyone else does. I'll ask her. It's a damned pickup truck, too! It can't be because it's easier. Why does she drive a damned pickup truck, anyway?*

Camila's students recognized her black mood today. Her ready smile wasn't so ready when Denise Herssy came in late for class. "Do you have a hall pass? Why are you so late? None of the other students were late..." On and on. Her class watched in amazement as she ripped into the poor Denise. Fortunately for Denise, Camila realized she was venting and that it had nothing whatsoever to do with her student being a little bit late. She immediately apologized to Denise, told her to take her seat and not let it happen again. She knew she had over-reacted and the reality of that embarrassed her; she realized the rest of the class was literally walking on eggshells so they wouldn't trip any of her buttons.

Camila's mind seemed riveted on her situation at home. Try as she might to focus on her present situation in the classroom, her thoughts kept drifting to the house on Goshen Road where poor Angie was trapped inside on beautiful summer days, fearful of whatever child predator was on the loose in this Godforsaken pretend-city, in this Godforsaken coal state where people couldn't even speak good English.

She missed Massachusetts. She missed Boston, its history, its color, its mix of cultures, languages and most of all she missed being near the sea. She had had no cod chowder since she left the state. There was no fresh maple syrup and no maple sugar candy from Vermont. Pennsylvania's version was a poor comparison to what she had enjoyed at home.

Besides that, the unexpected complications with her new husband shocked and appalled her. The episode at Joe Cleod's home haunted her. "Shut up and get in the car," INDEED! She complied to avoid making a scene. She didn't bring it up again because she wanted to digest and think about the experience. *Is this how men from West Virginia treat their wives?* From what she saw among her new acquaintances, she didn't think so. *What kind of man treats his wife like that? "Shut up and get in the car," indeed! Fuck you, Bevin Hardy, or Cleod, or whatever your name really is!*

The class had finished its project and Camila took the time to go over every paper, offering praise and suggestions. Then she gave them another assignment that would free her to return to her worries and woes.

His brother is a classic pig. He stinks. He looks vile. How could anyone leave a child with such a man? Poor Billene. No wonder she ran away! Camila had heard the stories of Bevin and Joe Cleod's father and the accusations that HE was a child predator. *It's awful to fall back on such a cliché, but the apple never really does fall all that far from the tree. Could Bevin be...? I couldn't have made such a horrible mistake. But maybe I did. The pressure of the rumors in Boston forced us to leave. Was he guilty of that murder, too? Angie and I should ditch this bastard and go home. I wonder if I could get my old job back...*

C3 ‰‰

Billene Parsons! That's my name. It's not Cleod at all! It's Billene Parsons. Her ride pitched up and down and circled round and round, a wooden pony on the anachronism of a 1927 carousel at the corner of San

Carlos and San Marcos Avenues in St. Augustine, Florida. "The oldest continuously occupied European settlement in the Unites States," their tour guide, Friar Bob had said earlier. Her dad had laughed at that, commenting on how carefully worded it was.

"That means," he said, "there were other settlements before this one but they were abandoned or failed for some reason — they weren't continuously occupied." Billene didn't care. She had never been outside the confines of Copperhead, West Virginia, except for the brief experience at Beckley. This trip to Florida had opened her eyes. *This is a big country! We drove all day to get here and this is only a small part of the USA.*

She had never seen an ocean or been to the beach. She smiled at the memory of how carefully her dad lathered her with sun-block. The sand stuck to her feet and she had to rinse them off before going back into the hotel. At the beach she saw schools of fish swimming together in the surf. "Them's mullet," a man told her, amused at her amazement. He stood in shallow water, throwing a circular woven net into the breaking waves. When he brought the net back in, it had fish in it. He called it a "cast net."

"Can I try to throw it once?" Billene wanted to know.

Bill Parsons smiled. "It might be a little too heavy for ya, kid. Maybe next time, okay?" They watched the man for awhile. The fish were small. "It's for bait," her dad told her. "In a little while he'll probably do a little surf fishing, maybe catch something bigger."

They continued down the beach. While Billene was picking up sea shells, Bill's cell phone went off, *beep, beep, beep.*

When Bill finished the call he said, "We need to go back to the hotel where it's quiet. I have to make some phone calls right away."

First, he called Dr. Evelyn Grayson, Child Protective Services in Beckley. After a short conversation, he said, "She wants to talk to you," and handed her the phone.

Dr. Grayson's cheerful words were belied by her tone of voice, which was concerned and grave. "Hi Honey. How's everything?"

Billene bubbled, "I'm great, Dr. Shrink. We're in St. Augustine, Florida. We took a tour and saw a big old hotel. I rode on a antique carousel. We went to the beach. I saw the ocean. There was a man fishing with a net of some kind. He was catching fish faster than I ever saw anyone catch fish. Tomorrow we're going to Disney World... Hey, Dr. Shrink?"

"Yes, Billene?"

"My name is Billene Parsons, not Cleod. I have a dad, a real dad."

"I'm glad you're having a good time. Let me talk to Mr. Parsons again, please."

After the discussion with Dr. Grayson, Bill called the sheriff's office in Copperhead. That conversation didn't leave him smiling but he shrugged it off, saying, "It's not a big deal." Then he called Maguire.

That evening for dinner they went to Barnacle Bill's on Castillo Drive, on the recommendation of Friar Bob, their tour guide. The restaurant was crowded and a little bit noisy. Their waitress, Debby, recommended the Caribbean Mango Mahi which they both ordered.

"Ya know, Dad, this is really great, but ya know what's really missing here?"

"What's that, Kiddo?"

"Sherry."

Chapter Twenty-Nine

Camila enjoyed chaperoning the girls' swim practice. The smell of the chlorine in the pool reminded her of her days at the YWCA in Boston where she herself had learned to swim. She noticed Jeannie Hardwick now had the regulation two-piece swimsuit.

Bernice Jackowski, the girl's swim coach, was in rare form, fresh from a workout in the gymnasium, her cheeks still slightly flushed and skin glistening. *The men would call that sweat, but ladies get a break for some reason.* Camila began resenting Jackowski's youth and form again but caught herself... *I was that age, once upon a time. I wonder if this is how the older women thought of me?* She forced herself to stop thinking about it.

Angie, hearing about the girl's swim team, wanted to come to the school on the afternoons they practiced and join them. Angie had been quite the promising swimmer in Boston, specializing in breaststroke. "Mom! I was on the swim team at my school in Arlington. Why not here? Copperhead has no YWCA, but the school has a swim team and it's practicing now, over the summer, so when the fall competitions come along they'll be in shape and ready to compete!"

Camila was very firm. "When school starts in the fall, you can join the swim team, if you still want to. For now, I want to keep you safe in the house. I don't want anybody to even see you outside the house until we get this all settled with the sexual predator nonsense." Bevin, to her amazement, agreed. *So Angie is home and safe in the house, I hope.*

Ever since she had turned on the car radio on the way to school this morning, something had been subtly churning in the back of her mind. Ray Peck, host of the morning news, talked of tonight's full moon, that the sky would be clear, the weather warm, but not too warm and "what a great evening it will be to watch the moon rise beyond the mountains to the east." *Something about full moons around here...*

Sherry hurried into the room, pulling a strap up over her shoulder as though she had just finished climbing into her swimsuit. "Sorry I'm late. I had some papers I had to finish looking at. The time goes by so fast when you're having fun, eh?" She glanced over at the lineup of girls ready for their racing dive. "Looks like I didn't miss anything. They're all still dry."

Camila furrowed her eyebrows and looked at Sherry. "There's a full moon, tonight. You going to go watch it?"

Sherry grinned back. "I'd love to but I can't leave my horses on a full moon. The farrier wanted to come over this evening and work on tweaking some of their shoes. I told him they get too jumpy under a full moon and that it would be better to wait a few days. You going to sit out on the porch this evening with a glass of red and watch it come up?"

Camila's grimace deepened slightly. "I can't, either. I have a planning meeting this evening. I brought an extra lunch. I won't even be home for dinner. Bevin will have to cook. That'll be a hoot. The new school year is coming quickly and this needs to be done well in advance. Bevin got out of it, though, so he'll be home watching over our daughter."

Camila barely noticed Sherry's forehead wrinkle slightly. "Some men can cook just as well as any woman," Sherry observed. "And some can't."

Camila's mind drifted back to her dissatisfaction with Bevin and her fear that he was the predator everyone was looking for. "The Neighborhood Watch thing seems to be going well," she said. "Have you heard anything about it, Sherry? Bevin has really gotten into it."

Sherry squirmed. "Some people think it's pointless, that the guy who's doing this stuff isn't from around here and isn't going to be coming back any time soon, especially since he was just here a short time ago. It's been twelve years, after all, since the last time and it could be another twelve years before it happens again, if it ever does. Others think it's a good idea and that with this community effort, they may well catch the guy. As for me, I don't have an opinion. It seems like a good thing, overall. What do you and Bevin think?"

Shifting her thinking again, or trying to, Camila was reluctant to share what she thought — that the criminal may well be her own husband. That led to the conundrum of how she was going to pack and get away without Bevin's interference. Her decision to go back to Boston and leave Bevin had been a struggle, but her inner conflict was finished. She was leaving, just not quite sure how or when. "I have mixed feelings about it. I think it would be interesting if we discover that someone involved in the Neighborhood Watch is actually the person we're looking for. He'd be out there, sort of actively searching for himself."

"That would be ironic." Sherry turned her face toward the swimmers, her head lowered, lips drawn down in a frown of determination and anger.

"Sherry, I know I've asked you this before, but you've been around Copperhead all your life. Do you have any idea who this could be?"

Sherry turned her frown back to Camila, narrowed her eyes briefly and said, "Can't really say, Camila. Sorry."

In silent resignation, Camila turned back to watch the swimmers. She didn't anticipate any problems with the girls. They were all good swimmers and Jackowski was right on top of things. If anyone got in trouble, she would be right there to pull them out of the water. *Sherry and I are only watching all this to satisfy state insurance regulations and bureaucratic paranoia. There was a drowning in a school swimming pool a few years ago in Charleston, but that kid was in the pool alone, against the rules and apparently cracked her head on the side of the pool or something...*

Camila's reaction to the appearance of her husband at the girl's swim practice — again — didn't take the edge off of her anger. As the girls finished their fifth lap, they crawled out of the swimming pool, saw him and started their pubescent cooing, "Oh! Mr. Hardy! It's so nice to see you." Jeannie Hardwick led the pack.

ଓଃ ଃ୦

Jeannie waited just inside the double glass entry doors of the school, at the end of the day, for her mother to come and get her. "Don't you even go outside the door till I get there. You hear?" Amanda's anxiety was clear and so were her instructions.

"Ah, Ma! I'll be at school. Nothing can happen to me there. It's right out in plain sight where anyone can see me."

"Stay inside the building till I get there. Even if I'm late. You wait inside. Understand?"

Jeannie fidgeted with the panic bar on the door. She pushed it open and watched it close. Then she pushed it open again and watched it again, making that click as it latched. She waited, as instructed, inside.

Jeannie didn't know why her mom was late and she was growing impatient. Mr. Roddy, the janitor, passed by several times, first pushing a large broom, then with a polishing machine that spun a soft disk on the floor, bringing it up to a bright shine as he passed. When he saw Jeannie still standing there after he had been working on the hall floor for almost half an hour, he stopped, turned off his polishing machine and approached her. "Your ride late, honey?"

"Sure is!" Jeannie felt downright sullen.

"Want me to call someone for you? Maybe they forgot to come for you?"

"I don't think my mom forgot. I'll just wait a little while longer; then, if you're still here, maybe you could call my mom?"

"Sure, honey. I'll do that for you. When I finish the floor, if you're still here, I'll call her and wait with you till she gets here. Okay?"

Mr. Roddy went back to his floor polishing. Jeannie kicked the door in frustration. She had an armload of books which she dumped on the floor in front of her, along with a wet towel rolled up with a wet swimsuit in it. *I need to get home and get this stuff hung out to dry so I can use it tomorrow. I don't want to bring a wet swimsuit to school.*

Just then, a blue minivan rolled to a stop in front of the school door. Bevin Hardy got out and approached the door. Jeannie was pleased to see him. His pinstripe suit and red tie were in perfect order. *He's always so spiffy. I bet Mr. Hardy will take me home.*

"Hi Jeannie!" *He even seems pleased to see me!* "I was wondering if I'd find you here. Is your mom late?"

"She sure is, Mr. Hardy. I don't know where she is, but I'm pretty sure she'll be along pretty quick."

Hardy stood there for a few seconds, glanced around, shuffled his feet a couple of times and said, "Ya know what, Jeannie? There's going to be a big full moon tonight. Did you know that? And it's going to start rising in just about half an hour."

Jeannie felt a little awkward. Hardy had never given her so much direct attention in the past. He had always been nice to her, but not like this. "No, I didn't know. I bet it's going to be pretty." *Gee! It seems like he's getting excited about it. He must like full moons.*

Hardy continued, "Ya know, Jeannie, I know a perfect place to watch it from. Suppose I give ya a ride home and on the way we can stop and watch the moon come up. How does that sound?"

Now it was Jeannie shuffling her feet and looking around. She wondered where Mr. Roddy had disappeared to and if he would be back soon. "My mom will be here pretty soon. If I don't wait for her she'll be mad at me."

"Your mom knows me. I organized the Neighborhood Watch and

I've been all over town helping other parents get involved in that. Come on along with me. We won't be too late. Then I'll get you right home. Whadya say?"

Bevin Hardy's big grin and charming manner were too much for Jeannie. She tucked her wet towel under her arm and said, "Okay. Let's go." She reached for her books, but Hardy picked them up and opened the door for her. Hand in hand they strolled toward his blue minivan. Hardy opened the van door for her but just as she was about to get in, her dad came swinging into the school's parking lot. When he saw her about to get into Hardy's car, he started honking the horn.

"Oh, Mr. Hardy, I'm so sorry. That's Dad. I'll have to go with him. I'll watch the moon from our front porch and I'll think of you. Okay?" *Gee! Mr. Hardy seems angry. I wonder what I did to make him mad.*

Jeannie walked to her father's car and opened the door. As she got in, she waved goodbye to Hardy who was standing there glowering. He waved at her father, got in the minivan, and drove off.

Jeannie was astounded when her father angrily demanded, "Exactly what was that all about?"

"That was just Mr. Hardy. You know him. Since Mom was late picking me up, he offered to give me a ride home." *I don't think I better tell him about watching the full moon coming up. He won't like that very much.*

"You have strict instructions to not get in anyone's car but ours. We've only known him a short time. Yes, we think we can trust him, but not with our daughter. For your own safety, you must listen to what we tell you and obey us. We want you to be safe and the only way we can be sure of that is if you DO what you're told."

"Yes, Dad. Sorry. It won't happen again." *Till the next time...* She smiled to herself in anticipation of when that might happen.

03 80

Angie Hardy, filled with boredom, perched on the swing on the screened porch in her stepfather's aunt's house on Goshen Road. *This has got to stop. I've read every book in the house, watched reruns on TV till I almost have them memorized. I started to learn to knit. This sucks. I wonder what happened to Billene. She was fun ... but a little scary, I guess. I wonder why she ran away and I wonder where she is.*

Bevin's minivan pulled into the driveway, a little faster than usual. "Hi, kid. How was your day? Boring as usual?"

"Yes." She put all the disgust into that she could. "Where's Mom?"

"She has a planning meeting tonight. She'll be a little late."

"That sucks." Bevin came up the stairs onto the porch, looking at her a bit oddly, Angie thought.

"Ya know, kid, there's supposed to be a big full moon tonight. Moon rise is in about thirty or forty minutes. I know the perfect place to watch it come up. Maybe that'll break up the boredom a little bit. Wanta go?"

"Sure. Why not."

Bevin backed the minivan out to face the rising mountain in front of them. "Nothing like watching the moon rise from the very top of the mountain. Makes ya feel like an Olympian god or something."

"Sounds great, Bevin. Let's go." The boredom dripped from her voice. Sarcasm seemed to come naturally to her and she relished it. They started up the road toward Chad's Knob but Bevin turned into the first driveway he came to, instead of continuing up the road. "What's this?" she wanted to know.

"I thought it might be fun to pick up my brother and bring him along, if he wants to go."

"He's creepy," Angie moaned. "But I guess so."

Joe was squatting over a cooler on the top step of the porch as they pulled in. He came up with a full beer bottle. As he removed the cap, he turned and waved. "Hi, Beaver. What's that cha got with ya?"

"This is my daughter, Angie."

"Step-daughter!" Angie said loudly.

Bevin laughed. "She hasn't quite accepted me yet, but she will soon." As he said that his expression changed from cheerful and charming to cold and sinister. "Angie, I'd like you to meet your Uncle Joe, my twin brother."

"Beaver! W'at chou doin'? You can't take her up there with you."

"I have to split anyway, Joe. The FBI came and took DNA samples a couple of days ago and it's just a matter of time before they come back and when they do, you won't be seein' no more of the one Beaver Cleod Hardy. It looks like Mexico for me."

Angie listened in astonishment and growing fear. *It's him! He's the bad guy everybody's trying to find. He even organized a Neighborhood Watch to hunt for himself. If he's in charge, he'll know where they're looking!*

"So it's you I've been hiding from all summer!" she exclaimed.

"'Fraid so, honey. Joe..." Hardy called through the window. "I cashed in my retirement yesterday. I got lots and lots of cash. Why don't you come along with me tonight then we'll both go to Mexico. We can be there, easy, in two days, if we share the driving."

Joe took a long swig from his beer bottle, nearly emptying it. "I don't think it's such a great idea, Beaver. They took my DNA a couple of days ago too, but I ain't done nothin' I can get in trouble for so they ain't goin' to find anything out there, about me. It's you they want."

"Come on, Joe. Ain't you had enough of those coal mines yet? Doesn't a nice little bit of nooky sound good to ya and then the beach in Cancun? Git in the car and quit fussin'."

Joe pitched his last beer bottle into the woods beside the cottage, glanced at the azalea bush where Billene used to hide from him and got in the car.

"Don't you want to git nothin' to bring along?" Bevin asked. "When we leave we're gonna be in a hurry."

Joe looked across Angie, trapped between them on the front seat. "I don't have much I wanta bring. We can stop on the way back and I'll stash a few things in the back of the car. This'll be nice. I always wanted to spend more time with you."

Angie started squirming. "Let me out of the car."

"That ain't gonna happen honey," Joe chortled as Bevin backed the minivan out of Joe's driveway.

"Let me out! Now!"

Bevin snapped a look at her and practically growled, "If you don't behave yourself, you're going to get hurt, sooner."

"You can't do this to me. I'm your daughter."

Bevin growled again in answer, "Step-daughter."

"My mom will kill you."

At that, both men started laughing almost uncontrollably.

03   80

Giuseppe Bartalucci, better known as Chigger, was glad to see the sun nearing the horizon. *Just a few more hours and it'll be dark. Then shortly after that, I can go home. The moon should be appearing any minute now. I wonder...* Just then he heard the engine of the minivan struggling up the mountain. He lifted his rifle, pulled back the bolt and shoved a cartridge into the chamber, clicked on the safety and hoisted the gun to watch through the telescopic sight. His favorite rifle, the 7mm magnum, had the range, the accuracy and the power to do anything he might want. The only drawback was it had bolt action instead of being semi-automatic like the military weapons he had used in the past. *This rifle may be a bit slower but it has more power and greater accuracy. With that, it doesn't need speed.*

As usual, when he shouldered the rifle with the probability of taking a life, his first assassination assignment snapped back to his mind. The target, a certain Asian military leader, had stood just over a mile away. Giuseppe, as he was known then, knew the man's wife and children from pictures he had seen in his briefing. He knew the man's face down to the tiny scar above his left eyebrow from an accident he had had as a boy. The moral arguments about murder had been argued in his mind endlessly. His Roman Catholic upbringing named what he was about to do exactly what it was — atrocity. He was about to kill a fellow human being, like a coward, from a distance, unknown to his victim, unseen by the victim's family. It was shallow, cold murder. Chigger shrugged off the memory with the only possible answer. It came from his Squad Leader, Lieutenant Commander Emanuel Hower Epson, a man of huge size, bald head and bawdy sense of humor. "Some men need killin.' It is you who will kill this one."

As the blue minivan crawled into view over the last stretch of the steep, uneven tire ruts, Chigger felt his lips draw down into a grimace of angry determination. He had waited for this moment for weeks. He had taken the time, weeks before, to sight in the rifle to this exact distance. The weapon's pristine condition left no excuse for failure other than Chigger's own reluctance to take a life. He waited while the minivan came to a stop.

That two men rode in the vehicle surprised him. That a twelve year old girl sat between them did not. The two men left the vehicle at the same time with the man on the right side of the car dragging the girl by the arm, to the front of the car. He held her by the shoulders while the driver came around and tore off her blouse.

He stood up with a grin to the other man, waving the torn cloth in the air. Chigger had his finger on the trigger, the man's head in the crosshairs. As he began to exert pressure on the trigger, he stopped in shocked amazement as an arrow, appearing apparently from nowhere, pierced the man's throat, passing just about halfway through. Chigger's mouth dropped open in amazement, but before he finished the gesture, a second arrow appeared in the man's throat from a slightly different direction. Bevin Cleod Hardy fell straight down on his face.

Angie, in shock, fell backward as Joe Cleod released her. She began screaming at the sight of her stepfather, eyes wide open, blood gushing from his mouth, apparently trying to say something as consciousness faded from his eyes. Over the hysterical shrieking, Chigger could hear Joe Cleod's shouts of rage. "Where are you? Who are you? What'd you do ta ma brother?"

Chigger sighted his rifle again — with Joe's head in the crosshairs this time. His finger was just beginning to give pressure to the trigger when to his surprise, another arrow appeared, this one in Joe's throat, passing just about half way through. Almost instantaneously, a second arrow appeared beside the first and Joe Cleod dropped to the ground making a sound, Chigger thought, similar to that of a piece of dung from the back end of a horse.

Angie's shrieks grew even more shrill. She was on her feet in a flash and headed at a dead run for the road down the mountain, screaming in full-fledged hysteria. *Too bad we couldn't have saved her that.* Chigger coldly contained his remorse. *What has to be has to be. Shit happens.* He waited a full twenty minutes before he rose to investigate the site. He reasoned it would take Angie half an hour to get home, even if she ran all the way. He would still have time to leave the scene without complications.

Chigger walked slowly and openly to the spot where the two dead men had fallen. As he did, another figure stepped out of cover from the other side of the clearing: the Keetowah. "Another was here," he announced, "to steal my kill!" He nudged the body of Bevin Hardy with his foot. "Look at the arrows. That one is mine — Cherokee. That one," indicating the other arrow, "is Shawnee. The brave who released it fled down the mountainside near where you were hiding. Did you see him?"

Chigger shook his head and said, "I did not, and thank you for doing this. I take no pleasure in this kind of work. I only do it because I am skilled."

"Not so skilled," The Keetowah laughed at him. "I stole *your* kill." He continued laughing as he disappeared into the brush. "Be well, my brother," he called out over his shoulder. "Go home. Drink wine with your family."

Chigger pulled out his cell phone and turned it on as he returned to the forest. When the signal indicator lit up, he texted, "PU," for "pick me up" and started down the mountain toward the road a few miles away to the west. Once the message was sent, he turned off the cell phone.

Chapter Thirty

Camila arrived home much later than she thought she would. Her wrist watch indicated almost 8:00. The full moon was climbing well above the eastern horizon and the sun had reached the edge of the earth in the west. *Dark soon. I hope Bevin has some food ready for me. I'm hungry.* She was surprised to find that Bevin's car was not parked in the driveway. Her surprise increased when she realized there were no lights on in the house. It looked as if no one was there yet.

Inside the front door, she switched on a light and heard sobs coming from upstairs. She found Angie wrapped in a blanket in the chair beside her bed. Camila snapped on the ceiling light in time to see Angie cover her head with the blanket.

"Angie, this isn't like you. What's wrong?" As she approached Angie, her daughter's sobbing escalated into hysterics. Camila wrapped her arms around Angie and pulled her into what hug she could get with the child still seated in the chair. "Hey, sweetheart. It can't be all that bad."

Angie rose from the chair and clung to her mother. "Yes it can, Mom!"

"Tell me." Camila's fear and anxiety were growing quickly, but she controlled herself, trying to maintain a calm exterior for her daughter's benefit. *Where is Bevin? What the hell's wrong here?* "Has Bevin been home yet?" She did her best to keep her voice on even keel, calm, assured, in control.

Angie squeezed her mother tighter and in a very high-pitched, but very soft voice, replied, "Yes."

"Where is he, honey? Do you know?"

Angie released her mother and returned to her chair. In the stark light of the ceiling bulb Camila could see she had been crying for some time. Her face was red and streaked with dirt and tears. It was only then that Camila noticed that her daughter's shirt was partly missing and she had scratches on her upper body. Camila seemed to feel the earth drop from beneath her. *How did her blouse get torn like that? ... and the dirt? My God! What's happened here?*

"He's ... He's on top of the mountain," Angie stammered. "I think he's dead." She gritted her teeth and her brow creased in fury as she ground out the words: "I *hope* he's dead!"

Camila could see that Angie was feeling safer, that fear was being replaced, thankfully, with rage. Camila went to the bathroom and fetched a warm wet wash cloth. She hoped that Angie was calming down enough that maybe she would tell her what happened. As she wiped the tears and dirt from Angie's cheeks, she cooed softly to try to ease her daughter's trauma. *Dead? Bevin? On top of the mountain?*

"Angie?"

"Bevin is the guy everybody's been looking for. He's dead. On top of the mountain. We should call the police."

CƷ   ℇᴐ

Deputy Joe Perry smiled as he sipped a beer and examined his rear deck, which overlooked the New River. He had built the deck with his own hands while his wife, Corky, uncharacteristically silent, kept him supplied with cold drinks, the occasional snacks and a quirky smile that said, "I'm not going to say a single word." She was surprised and pleased when the deck was finished and as proud of it as he was. She even helped with the final step, staining the wooden surface with water sealer. He was about to take a bite of the chicken he just finished barbecuing when the phone rang. It was Sheriff Billy Rankin.

"Joe, I know you're off for the weekend. I hate to bother you. Can you come?"

"Well, Sheriff. I'm about to bite into some chicken that's been cooking for the last couple of hours and I've drunk about two bottles of beer. You still want me?"

"Joe, I'm awful sorry, but I think we got another body on Chad's Knob. I'll come get you. I'll drive. Please be in uniform and bring your side arm. I'll be there in ten minutes." Without ceremony the sheriff hung up.

"Corky, I'm sorry. I gotta go. This sounds serious..."

By the time they arrived at the top of the mountain, it was almost nine o'clock. The moon was ten to fifteen degrees above the horizon. Perry kept his amused comments to himself as he watched the sheriff maneuver the patrol car over the rough ruts of Goshen Trail, near the top of the mountain, cussing at every unexpected bump. "I sure hope we don't damage the car on this miserable mountain trail," Rankin muttered.

"We'll be okay. Just try to keep the tires out of the ruts so we don't bottom out too much."

As they cleared the peak, coming into the small clearing at Chad's Knob, Perry could see Hardy's blue minivan with the passenger door open and the dome light still on, though rather dim. Rankin stopped the patrol car behind the minivan and both got out of the car, still not seeing anything other than the blue minivan. Perry began walking forward on the right side with Rankin pacing him on the left, both with one hand on their side arms. Both men aimed their flashlights into the interior of the van, noticing nothing out of the ordinary. Rankin proceeded to the front of the van, ahead of Perry.

Suddenly Rankin exclaimed, "Holy shit!" Bevin Hardy and Joe Cleod lay stretched out on the ground, both in awkward positions, both the color of death. The arrows remained in their throats: two arrows each, above puddles of blood seeping into the rough mountain soil. Rankin started making cellphone calls — ambulance, State Police, FBI, his wife.

Perry gave a brief thought to his barbecued chicken. *This is going to take awhile.* He called his wife.

Joe Perry didn't get home till after midnight. He interviewed Camila Hardy at the hospital in Beckley, where she had taken Angie after learning what had happened to her. He tried to interview Angie but she refused to talk to him. He stayed with Camila for a while, trying to help her understand what had happened. He considered visiting some of the other parents but the hour was growing late. The FBI didn't show up, but the State Police did, with bloodhounds and their crime unit, hoping to find some evidence to track down the person who had brought the child predators to justice. Perry hoped they failed.

The only trail they found led down the side of the mountain to the old dirt road running through the valley. They lost it there.

The thought that stayed with Joe Perry all the way home and through the next few days was, "The people of Copperhead can still take care of their own problems."

C3   80

Sherry Paulus's computer was having hiccups. Her efforts at revis-
ing some lesson plans for the following week was interrupted, to her
great frustration, first by the computer acting up and second by the
knock on her door. She was surprised to find Deputy Joe Perry at her
door with two men in black suits. Joe's expression was of determination. The men in the suits seemed impassive.

"Good morning Ms. Paulus," Joe began. "Mind if I ask you some
questions?"

Sherry's frustration couldn't be missed. One thing Sherry was
known for in Copperhead — being open about her feelings and impressions — endeared her to some and intimidated others. Joe Perry had
known her all his life and he was not intimidated. "Who are the guys in
the suits?" she demanded.

"I'm sorry Ms. Paulus..."

Sherry cut him off. "You been calling me Sherry all your life. Why
the Ms. Paulus stuff now? Have a seat, Joe, after you introduce the
suits."

Joe took off his hat and said, "Sherry, this is Special Agent Matthew
Brown and his partner, Special Agent William Montgomery, of the FBI.
Gentlemen, this is Sherry Paulus."

"Thank you, Joe. And why is the FBI calling on little ole me?" Sherry hoped her smile wouldn't seem too sarcastic.

They took seats in Sherry's modest living room and Joe opened a
folder, pulling out a sheaf of photographs. He handed them to Sherry,
saying, "There was another incident at Chad's Knob last night. Two
men were killed. We found these arrows in them." He indicated the
photographs. "Did you make these arrows?"

The photographs showed only the ends with the feathers and the
ends with the arrowheads, but not what they were embedded in. Sherry
studied the photographs and after a few minutes she looked Joe straight
in the eye and said, "Two of these four arrows are made with the Shawnee design. I make arrows like this and sell them all over the place. You
can find them at Tamarack, the Indian Crafts shop in Charleston, and
some of the truck stops, gift stores, further north. I could have made
them. These other two, I think may be Cherokee designs. I don't make
arrows like those. One thing, though, the arrows I make are decorative.
They are not weapons."

Joe scratched his head and turned to Montgomery. "Do you have
any questions, gentlemen?"

Matthew Brown broke the silence. "Our background work on you indicated you were a champion archer at one time. Do you still compete?"

Sherry chuckled. "I quit archery when I was in grade school. I embarrassed an upperclassman who I had a crush on and I felt awful about it. I put down my bow and never picked it up again. In fact, I got rid of it long ago. I don't even own a bow today."

She involuntarily glanced at the wood-burning stove in the corner of the living room where only last night she had burned a pile of bill stubs. Since her shredder quit working, she burned her bill stubs and she liked to put a little wood under them to keep the fire going until all the paper was gone. Last night, she burned bill stubs and the bow she made for her ritual kill, after chopping it into one- or two-inch lengths. The bow string, made from sinew, was gone as well. She frowned slightly at the memory of burning the rubber gloves she had used to make those arrows. They were unwieldy and made working with her hands more difficult. They also stank when she burned them. Her smooth-bottomed moccasins were in her closet with her other shoes. The smell of deer and rabbit dung was not strong, but when she noticed it, she thought of the forest, not of blood and vengeance.

"What were these arrows used for?" Her question was benign, her expression pure innocence.

William Montgomery ignored her question. "Ms. Paulus, how many of these arrows do you suppose you sold over the last few months?"

"You'd have to check with the stores," Sherry answered. "I put about three dozen arrows out there and I've been getting calls for more. I have a small stash right here, right now. You want to see them?" She rose.

"I don't think that will be necessary," Joe Perry said. "Do you guys want a sample?"

When they left, Sherry had one less arrow for her retail outlets.

のみ な

On the night of the full moon, two dead men with arrows in their throats stretched their bodies under the pale light. Daniel Maguire personally swung by the old dirt road at the bottom of the valley, below the peak and picked up Giuseppe Bartalucci. Neither of them spoke until they arrived at Maguire's desk, the kitchen table, at his residence on Jessica Lane. Maguire set a wine glass in front of Chigger, popped the cork from a fresh bottle of Fatascia Almanera Sicilia and poured them both a full glass. "To a job completed," Maguire toasted.

Chigger lifted the glass, swirled the wine around slightly, took a whiff and lifted it to his lips. After a small taste, he put the glass back on the table and said, "Yes. The job is done, but I had nothing to do with it. I didn't fire a shot, lift a knife, swing a club; nothing. I only watched it happen."

Maguire's surprise was marginal. "So tell me what you saw."

Chigger described the scene, the arrows, the dead men and the Keetowah complaining about another stealing his kill. Maguire's smile as Chigger described what happened puzzled him. "I don't understand why you're smiling. You hired me, at great expense, to do a job. You put up with nothing happening for weeks and when something did happen, it was others who did what you're paying me to do. But you are smiling."

Maguire took a deep swallow of his favorite wine and returned the glass to the table. "I hired you, I suppose, because I had lost my faith in the ability of the people of this backwoods community to handle their own problems. I'm smiling because my faith in them has been restored. In Copperhead, West Virginia, from the time white men first came to these woods, we solved our own problems because outside authorities were always too busy to be bothered with us. I'm happy that I now know that we can still solve our own problems. The Keetowah was an unexpected friend."

Chigger tasted the wine again and joined Maguire in the smile. "Yes. I was delighted to meet him — a totally unique individual. I wonder where he'll go now, or if he'll stay on the mountain. He seems safe enough. The other man was completely unexpected and it was an interesting coincidence that he used Native American weapons as well. I wonder who he was."

Maguire, as always, showed interest in the Native American culture that once thrived in his homeland. " I think the white man always gave too little credit to the Native American women. Their men were very fierce and proud fighters — warriors — but the women were stronger, fiercer and more determined than their men. Maybe you should wonder who was that squaw, rather than who was the brave."

Chigger smiled a little wider. "Is there something you know that you aren't telling me?"

Maguire replied, "It's only conjecture. I think it was a certain Shawnee squaw, who I know. She was very smart about how she did this, if it was her."

C8　80

Camila felt as though she had been beaten up, kicked repeatedly and thrown down a two-story staircase. Her head hurt. Her back hurt. Her eyes were sore from crying. Her cheeks felt that they had been burned and scarred by her tears and she would never again be the same. How could she have been so easily fooled to marry a child predator whose main interest was more than likely her daughter than herself?

But there were consolations: her new ride was a Prius 3. She loved it. The police had given her the money they found in Bevin's blue mini-van, some $42,000 in cash. *Nice that they were honest about that. They could easily have kept it.* She paid cash for the Prius, trading both her old Bonneville and Bevin's minivan.

There were very few guests at the funeral and those that came, Ca-mila suspected, came more out of morbid curiosity than respect. There was no mortuary in Copperhead, so the funeral was held at Beckley. Both men were buried on the hilltop, south of Copperhead, in the small graveyard overlooking the New River and I-64. She paid for the funer-als not out of respect but in gratitude that they were both dead — and to be free of any obligation connected with the matter, *forever, from now on. The son of a bitch is dead! Thank God!*

When Camila told Angie they were going to go back to Boston, her daughter was overjoyed. "Thank God we're leaving this place! The only thing I liked here was Billene and she's long gone. I hope she's safe."

"She is, Angie. Would you like to see her before we leave? She's liv-ing in Beckley with her real father."

"I think I just want to go home."

Camila arranged for the movers to arrive in Boston three days after she did, to give her a chance to find a place to put her furniture. She hired a realtor from Beckley to sell the land and house and she was sur-prised to learn she was also now the owner of Joe Cleod's cottage, fur-ther up the road. Bevin was his only heir and she was Bevin's only heir. *What a mixed blessing this is! To inherit all this money from these two vile people! Maybe I should just give it away. Naah. I don't think so.*

The road to Boston began with the steep ramp up to I-64. As they started across the bridge, Angie called out, "Look, Mom. The valley is full of clouds, just like when we came here. It's the valley where the clouds sleep."

Camila bit her tongue to stop her response, *Yes, Angie, the valley where the Cleods sleep.*

CR 80

A little over a year later, Sherry attended a Native American Festival in St. Augustine, Florida, with her new husband, Bill Parsons, and her stepdaughter, Billene. The event was hosted in a large open field. Na-tive Americans attended from all over the United States and even some from Canada. One of the booths attracted Sherry's attention and the three of them stopped at it. The Indian claimed to be Cherokee. He was tall, gaunt and much older than Sherry and Bill. His weathered skin sang of the sun and the outdoors. The information poster at the entrance to his tent said he had long lived outdoors after the manner of his people but grew weary of the isolation. Sherry felt drawn to learn about this interesting man. As she engaged him in conversation, she picked up an arrow he had made from the wild things of nature. It was a Cherokee arrow. She openly admired its craftsmanship and art. The conversation meandered, leading Sherry to reveal her own Shawnee background and that she crafted arrows from her own people's designs to sell in retail outlets.

The Indian smiled. "Then you might be interested in seeing this arrow." He indicated a collection of arrows on the other side of his table. He picked one up and handed it to her. "It's a Shawnee design. I was lucky to find one."

"And where did you find one?" Sherry pressed the man.

His expression turned from friendly to serious. His gaze became slightly less than a glare when he answered, "On a mountain top, near Copperhead, West Virginia, a little over a year ago. Why do you ask?"

The realization of who he was crashed through Sherry's mind like water gushing from a broken dam. She stared at him with growing understanding, then held out her hand in greeting and said, "I'm glad to finally meet you. I am Alsoomse, of the Shawnee. This is the design of my arrows."

The Keetowah Cherokee raised his eyes from the arrows he had made and surveyed this woman whom he now knew. "My name is Kana'ti. I am proud to know you, Alsoomse. You are as good with the bow as I am, but you stole my kill."

Sherry's eyes grew fierce as she returned the Keetowah's gaze. "I think maybe, you stole mine!"

"In either case," the Keetowah smiled. "Our designs were successful. May the need not rise again. The Cherokee and the Shawnee now live in peace. We do not dispute such things."

Bill Parsons had heard some of this cryptic exchange. Billene was studying Indian paintings in the next tent by then, and heard none of it. While he did not interfere at the moment, later when they were alone he asked, "You and that Cherokee were arguing about stealing each others' kill. What were you talking about?"

She was silent for just a moment before answering, "We were talking about someone who shouldn't have pissed me off. Let's leave it at that. These are things of the past that no longer matter."

"Someday, maybe you will tell me?" Bill Parsons persisted.

"Someday, maybe I will."

About the Author

Robert G. Makin found his life paths growing up on Laurel Mountain. There he became friends with Elves and Flying Squirrels, did spelunking at Wild Cat Rocks and listened at the feet of his grandfathers to the stories of the Railroad, the Steel Mills and the Old Country. Bits and pieces of Old German and ancient Scottish Gaelic still creep into his conversation from those days gone by. A degree in Fanciful Literature from Indiana University of Pennsylvania fueled his drive to learn more about Elven History and their social structure. He sought fulfillment at Lancaster Theological Seminary of the United Church of Christ where he discovered Essenism, some of the precursors of Biblical History and the stories told to Abraham as Abraham sat at the feet of his grandfathers. They were stories of Nanna, Ningur, Inanna, Ya and Enlil, at the birth of Human Kind. Makin found that there is no history quite like oral history, nor quite as honest. Some truths have been politically incorrect for millennia and forbidden from written histories. Some truths have been corrected and updated to fit what's popular. Makin has found them hidden in Social Artifacts and takes pleasure in their unraveling and revelation.

Makin earned his bread for many years by selling opinions. Today he spends his time, sharing his love for and the history of St. Augustine, Florida with visitors from all over the world who come to hear his tales. In his books, Makin expresses the exuberant mysticism of the unknown, the what-if's, the maybe's and the things that very well may have been, like friendships with Flying Squirrels and Elves.

Other Books by
Robert G. Makin
Available at Amazon, Barnes & Noble and other book sellers

Strathnaver Legends

The heart of a quiet, peaceful village, ripped open by the remorseless vitriol of a sadistic predator drives kith and kin on a hunt for the hunter. Falling in with unknown races and cultures, they are forced to overcome prejudice and distrust in their drive for a common interest, to live in freedom from terror.

Aleister Through The Looking Glass

This is a children's book written for children over the age of 30. Starving-Writer Aleister Smiley takes a job returning unread manuscripts and depositing reading fees. He shortly finds himself whisked into Never Ever Land where he can Never Ever be published. Provinces of Never Ever Land parody the plight of the writer in this new age of formula loving editors, agents and publishers.

Return to Masada

The historic Battle of Masada has become a symbol of freedom, hope and courage to die, if necessary, for one's principles. Makin delivers a new version of this famous "David and Goliath" struggle of the Jewish people against the Roman Army.

The Faces of Inanna

A special fraternity of men, "Watchers," formed in ancient times by the old gods to monitor the development of human culture, comes into conflict, in modern times, with a daughter of one of their creators. Johnny Lewis, having moved on from his days in *Return to Masada*, follows through on his commitment to become one with the fraternity. As a member of the ancient enclave, he is sent to help resolve an enigmatic problem, barely understood by the modern fraternity. His solution leads him in a whole new direction. He finds Inanna irresistible, impulsive and without discipline.

If the old gods were indeed immortal, as the people of Sumer said in their Cuneiform writing, then they are still among us. Treat well the stranger in your midst, for it may be a god or an angel...

www.ingramcontent.com/pod-product-compliance
Lightning Source LLC
Chambersburg PA
CBHW050357030726
47503CB00006B/1902